W9-BFJ-165

EXTRA LIFE

EXTRA LIFE

DEREK NIKITAS

The following is a work of fiction. Names, characters, places, events and incidents
are either the product of the author's imagination or used in an entirely fictitious
manner. Any resemblance to actual persons, living or dead, is entirely coincidental.

Copyright © 2015 by Derek Nikitas
Cover design by The Cover Collection
Interior design by E.M. Tippetts Book Designs

ISBN 978-1-940610-53-5
eISBN 978-1-940610-79-5
Library of Congress Control Number: 2015946259

First hardcover publication: October 2015

POLIS BOOKS

Hoboken, NJ 07030
www.PolisBooks.com

ALSO BY DEREK NIKITAS

Pyres
The Long Division

For Gavin

DAY ONE

8:10 A.M.

EVERY YEAR, TOURISTS swarm my town. Sure, our Atlantic beaches are sweet, but people should know, just under the surface lurk sharks. If you're not careful, you'll get a jellyfish sting, you'll get caught in a riptide. Years ago, hurricane waters drowned a thousand homes and raised buried caskets to the surface. True story. We've got miles of beachfront boardwalk just aching for Instagram, but the flip side is flood and blood and fear.

Cape Fear, that is.

For the last thirty years, almost twice as long as I've been around, Cape Fear, North Carolina has been the backdrop for a hundred creep-show TV series and movies. Believe it or not, it's the biggest US production hot spot after LA and Manhattan, probably because we're a post-apocalyptic ghost town after the tourists abandon us for winter.

Nowheresville, just east of the Twilight Zone.

The whole Cape Fear movie scene started in the early Eighties when they came here to make *The Kindling*. You know, the one where

1

Drew Barrymore is still *E.T.*-era cute, and she starts people on fire with her brain? A few cheap special effects struck box office gold. Because of that success, a movie mogul and uber-producer named Marv Parker got delivered his first truckload of cash and built his local empire, Silver Screen Studios, right here in town.

You've seen some of our homegrown horror shows. There was that messed up flick with the kid who finds a human ear in his yard and the villain with the oxygen mask. Or the one actually called *Cape Fear*, with Robert De Niro as a tattooed psycho who's in love with his cigarette lighter. Also, *A Walk to Remember*.

In the Nineties, Silver Screen did a slew of teen slashers. *I Know What You Did Last Summer, Prank Call, Step Into the Light 1* through *4*, you name it. My real-life high school pops up in the backdrop of a whole lot of shots, but always with a new makeover, a new fictional name.

My dad and I used to catch showings at the old-school Pastime Playhouse before it burned down. We'd point at the screen and whisper, *"look, look,"* whenever a familiar Cape Fear location did a cameo. Even the Pastime Playhouse *itself* showed up on screen a couple times with its giant clock facade, tingling everyone in the audience with that squirmy sense of being in and out of time and body, real and not real. *There is where we are, but we are not there.* More fun than whatever the actual movie was, honestly.

I can spot my city in just about any Halloween horror marathon. A string of films all out of their proper release-year order, so my sense of time gets twisted inside out and backward, like that chimp they put through the faulty teleporter in *Revenge of the Replicons* (another Cape Fear classic).

But around here there's a whole other level of darkness that doesn't quite show up on celluloid or digital. I mean, you probably already heard about the Pastime Playhouse tragedy. It was an international scandal. Everybody knows the premise, but there are always facts below the surface and between the lines, things you couldn't know.

Like, just for example, that movie *The Crow*, from twenty years ago. Remember? Yeah, way before my time, too, but it's the one where Brandon Lee, son of martial arts legend Bruce Lee, plays the goth dude who comes back from the dead to avenge his own murder, jump-starting the whole dark superhero/comic book adaptation craze?

What if I told you Brandon Lee was *killed* on set at Silver Screen Studios, right here in Cape Fear? What if I said he was shot in the stomach by a malfunctioning blank cartridge that was supposed to be harmless? What if I told you he took his mortal wound right at the exact moment when his character was supposed to die?

You'd call me crazy or at least a liar. Because, duh, obviously Brandon Lee is alive and well. *Obviously* he went on to star in two smash-hit *Crow* sequels, not to mention *Speed* and *The Matrix I-III*.

But just try to imagine for a second if Brandon Lee really *was* killed on the set of that movie. Imagine all those future leading-man roles of his went instead to, I don't know, some doof like Keanu Reeves. Imagine Brandon Lee's been dead for two decades.

Ridiculous?

Maybe here in this life, maybe as far as *you* know. But in another universe, something like that could've happened. In theory, *anything* could've happened, and probably did. That's the kind of deep down, spun-around, terrifying truth that trumps all the monster movies getting filmed here in Cape Fear.

Sometimes I forget what's real around this place and what isn't. I admit it. There's a certain slipperiness of memory. I get confused a lot, which makes me sound like a nursing home geezer with dementia, when actually I'm a sixteen-year-old high school junior. The thing is, I've lived a lot of lives over my short time in this world, and it all traces back to that morning I was ten minutes late for school.

(See, I was just about to toss y'all a *Back to the Future* reference, how I was running late that morning and sorry I couldn't hitch a skateboard ride off the back of a truck like Michael J. Fox. Except that zinger would've went *woosh*, right over your head, even if you did catch the movie. Because where you come from, it's not called *Back to the Future*. It's called *Spaceman from Pluto*, starring Eric Stoltz, and it was stinker nobody bothered to go see.)

So, yeah. That morning, late for school but not in any hurry. I wasn't going to sweat it, even on a muggy coastal morning dusted all over with pollen. I'd been in way worse trouble than a tardy slip. Like especially that trespassing and vandalism arrest that got me tossed out of public school in the first place. What a punishment, right? Kinda-sorta expelled, forced to enroll in an exclusive private school that's as ritzy as Cape Fear gets.

But that was two years back, my freshman year, and I was now fully rehabilitated, partly because of the positive influence of my best friend, Conrad Bower. And Conrad's house was where I was headed that morning.

I found him pacing the creaky wood floors of his plantation porch, adjusting his shouldered backpack because the thing was ballooning with junk. His house was in the antebellum district off Market Street. An imposing house with peeling white paint, it was shadowed by trees strewn with Spanish moss like a creepy text font. Way too much house for just my man Connie and his mom, but it wasn't supposed to be just the two of them.

"Crap, Russ, crap—we're late," he said to me, all White Rabbit. My full name is Horace Vale, *Horace* after my maternal great-grandfather, a dusty history hand-me-down. *Russ* was better, a sleazy Seventies exploitation filmmaker name. The kind of name even dogs could pronounce.

"You could've taken off without me, you know," I told him.

"No, not hardly. How many times did you press snooze?"

"I don't know—two or three?" I said.

4

"And what time did you get up?"

"I don't know—seven-fifty?"

"That doesn't add up," he decided. "Your alarm is set for seven and each delay is nine minutes, so two or three delays—"

"I get it. My math sucks, and we're late for school, so let's move."

Connie made it all the way down two porch steps before he stopped and said, "I mean, what if it was something serious that held you up, an accident or something, and you needed my help? I'd want to know. Or you'd get here and I wouldn't be around. What would you think? "

On the sidewalk, I did my best *let's-go* lean.

But then Connie did it anyway, his usual deal. He scurried back up the steps, jiggled the doorknob to check that it was locked. This time of day, his mom was still gone on her nursing shift at New Hanover Regional, so it was Connie's job to make sure the house was secure.

He hesitated, as usual, unlocked the door, and told me he'd be right back. He would now comb through his house testing window locks, oven dials, the freezer door—*check, check, check*—making sure he hadn't forgotten any book, pen, or touchscreen device he could've conceivably shoved into his backpack.

Every morning, I was supposed to budget time for this. It used to irritate the crap out of me, but we all have our morning rituals. Mine was fixing a hot mug of coffee for my dad and marching it up the steep attic steps to his office, where he'd be slumped asleep over his desk in front of a triptych of computer monitors, debugging software.

This chore started two months earlier after Dad was laid off from his techie software job at Rush Fiberoptics, where he applied Game Theory and Quantum Mechanics to software applications. What was still sci-fi in reality my Dad could make doable in cyberspace— prototype trial runs for the eventual real deal, when the tech finally caught up to his imagination. He was freelance now—and by *freelance*

I mean just farting around for free.

I'd wake Dad with the java delivery, then head back down to the kitchen for a kale smoothie debriefing with Mom, fresh from her dawn jog. We'd consult the giant white board where our weekly schedules were laid out in marker, moment by moment. Dry-erase marker, but if I dared to actually erase anything, I risked being sentenced to a five-mile jog-along with Mom.

Every morning the same, like *Groundhog's Day*.

So now, while I waited for Connie to finish indulging his OCD, I fished my cell from my cargo shorts and scanned the recent texts. All seven were from Connie, minutes before I arrived. *Russ, dude, where r u?* and so forth.

It always gave me a chill, reading an old text after you've already talked to the sender, you know? A strange blip in time—the past flashing back on you. Like how my grandma still had Grandpa talking on her answering machine message, even though he died five years ago.

Brooding too much on the shadowy side of things could make you downright mental, like my friend Conrad here. His house-check compulsion was a thing I didn't bitch about or chide him for because it had to do with his dad. Connie's father wasn't holed away in an attic like mine. He was dead—Afghanistan, helicopter—and these safety checks were how Conrad fit that terrible fact into place, every morning of his life.

I couldn't imagine what it was like, even if Connie and I were close. He and I might not have even been friends if I hadn't at first been paying penance for a shitty prank I played on him once, and also if we weren't both such ridiculous movie buffs, especially the classic ones before CGI spoiled all the fun of questionable practical effects. We weren't Luddites—I mean, we caught all the latest stuff, but we'd also seen *Evil Dead III: Army of Darkness* so many times we could play dialog karaoke with the mute on. "*Klaatu Barada Necktie*" and etcetera.

(Connie would mention that gibberish *Evil Dead* line is actually a reference to a major plot point in a Fifties space-robot movie called *The Day the Earth Stood Still*. We could do this all day, really, but you can just add these movies to your queue for later.)

We barely ever watched a movie apart, and we hardly ever skipped our three-hour post-credits debate, even after the crappiest flicks. Sometimes we even recorded our own commentary tracks. Yep, we were *that* in love with our own opinions—especially Connie with his plot logic nit-picks, his *"how could the mother possibly not remember giving birth to twins, especially if one was a werewolf?"*

The difference between us was, I was a wannabe filmmaker. I loved the indie/hand-held/slice-of-life/stark reality stuff, the grassroots, DIY, guerrilla-shoot tactics. Connie was a fanboy who binged on sci-fi and fantasy, bursting with special effects and wonky philosophy—his current obsession being that *SyFy* show about the teens from all different time periods mysteriously awakening from cryogenic sleep inside the same boldly-going spacecraft. He had elaborate theories about how the show would turn out.

Honestly, I wasn't exactly eager to earn my geek badge, not in a public ceremony, anyway, but at least Connie's viewing taste was a step up from Cape Fear's most popular current television output—the CW's *Cape Twilight Blues*. It wasn't even a horror show, just a teen soap opera, pretty much the first wholesome series they've made around here in years, if you think a bunch of snarky, back-stabbing, bed-hopping, twenty-something supermodels pretending to be teenagers is *wholesome*.

Over the last two seasons, just about every glossy magazine in the world had a cover spread of one of the six dreamy stars of *Cape Twilight*. Every dude I knew had a secret crush on the show's lead actresses—Morgana Avalon or Clarice Louise-Best, or both, or neither, depending on the most recent episode.

I wish I was above all the hype. But in a town like Cape Fear, living that close to shimmering star power, when I saw Morgana or Clarice or even Bobby Keene-Parker in the flesh, squeezing oranges at the Harris Teeter or seated at a movie two rows behind me? It seemed like more than this town deserved, a permanent backstage pass. I always felt on the verge of breakout fame myself, and that's exactly the type of hunger that can turn you into a cannibal.

And I had the taste for it, bad. Like, when I think about the first home video I ever shot: eight years old, in the backyard with a setup on a tripod, and my dad's supposed to be watching me. I got it all worked out. I'm fixing to jump off the roof onto a trampoline, then bounce into our pool, get it all on tape, send it to *America's Funniest Videos,* and win ten thousand bucks.

Well, I hit the aluminum pool rim and broke my arm in two places. I edited out the part when I'm rolling around in agony, just so it would still be funny. *AFV* actually *did* run it, as part of one of those musical montages where they show twenty-nine other trampoline mishaps in thirty second. My *one second* of fame.

And no cash prize. Those only go to genius pets and slapstick babies.

Sorry, I took a few detours there. Let me wind us back to the starting point.

So, time's ticking, and finally Connie stumbled back out of his house looking dazed. The humidity was already making his glasses slip down his nose. "Ready?" he said, like *I* was the hold-up. For an answer, I slapped a rolled stack of printed pages to his chest. Three-hole punched, clasped with two brads. Connie grabbed it, gulping melodramatically.

The pages were my original short movie script, a dialog sketch with just two actors. My big Broadcasting class project. Connie was going to play a fictional guy planning to triumphantly pull off the same motorcycle stunt that killed his daredevil father. The scenario

8

goes like this: he's having lunch one last time with his female friend since Kindergarten, he's desperate to tell her that he's in love with her, that he's doing the jump for her, because it might be his last chance to spill his guts, but she's too wrapped up in her college scholarship prospects to notice his inner crisis—you get the idea.

This video project was the only school assignment that got me pumped, made me wish I could fast-forward through the day and get the camera rolling. It was going to be my contest entry for the internship at Silver Screen Studios, my *future*.

"Your lines are all highlighted in green," I told Connie.

"We're really going to go through with this?" he said, leafing through the pages. His brown and white bowling shirt would have to settle for his costume, since there was neither time nor budget for a change.

"Right after school. I got permission to shoot at The Silver Bullet and everything."

"Shoot what bullet?" he asked.

"The *diner*, the one called The Silver Bullet," I said. We'd been talking about it for weeks.

I knew what Connie was doing. He was just hoping if he pretended the planning never happened, the inevitable would just disappear. But I wasn't about to back down. Yeah, I admit my dead-dad-daredevil storyline cut a little too close to Connie's real-life tragedy. But all that was off-camera, since I didn't have the budget or know-how to record the actual motorcycle stunt anyway.

Really, the stunt-boy character was more me than him, or at least a mash-up of the two of us. Besides, acting out the part would be good for Connie, therapeutic. He'd already agreed in theory. I wrote this part for him, to *help* him, and he knew it.

"Just study your lines. You don't need to act. You just need to *be*."

"But who's going to do the other part, the girl?"

"Leave that up to me. This thing's in the can by sundown."

He wasn't really listening. Something else seemed to be on his mind. He shot a glance back toward his second-story bedroom window.

"You locked the front door, Connie, I promise."

"No, it's not that," he said. "More like—déjà vu. Like we did this before."

"It's just performance jitters," I assured him, and off we went.

8:30 Λ.M.

ΛT PORT CITУ Academy, morning bells clanged at 8:20 every day. Televised announcements went live at 8:25. On every monitor in every homeroom beamed the sweet, sweet smile of Savannah Lark, our in-house anchor girl.

Five minutes after Morning Broadcast started, ten minutes late for class, I showed up to Geek Central, the Media Lab. It was windowless, dimmed for taping, the only lights cast on Savannah at the news desk. She read from the monitor, luring volunteers for the Fundraising Committee's annual bake-off.

Mr. Yesterly, our media teacher, stood by the camera with his bulging earphones cockeyed on his head. He aimed two fingers at the kid cuing the pre-recorded tapes at the control deck. Sadly, the tape that ran alongside the sports highlights was a completely unrelated clip of volunteer seniors scooping poop at the Humane Society.

"*Crap*—tape *three*," Mr. Yesterly whispered hoarsely. "Tape *three*."

The control deck kid panicked. His fingers went all spidery, but he couldn't manage to actually press a button. So I slid in, tagged *stop*,

11

loaded the proper clip. Just like that.

Paige Davis, the five-foot junior videographer, was tiptoe on a stool as usual. She looked away from the viewfinder long enough to frown at me from under the rim of her baseball cap. She snapped a grape-sized gum bubble, then looked away.

Like Yesterly's screw up was *my* fault, somehow.

In a way I could see Paige's point. After all, I *was* the news director, the one who was supposed to be sitting in the empty canvas chair beside her. I earned my title fair and square. Problem was, if you were director, you were supposed to show up for the gig fifteen minutes *early*, minimum. Not five minutes late.

The daily news report was over after the newest installment of Vice Principal Skagg's thirty-second PSA series. This time it was Skagg's "friendly reminder" about time management and how it's a shame nobody wears wristwatches anymore.

After that, Savannah Lark signed off with a flip of her bangs.

Golden tresses, sharp arched eyebrows, and ripe pink lips that spoke every word of news like retelling a mind-blowing dream she had the night before. Girls like her could make smart guys do dumbass things.

Yeah, I know what you're thinking. I'm your typical sad sack, out of my league, pining after the homecoming queen. But Savannah wasn't that. She was on the modern dance team instead of the cheerleading squad, and she sewed her own clothes—fabrics culled from secondhand drapes and upholstery. I even heard a rumor she read books, *for entertainment.*

Plus she had a legit talent agent who landed her a national zit cream commercial when she was only fourteen—and, even crazier, nobody at school made fun of her about it. Last season, she did a walk-on role in *Cape Twilight Blues*, Joe Malone's squeeze-of-the-week. Her only line was, "I love it when you diss her like that, Joey Baby."

She was already holding her proverbial one-way ticket to Hollywood. And I was gunning to reserve the seat beside her, all too eager. I was going to be her muse, even if she didn't know it yet. Heck, I even hammered out my own original episode of *Cape Twilight* just to see if I could write outside my comfort zone. I write a lot of things, but this one was a spec script, which means some nobody dude like me types up a plot for free, hoping it'll help me break into the business someday.

The script was only to see if I could build a sturdy plot, maybe impress Savannah. I outlined it for weeks, rushed a draft in a few days. Seriously, once you've got the story, the lame-ass dialog just writes itself. The script was mostly a joke. I made two copies, gave one to Connie and put the other in a drawer, then flaked on the follow-through revisions.

"Lights," somebody barked. Even though the spotlight darkened, I could swear Savannah still glowed for a few seconds longer.

I sucked up my nerves and headed her way.

She stood up and started unbuttoning her blouse. Don't get excited: the blouse was a costume for the news broadcast, but when she slipped it off her shoulders, man, even though I knew her regular striped V-neck tee was underneath, I couldn't help but stumble over the snake pit of wires and cords in my path.

Luckily, being three or four notches below a girl like Savannah, I didn't have to fret about how I was coming off. I could trip over myself, almost do a face-plant, and it would be no biggie.

That was the advantage I had over all the jocks and slick pretty boys. *Nobody* at Port City Academy had the gall to step up to Savannah Lark but me. It was part of my job description. I was the behind-the-scenes guy, the wind beneath her wings, so to speak.

"Great show, Savannah. Your timing was impeccable," I said. "Hey, I've been meaning to ask, you know the Young Auteur competition Mr. Yesterly's been talking about the last couple months?"

"Sure, the short film contest," she said, hooking her purse strap over her shoulder.

"I've been working on a script," I explained. "I really think I got something special. I'd love you to read it, obviously with an eye on the female lead. It's something juicy that you could definitely put on your demo reel. Seriously get noticed if you put the right spin on it, you know?"

She had her phone in both hands, thumbing through text messages.

"You could get it done in like a matter of hours," I said, urging her copy of the script toward her. All her lines were highlighted in pink. "I've broken down the shots so you wouldn't even have to memorize the script all at once."

"'Take the Leap?'" she asked, reading the title aloud.

"It's just a place-holder title right now. We'd shoot this afternoon."

"*This* afternoon?"

"Total short notice, but I had to be sure every line sung. You'll see."

"But I thought the submission deadline was today," she said.

"Monday afternoon. I'll edit it this weekend."

She smiled like you do at a kid who's done a totally obvious magic trick. "I appreciate this, Russ. I'll have to see how my day goes from here…"

"We're going to shoot at the Silver Bullet diner. You wouldn't even have to change what you're wearing. You'd be so perfect, Savannah, I really can't imagine anyone else for the role."

"Tell you what," she said. "Give me your number, and I'll text you before school's over if I'm good to go."

Score. I mean, tentative score. Conditionally, if all went according to plan. But, *score.*

She pressed the digits into her touchscreen while I recited them.

Her mixed berry-scented perfume smelled of sweet promise. That

14

afternoon, I'd capture her starlight on digital video. I'd win myself a summer internship behind the gates of Silver Screen Studios, and spend the next three months proving my creative genius to the big wigs.

I didn't want to plan any further than that, limit my options.

I got a little distracted watching Savannah walk away, so Paige Davis had to punch my shoulder to get my attention. Then she had to hike up her chin to see me over the brim of her 2011 pink ribbon 5K walk-a-thon baseball cap.

She said, "I thought the director was the one who did the *don't text me, I'll text you* routine, not the other way around."

"You're a walking spycam," I said.

She plucked Savannah's wireless mic from the desktop and showed it to me. "Guilty. I recorded the whole thing, so y'all could keep it as a memento of whatever."

"You *recorded* our conversation?"

"You mean your monologue?" Paige asked. "No, I didn't. I was kidding."

"You watch. She'll fall in love with the script. She'll do the shoot."

"I'm positive you're right," Paige said. Sarcasm so light you could never call her out on it. It went like this with Paige and me. Years ago we were on the same community little league team. Then, after I enrolled at Port City Academy, we wound up together in just about every extracurricular club. *Friends* was maybe too strong a word, but we crossed paths and partnered up for projects more times than I could count. She was like a yappy little dog—too cute and predictable to really annoy me much.

Truth is, I looked forward to our bickering. Paige's quips kept me honest. I loved to see her trying so hard to win against me in everything, even if she succeeded more than half the time. Most kids at Port City Academy weren't worth her scathing critiques, is what I told myself. Noble adversaries made your wins more delicious and

15

seasoned your losses with just the right bitter flavor.

There was also the other reason you couldn't really dislike Paige. Like Connie, she was a survivor of Cape Fear's dark dragging undertow. Two years back, her older brother killed himself just before his high school graduation. Pills. It wasn't anything she talked about, but everybody knew.

I remembered her brother at our baseball games, cheering her on from the bleachers. A knee injury kept him out of varsity so Paige was his backup plan. I didn't hear the news until summer was over, until the gossip and funeral and the earliest stages of grief had already passed.

At school, Paige came back with a vengeance, like his suicide was totally wiped from her memory. She *seemed* the same, not post-traumatic neurotic. Maybe even *more* focused than before, but there was this cloud in her life, this thing that was her identity—The Girl Whose Brother Killed Himself—even if she totally rejected that label with everything she did.

But you can't catch a person's pain from just brushing against her in a crowd. Most people in our class, even the teachers, handled Paige like her latent family illness could relapse with the slightest exposure, like one unkind word could kill her. Only a few of us knew she needed worthy frenemies to thrive.

Paige's dead brother, Conrad's dead dad. I didn't know exactly why I got caught up with these tragic family histories. Maybe because I'd gotten mostly a free ride in life and I felt the pang of privilege. Or maybe I wanted to appreciate their pain because it could help the intensity and authenticity of my scriptwriting, and of living life in general. It helped me prep for whatever twists might come my way.

Isn't that what great art is? A test drive for living? Play it out till you get it right? And if I managed to catch a clean stretch of truth, my movies could help somebody's suffering. Maybe even my friends'.

I don't know.

"I need to ask a big favor, Paige," I said.

"You want me to run camera for you this afternoon," she guessed.

"I'd like you to be my *cinematographer*, yes."

"Ooooh, fancy. *I'll have to see how my day goes from here.*"

"Very funny."

"She didn't even trade you her number, dude. That's a bad sign."

"I'll call you if she sets a time. *When* she sets a time."

"That's the spirit," she said, smacking my arm again. "Oh, and by the way, Savannah was right."

"About what?" I asked.

With her *gotcha* grin, Paige delivered the news: "The deadline for the film project *is* today, Hitchcock."

Today. I got the stupid deadline wrong, even after hearing it from Savannah's own lips three times a week during the morning broadcasts. I thought it was on Monday. I even wrote it wrong on my mom's kitchen white board. You get a date fixed, you just can't shake it. The perfect scheme starts to topple, and I'm scrambling to get a hold of it, thinking *this* is the worst of what could possibly go wrong.

I had to plead my case with Mr. Yesterly. His office was only a few steps away, a fish-bowl cubicle inside the media studio. Just as I came in, he dribbled hot tea from a mug onto his hand and hissed at the pain.

"Guess I won't be drinking that for a while," he said. He uncapped a bottle of aspirin with his thumb and tossed a few in his mouth.

"You all right, Mr. Yes?"

"Under the weather." He rubbed his left shoulder and scrunched his face.

"You shouldn't pump iron so much."

"Ha—that'll be the day."

George Yesterly was a nice enough guy, but it was crazy to think he used to be actual on-air broadcasting talent back in his prime. He did time at WCPF, the local NBC affiliate, then got promoted to Atlanta and spent three years doing roaming street reportage there. But then, for whatever reason, he jumped ship and came back to Cape Fear to teach.

Nervous breakdown was the rumor.

Even more bizarre was knowing this chubby dude with the fishing vest and the low-tide hairline grew up with my mom. *Asked her to the prom*, in fact, although she turned him down. Awkward. Sort of a stalker scenario before there was a word for it. Hang-up phone calls, freaky anonymous love poems slipped into her locker, way back in the day.

Mom could laugh about it now, seeing Yesterly's name on my report card. Not that he ever once let on that he knew I was her kid, even though he *had to* know, and I bet the dude still carried the torch for Madeline Belmont. I figured maybe he'd even cut me some slack, considering.

Use whatever advantages you've got, as Mom herself would say.

"I wanted to ask you about the deadline on the Young Auteurs project," I said. "For some reason I had it in my head that it was Monday. I'm just finishing up the final edits on the footage…"

Yesterly flashed his crossing-guard *stop* hand. "I can't, Russ. It's for your own good, and I'm sure you'll agree if you reflect on it. Firm deadlines are an indispensable part of this profession."

"Honestly, Mr. Yes? I don't want to be a news director. I want to do movies, and I truly believe this internship with Silver Screens is going to put me right where I need to be."

"Well, you haven't won it, yet," he warned. "You've got to put *yourself* where you need to be. And please understand, this morning was your third tardy. If you're late once more, I'm going to be forced to transfer your director status to another student I can trust to get the job done."

He didn't need to say who he meant. A certain snarky redhead who just *loved* to win.

"I'll be on time from now on," I promised. "Twenty minutes early."

"I'm glad to hear it. Get yourself organized, and you'll be unstoppable."

"But about the film competition?" Thirty seconds to plead my case before the first period bell rang. I didn't want to have to mention the distant past: Yesterly's own junior year, when he stole my mother's beach towel while she was taking a dip in the ocean. Allegedly. Going over those reruns would be awkward for both of us.

"Aw, Russ—" he groaned.

"Please, Mr. Yes, hear me out. I wasn't sure if you set the deadline yourself, to provide like a buffer, or if it was studio-imposed, because if there's any wiggle room at all, first thing Monday morning, or, if you want, I could even bring it around your house this weekend."

"I'm sorry, Russ. The deadline is four-thirty. That's when I'm leaving with the entries I have. There are other area high schools, and all of them are adhering to the deadline. I've got my own responsibilities to uphold."

He *did* look genuinely sick to his stomach about it. The poor guy knew I was a shoe-in.

"If I brought it by the studio myself, on Monday, do you think they'd—"

The bell cut me off, time up.

"See, this is what I'm talking about, Russ," he said. "You can't go calling in favors all the time. You've got the talent. You've got the ambition. I'm sorry to have to be straight with you."

I put my face in my hands and said, "I get it. No favoritism."

"I'm glad," he said, wincing a little. "I know you'll learn from this for next time."

"Mr. Yes?" I asked, showing him my best tortured, defeated look. "Could I have a tardy slip? I'm late for math."

1:00 P.M.

TIME WAS NEVER on my side. All the work I did convincing Savannah, corralling Conrad and Paige for this film shoot of mine? It didn't mean squat now. If I had a way to contact Savannah, I'd have called the whole deal off. But our line of communication ran in only one direction.

So instead, every chance I got, I checked my cell for a text from her.

Those chances were few, since most teachers had a phone confiscation policy. The phone had to stay in my locker until lunch break, and all I did was think about getting back to it. Hooked on the hope of that little blinking signal: *new message*.

All through lunch I kept the cell on the table, right by my hand. Across from me, Conrad couldn't start eating till all his green beans were leveled flat in one compartment of his divider tray. His conversation fixation this week was interplanetary colonization, and he was asking me, "So would you do it? Would you volunteer to take the interstellar *Mayflower* to a habitable planet?"

I played along. "Sounds like fun. Why not?"

"Because it'll take *light years*. You'd live the rest of your life on a spaceship, and so would your kids. It would take, like *ten generations* to get there. By then you'd be ancient history."

"Does the ship have a movie theater? Would Savannah be there, because making ancestors with her…"

Conrad frowned at his lunch tray. "This isn't about girls and movies," he said.

"You're only thinking about this because of that stupid *Uncharted Cosmos* show. Your zero-gravity sex dreams with that Manic Pixie Dream Girl in space spandex. You know, I think you're actually happy my video shoot fell through."

"No," he said. "I wanted to see you win the internship."

"Did you even read the script?"

He nodded inconclusively, and then went back to his musing. "Warp speed isn't so much moving as it is shrinking space," he said, slowly crushing his empty milk carton as if to demonstrate. I wasn't even sure he was talking to me.

Sometimes he'd fall into these hypnotic states. He'd answer your questions, but only on autopilot. I was used to this behavior from my dad, who did what he called *thought experiments* for a living, at least before he got canned. Government contract stuff, supposedly. Maybe even military.

Connie was on Dad's wavelength. He liked to think my dad secretly knew the status of every nuclear warhead in China and could safely wrangle us all into an underground bunker while the world above was blasted to ash and permanent shadows. Seriously doubtful. Connie probably wanted to think of my father as heroic like his was, but Kasper Vale only worked in his slippers, gawking at the harmless glow of his computer monitor.

"Savannah's probably not even going to call," I said. "You're off the hook."

"I would've done your video shoot," Connie said.

"Maybe it's time to revisit the radio tower idea I had?"

Connie grabbed the edges of the lunch table. "No freaking way," he said.

Just the thought of heights could set him off, even if he wasn't the one in danger. My first video brainstorm before I came up with the diner scene was to climb the WCPF radio tower down by the river, all the way to the top, recording the whole event on a camera mounted to a bike helmet I'd be wearing.

Why? I don't know. It was the next logical step in a series of stunts that started with the *AFV* trampoline thing, a chance to redeem myself, even if it was more of a performance art piece than a *story*. But Connie vetoed the idea every time I mentioned it. Listening to him moan about the iffy legality and the threat of death took almost all the thrill away.

There was a reason my parents loved me hanging around with him. He was the nagging good angel on my shoulder, drowning out the little devil that had my other ear.

"Wait," I said. "You want me to strap into a warp-speed space ship and risk getting my molecules ripped apart, but climbing up the side of a radio tower is too risky?"

"I was talking theoretically. You're actually..."

Just then, there was a buzz on the tabletop and his eyes darted toward my cell. On the touchscreen was the graphic of the dancing envelope, opening and shutting.

And that promising (1), written in bold, arresting, unopened-message blue font.

It was exactly one in the afternoon, an hour till the end of school. Eager, I clicked the message icon. The sender's phone number was *unknown*, but there it was, an eyeful of bittersweet:

ok 2:30 slvr bullet gr8 script! —sl

Sweet Savannah was in for the video shoot, now that I was going to miss the contest deadline. Didn't matter. The neon marquee lights went bright in my head anyway. At that moment it suddenly didn't matter whether my movie ever got screened. With Savannah as my star, I was going to make this movie happen, no matter what. The Silver Screen internship could go to some other hack for all I cared. I was free, gonzo, original. Independent. I'd find my own path to success with Savannah Lark as my beacon.

"She's in!" I said. "2:30 at the Silver Bullet diner."

Connie dropped his fork.

"Don't flake on me here, Connie. *She's in.* Savannah."

"What about your cinematographer?"

I was already on my feet. "Where's Paige this period?"

"How should I know?"

"Because you memorize everybody's schedule for some weird reason."

"Fine," he said. "Gym class."

Before I left, I tousled his hair and said, "Eat your peas, young man. You look greener than they do." A little reassurance. Acting in my video project was going to be great therapy for him. It was the least I could do. Having my own personal Jiminy Cricket talking me down from ledges was nice and all, but the cricket had to cut loose a bit himself. Balance in all things.

Off I went to find Paige. She was the best digital video stylist at Port City—probably *any* school in the area—and I needed to secure her services. Even it if meant risking detention to sneak outside to the track.

When I got out there, her class was running laps. I climbed the vertical cross-beams on the back end of a set of bleachers overlooking the track. Never mind the normal route. If there was something to climb, I was on it. Getting a bird's-eye view wasn't worth it without the burning muscles and adrenaline rush.

Turns out Paige was already done with her jog, pacing in the grass nearby, gasping for air. Weird to see her in shorts, her pale freckled legs. Trust me, this girl was usually all about figure-blurring long and baggy cargo pants.

So here's the deal with Paige Davis and me. Back in little league, we were the two top pitchers for the Ghering Chemicals-sponsored team. My mother, who happened to be the Southeast Regional Assistant Director at Ghering, coached us into the county playoffs.

Last game, down to the wire, Paige on the mound. The Firecracker, they called her. She lit the fuse and the cracker popped hard when it struck the catcher's mitt. But late in the game she got winded and allowed too many hits. So Mom put me in. I was good. I was all about The Game back then. Daily pro stats in the newspaper. Baseball cards filed away alphabetically in binders.

Because my parents went to college in Boston (MIT), I was a Red Sox fanatic, and my prize card was a Curt Schilling. 2004: the year Curt helped pitch away The Yankee Curse and finally win the World Series, all with a torn ankle tendon bleeding his white sock red. I kept the Curt card under my hat for good luck. It was sweat-soggy and stank of hair, but whatever.

My first fastball took flight, and a half second later, some bruiser from Market Auto Body grand-slammed it through the windshield of a Cherokee in the parking lot.

So, yeah, we lost. In the dugout, I crumpled the stupid Curt card and tossed it in the trash. Nobody would talk to me. Almost nobody. Paige sat down, punched me in the shoulder, and said, "Cheer up, Charlie. They woulda lost if I didn't load the bases."

I probably shouldn't have said "you're right," but I did.

So now, before I could scramble down the bleachers the regular way to talk to Paige, some tall chick in a tennis skirt came cat-walking off the track toward her. One of those girls who always looked like she just sniffed a fart and was eager to lay blame.

The girl said something to Paige. Whatever it was made Paige hike her shoulders and suck in her breath. I froze in place, close enough now to hear what they were talking about.

"I'm just saying, you're fast, like the boys," Tennis Skirt said, hitching her hip. "I didn't mean to call y'all out or nothing."

Paige folded her arms across her chest. "What do you mean, *call me out*?"

Just then, Tennis Skirt's male minion trotted up behind her. You know this dude: the one who's always adjusting his cup, even when he's not wearing one? He had bleach blond hair, buzzed on the sides, spiked on top. A classic style I liked to call *The Asshat*.

Asshat toed Tennis Skirt in the back of her knee to get her attention. She swore and swatted him, but he just laughed and said, "I let you get half a lap ahead of me and here you are flirting with some other guy?"

He nodded at Paige to show who he meant.

They found themselves hilarious. Paige stood her ground, silent, taking it.

"I heard y'all hang out with homeless chicks downtown," Tennis Skirt said to Paige.

"I volunteer at a women's shelter if that's what you mean," Paige said.

Asshat grinned, tongue jabbing his inner cheek. He said, "That's pretty kinky, dude."

Paige didn't respond, which freaked me out. Never had I ever hurled an insult at Paige that she didn't fling straight back at me. So to see her helpless, it was disorienting. I could suddenly feel the rotation of the earth.

I stepped onto the bottom bench of the aluminum bleachers. My shoes made a dramatic laser-gun echo. Asshat took notice of me and announced, "Look at that, it's the gay and lesbian alliance."

"Hate speech?" I asked him. "Seriously?"

Asshat's biceps pulsed left/right, left/right.

Coach Belk was nowhere around, I noticed. She was notorious for random smoke breaks, and this was conveniently one of those times. We'd have to fend for ourselves.

"Got a problem, Vale?" Asshat asked me.

"Your whole shtick is tired. A good insult's got to be clever."

"Russ," Paige growled, somehow behind me now. Without even really realizing, I'd jumped down off the bleachers and nearly chested up to the Asshat.

"So y'all admit you and her are gay together?" he said.

Strike one, Chief. Even Tennis Skirt rolled her eyes at that lame crack. I could see it, how the realization of his own lameness cranked through Asshat's head like a penny through a boardwalk coin-press machine.

Noting that my forehead didn't quite clear the height of his chin, I said, "I'm not going to dignify your prejudices, son. You shouldn't judge and you can't change a person, so what's your motivation?"

Asshat took hard breaths through his nostrils. Half the class was through with the mile run and was now converging around our late-breaking event. A few had their phones out, ready to snap mementos for instant upload.

Glancing back, I found myself alone against the enemy. Paige was storming off toward the school, already halfway gone. So much for her support.

When I turned back to Asshat, I saw instead a beautifully composed close-up shot of knuckles. It was Asshat's fist, barreling at my face. Flash bulbs burst all at once, and the fresh-mowed grass tasted just like sprout-and-hummus wraps.

1:50 P.M.

ONE PUNCH FROM Asshat, and I'm snoozing for a good thirty seconds. A while after the "fight," I found myself alone in a Port City Academy administrative conference room full of fake potted plants. I leaned back with an ice pack patched over my throbbing left eye socket, waiting for the verdict.

The clock made its ascent toward two p.m.

My cell phone jolted with a text. Four characters from Paige Davis: *WTF?*

I thumbed out a response: *did I win ur favor?*

ur an idiot

still need your mad camera skillz! I sent.

Radio silence from Paige after that.

The conference room door eased open with a light-knuckle tap. I was expecting the vice principal, but it was Dad instead. Kasper Vale, escaped from his attic habitat, in sweat pants and a flannel, nursing a travel mug from an Azalea Festival ten years ago. His eyes were a little blinky from the unexpected run-in with natural sunlight. Mom

28

was usually the contact parent for my fiascoes, but she had a drug company to manage. With no job, it appeared Dad would be pinch-hitting today.

"How you holding up?" he asked me.

"I didn't know they were going to call you in."

"You're supposed to say, 'You should see the other guy.'"

"The other guy is subhuman, and I didn't hit him," I said. Had to make my innocence known right away, since my track record liked to testify against me. In my defense, I'd been red flag free for over a year. My last and only misstep at Port City Academy was that terrible prank on Connie before we were friends.

Vice Principal Skaggs came in and slapped a file folder onto the table top: *Vale, Horace* written on the tab.

My rap sheet, thick enough to include my riotous days in public school, i.e. my freshman-year misdemeanor arrest for breaking into the high school's sports equipment shed, stealing the alligator mascot costume and hanging it by its legs, bungee-style, from the nearby pedestrian bridge that arched over Market Street. This was sadly a step down from my original plan to get dressed in the costume and dangle *myself* from the bridge. In the moment of truth, I couldn't bet my life on my knot-tying skills after only a two-week stint in Boy Scouts.

I had two accomplices, dipshits I didn't associate with anymore. One of them brought the video recording to the police and set loose the process that landed me in private school. I'm sure all the sordid details were available in Skaggs' file, indicting me before I could even get a fair hearing.

After the necessary handshake, Skaggs gave Dad his best Crest-whitened smile and said, "I believe Mrs. Vale will be joining us in a moment?"

"She will?" Dad and I said, tensing up, in unison.

As Skaggs predicted, Mom blustered in. She shouted, "gotta go," into her cell phone and thumbed away the call. Whipped her attention straight at me. Her busy hands tried to decide whether they'd throttle my neck or pet my head. "Let me see it," she demanded.

When I showed her my eye, she hissed and shook her head. Finally Mom noticed her husband slouching in the corner. She said, "Kasper," like he really was a friendly ghost.

He raised his plastic mug to salute her. "I didn't think you'd be able to get away from work."

Because Mom was top brass for a leading manufacturer of FDA-approved chemical mood-enhancers, dysfunction-solvers and ache/pain-reducers. A six-figure shyster, a *drug dealer*, but I learned to treat her career with a little cognitive dissonance. After all, her salary bought the most innovative, hands-on, private education a short attention span like mine could appreciate.

The wall clock read 2:05 p.m. It would take at least fifteen minutes to get down to the Silver Bullet diner and keep my hard-won videotaping appointment with Savannah Lark. Ten minutes to wrap up this parent conference.

"My son was obviously not the aggressor here," Mom was saying.

"We've found it incredibly difficult to get to the truth in situations like this," Skaggs explained. "So we've adopted a Zero Tolerance policy on bullying and violence."

Mom's phone rang, but she shoved her hand into her purse and silenced it. "So let me get this straight," she said. "A kid can walk up to another kid in this school and sucker punch him—*which is what happened*—and the *victim* gets punished? What sense does that make?"

"Madeline, we don't need to get angry here," Dad cautioned.

The glare she gave Dad was about as cold as my ice pack.

"I'm just saying," Dad suggested. "Maybe if we brought the boys together and had them apologize to each other?" It was the same solution Dad offered the first time I got in trouble with Skaggs—

30

shake hands and make up. But that time the truce was with Connie, who turned out to be my perfect counterweight. That was different. Guaranteed no *way* I'd have a change of heart and find myself buddying-up with Asshat.

"I'm unconvinced that you could charge tuition and enforce a suspension simultaneously. I'd hate to involve legal counsel to work it out," Mom told Skaggs.

So much for a ten-minute resolution. To distract myself from the countdown, I zoned on a view through the office window—the steel Cape Fear Memorial Bridge stretching over the river with its two vertical lift towers. There weren't many high places in my town, but this was one. My legs shuddered with the urge to climb one of those towers. My palms got moist. If only there was a zip-line from one to the other—a stunt to trip all the breakers in my nervous system. It wasn't a suicidal urge, and it wasn't fearlessness. It was the opposite of both, a siren call upward from the mundane ground, rising to where I could feel terrifyingly alive.

Two-thirty was when they finally wrapped it up, having decided jack squat except that I was partially at fault for antagonizing the zoo animals. Once again, I was facing expulsion or at least suspension: big skull-and-crossbones marks on any college app. It was like I hadn't cleaned up my act at all. I wanted to yell *objection!* I wanted Connie or Paige there to speak as character witnesses on my behalf.

As soon as the VP said, "Welp, that's it for now," I scrammed, left the liquefied ice pack at the main desk.

My shoes squealed on the hallway floor. I was in the clear, but just as I rushed past the drinking fountain, someone lurched out of the men's room, straight into my path. I saw the fishing vest first, then my broadcasting teacher George Yesterly's panicked eyes.

We collided, and each of us took a seat on the floor. His fall was less graceful than mine. Poor Yesterly, with his chalky skin and body heat, looked worse than Paige's gym class after their mile run on the track. I suddenly wanted a shower to wash away whatever might be catching.

"Oh, man, I'm sorry, Mr. Yes," I said.

"No, Russ, no—it's fine. I wasn't looking where..." His voice trailed off. Something over my shoulder had grabbed his attention.

Mom's shoe heels clapped up behind me, and Yesterly watched her approach with a dumbstruck slow blink. I felt bad for him—this chance run-in with The One That Got Away, just as he was dying from the plague.

"Horace, really," Mom scolded me. With both hands, she hoisted Yesterly up by the elbow, even though he outweighed her by a hundred pounds, easy. She had no idea who he was.

"Madeline..." Yesterly said.

Mom cocked her head, took a step back from the frumpy dude she just rescued. Then it registered for her. "George?" she said. She almost put her hand over her mouth.

Yesterly leaned against the wall to stop himself from falling again. When Dad and VP Skaggs arrived on the scene, Skaggs squeezed in to assess damages. "Are you all right, Mr. Yesterly? Any injuries?" he asked, apparently eager for something else to pin on me—assaulting a faculty member.

Yesterly shook his head. "No—no—that was completely my fault. I'm, uh, I've go this blood sugar issue. Damn thing has gotten the best of me today. I'll be fine if I just get something, something sweet..."

"Oh, dear. Let's get you some Pepsi and send you home," Skaggs said, leading Yesterly away. As they departed, Skaggs said to my parents, "We'll be in touch very soon, get this whole business worked out."

Mom gave a tight little noncommittal nod. For the first time in forever she seemed at a loss for actual words. Then I realized why. Misty watercolor memories of George Yesterly, the creepy kid who used to follow her home from school.

A sudden plan blurted from my mouth. "Mr. Yes—what about the Young Auteurs project? The deadline?"

Yesterly looked back at me, haggard. Then he looked at my mother and there was the passing glimmer, the sad smile.

"I was going to bring you my finished entry by four-thirty," I explained. "Still got some last minute edits. But if you're going home early…"

"M-monday morning," Yesterly said. "First thing."

Score. *Use whatever advantages you've got.*

2:40 P.M.

BACK IN THE game, my victory was laid out before me. Except I was already ten minutes late and counting. Story of my life.

"In the best of all possible worlds…" Dad was saying, just as he slowed his car for a yellow light that he totally could've made. "You'd be lauded for sticking to your principles."

"*Green*, Dad," I said from the passenger side the instant the signal turned. With Dr. Kasper Vale, you gotta cut him off before he really gets going or next thing you know he'll find a parking spot and start in on a two-hour theoretical physics lecture. He could turn anything into numbers. If you didn't shut him down fast enough, he'd analyze all your lofty metaphysical notions about love and ambition into the analogous functioning of human neurological and artificial information systems. It's a wonder I even exist if this was his mating call with Mom.

When we finally reached Conrad's house, I hit the sidewalk before Dad even full-stopped on the street outside. I promised to be home before dark, then bounded up the porch steps, leaving Dad to

34

wax philosophic by himself.

I failed to spot Paige until she said, "Y'all're lucky I can predict your every move."

She was propping up a porch banister, half-hidden by overgrown shrubbery. Her Canon HD digital camera was in its carrying case, strapped across her chest.

"You're here!" I shouted. "Thank you, thank you, *thank you!*" Without her, I might've rushed down to the diner minus a camera, or a person to run it. Some brilliant short film *that* would've made.

"I decided to take pity on you," she said.

"Good, because I'm *this close* to getting expelled because of you."

"Because of me?" she said, curling her lip. "I didn't punch you."

"Might've been nice if you stuck around to explain what happened."

"Maybe," she said, and shrugged it off. "Looks like you tried on every shade of eyeliner at once. And don't you dare blame me for the black eye."

"That guy was a dick. Don't let people talk to you like that," I said. "It builds up and poisons you. Douchebags can't be allowed to make you feel ashamed of who you are."

That pitying smirk of hers again. "Thank you, Mr. Public Service Announcement. But you really don't get it at all."

"Get what?"

Connie eased open the screen door, tested the porch with the toe of his sneaker, then pulled it back inside. He quietly counted off to ten, one of his stress management techniques.

"Hate to rush order, Con," I said, "but we're already fifteen minutes late."

"I was beginning to think you weren't coming," he said.

"Sorry to disappoint, but we're doing this. You *owe* me."

Paige gave me the stink-eye for that remark, but it was true.

Why? Let's face it, Connie was my hundred-pound ball-and-chain. Half my day revolved around accommodating his issues. Take for instance the reason I couldn't have Dad drive us to the diner: Connie was deathly afraid of moving vehicles. He hadn't been inside one in more than a year.

"Don't blame me if my bad acting ruins the shoot," Connie said. When he finally came out, he was still lugging his overstuffed backpack. I didn't have time to argue about how much that extra weight would slow us down.

"You'll be spectacular," I assured him.

"I need to real quick make sure the fire alarm is working. If I don't check it now—"

"We gotta *go*," I pleaded. "Savannah will split if something better comes along."

"Class act, she is," Paige said.

My groveling didn't matter because Connie was gone from earshot already, deep inside his house.

"Crap," I said.

"He clearly doesn't want to do this," Paige advised.

"Yes he does."

"*Um*, no he doesn't."

"I know him better than you. Better than he knows himself, probably."

"Hmmm…" she said.

"What's *hmmm*?"

"Nothing. It's just you said something a minute ago about not making people feel ashamed of who they are."

I let her win the debate because there was no time to lose. A mad dash downtown would've been nice, but I settled for a power-walk, the fastest Connie could go, and Paige *would* go. Ten minutes later we were sweaty and passing fast along the riverside shops toward the Silver Bullet, an aluminum-sided dining car rounded off for aerodynamics. Not that it needed speed. It hadn't moved in decades.

Parked at the curb outside the diner was a Phantom Gray Aston Martin Rapide. James Bond's preferred ride, a price tag close to a quarter million dollars. Only a slick young television star would have the cash-'n-cojones to drive a car like that in a town like this. In fact, I knew from town gossip and *Entertainment Tonight* exactly whose it was.

"That's Bobby's car," I said.

"Bobby who?" Paige asked.

"Keene-Parker, from *Cape Twilight Blues*." He was one of the show's Big Six Heartthrobs and Hotties. Lately, he was scoring praise from the press because his character came out of the closet in a mid-season shocker. This, after having slept with all the female leads and many female guest stars, but shock value was apparently more important than character continuity on *Cape Twilight*.

Paige shrugged, immune to celebrity. "Selling that car could feed an entire African country for generations," she pointed out.

My worry was more immediate. I rushed inside the diner, half-a-freaking-hour-late. The booths were mostly empty, but Savannah sat in the back, close to the neon bubbling jukebox. She had a windowed backdrop of the USS North Carolina docked on the far side of the river. Perfect framing.

Except, just as I feared, someone else was in her booth. Some dude with expertly sculpted hair and that stomachache posture that so many cinematic *bad boys* liked to affect. Bobby Keene-Parker.

In a booth. At my diner. With Savannah. My Savannah.

I took a long breath. It was vital to be chill about big-name actors if I wanted to make movies, right? These guys weren't untouchable royalty. They were my tools, my raw materials. And, frankly, Bobby was a pretty dull tool. Everybody assumed he got his acting gigs passed to him on a platter because his father was Marv Parker, president of Silver Screen Studios and executive producer of *Cape Twilight*.

When I got close enough to take their dessert orders, Savannah

37

looked up and said "*Heeeey…*" all drawn out, like she hadn't expected me, or couldn't remember my name. If she noticed the black eye, she didn't let on.

Bobby was in the middle of talking about snorkeling in the Caribbean or something. He had the leftover crumbs of a burger and fries on his plate, while Savannah had an untouched house salad on hers.

"Savannah, y'all didn't tell me you invited Bob Parker to the shoot, *ha-ha*," I quipped, shoving out my unsteady hand for a shake with stardom. "Horace Vale, director."

Bobby gave me his signature squint.

"Savannah and I were just getting ready to shoot a scene," I said.

Behind me, Paige and Connie took a booth near the entrance, as far away from us as possible. I'd seen kids in my dentist's waiting room who looked more optimistic than Connie did.

"Sorry I'm late," I went on. "Trouble at school. A fight. Could get suspended. So, uh, I guess you know each other from Savannah's guest stint on the show?"

Bobby's squint got even tighter. The three strands of black hair dangling over his left eye did their trademarked twitch. He said, "No kidding? You were on *Cape*?"

"Season two, episode three," I answered for her. "Your birthday party?"

"I was just an extra, really," Savannah said. She took an adorable little puckered sip from her straw and rolled her eyes at herself.

"I thought I recognized you," Bobby said to her. "Something told me when y'all walked in here—*you know that girl. Go sit with her. So I did.*"

Savannah melted two full inches in her seat.

Bobby popped a cigarette between his lips, grinned, produced a flip-top lighter, and lit it. The lighter was embossed: *The Kindling*, in glowing fire-orange letters.

"Swag from your dad's old movie?" I pointed out, nodding at the tie-in product. *The Kindling* was Marv Parker's first production in Cape Fear, the pyrokinetic picture that started it all. Bobby Parker wasn't even born yet when it was made.

Just then, Sally the afternoon waitresses came out of the kitchen.

With a wink, she yelled to me, "Heya, sugar, y'all best get that movie goin' before the dinnertime crowd rolls in. Do I look glamorous enough for my cameo?" She propped her hair with her palm and laughed at herself.

"Perfect," I said.

Bobby raised his cigarette and said to Sally, "burger was great, as always."

"That's lovely, darling," Sally said. "Now put out that cancer stick."

"Sorry, ma'am," he said with only the slightest local drawl.

"We doing this, or what?" Paige said. She was at my shoulder suddenly, again, jiggling the little camera clutched in her hand. Her complete disinterest in Bobby Parker was a marvelous thing to behold.

Bobby slung his arm over the seat back and looked toward the exit behind him, gauging the efficiency of his escape route, no doubt. My window of opportunity was shutting fast.

I said, "Bobby—I hope you don't mind if I call you that—I wanted to say I've been watching *Cape Twilight* since day one, and I'm fascinated by how your acting took on a total 'nother layer of depth this season. You're a natural, obviously, but after last season's finale, you really blossomed…"

Bobby grabbed his *The Kindling* lighter and flicked it open and shut repeatedly, a scrape like sharpening a butcher knife. I could tell he was the type who loved soaking in compliments, but hated the time investment it took to listen to them.

I went on… "The coming-out-of-the-closet plot—you've seen it done before—but never quite so poignantly, especially in a teen drama with, you know, a fairly light touch. It takes tremendous bravery."

Savannah was struggling to keep her chipper facade. She was digging through her purse, possibly for pepper spray in case I was fixing to say something really stupid and needed to be stopped. I was big-time flubbing this monologue. The camera was not going to roll this afternoon, and Sally the waitress and I were the only ones who'd be disappointed.

"I ain't gay, you know," Bobby said.

"I wasn't—" I said. "I'm talking about your acting. The way you became the character at a level I've never..." Then I remembered why I brought up the show in the first place. "Hold on," I said.

Connie had something I needed. When I lunged for him, he flinched backward and planted his butt on one of the stools at the lunch counter. I grabbed him by both shoulders and forced him to look at me. "Connie, please tell me you brought a copy of that *Cape Twilight* spec script I gave you."

His eyes shuddered in their sockets. "I- I think so. Are we still shooting? Maybe you should ask that Bobby guy to play my part," he suggested.

A brilliant idea, *if* we were living in a fantasy where all my whims were instantly indulged. But in this reality, Bobby was slapping down some bills, sliding out of the booth. He'd be gone in another minute by the looks of it.

"Never mind my short film for a second," I said to Connie, through gritted teeth. "I'm talking about the *Cape Twilight* script. Do you have it?"

Connie slid his backpack onto the counter, unzipped it. He pushed both hands in the bag and rooted around with the slow precision of a surgeon in an open chest cavity.

Bobby was already swaggering toward us on his way to the exit. But then he paused, turned to Savannah, and asked, "So how bout that tour?"

Without hesitation, my leading lady poured herself out of the booth. She was going to leave with him. When she saw my anguish, she found it in her heart to explain. "We're just going to look around the sets at Silver Screens, me and Bobby. All my shoots were on location so I've never actually been on the lot before. Isn't this exciting?"

Bobby said to me, "Good to meet you, Mike. Good luck with it all."

I would've choked if Connie hadn't saved me. He found the prized script—a wrinkled mess of papers stained with soda can rings. I caught it in both hands.

"Something I… wanted… to show you," I explained, and offered the script over to Bobby. He didn't reach for it. He looked at the pages, then at me. Suddenly, my so-called genius move stank of desperate stalkerdom.

"What's that?" Bobby asked. "Another spec script?"

"I—uh—"

"Know how many of these I see in a week, Mike?"

"It's Russ."

"Whatever. I don't actually read these things, but the producers do. Every single one of them's got a sweet-ass storyline about my character earning acceptance for *who he is*. I'm sick of it. Want to guess why that gay plot twist crap ever got written into the show in the first place?"

"Social consciousness?" I ventured.

Bobby snorted. "*Because*," he said, "my fat fascist father thought it would be hilarious to humiliate me. Show the world I'd do anything for a buck."

"Being a huge TV star must be *incredibly* humbling," Paige said, mostly to herself.

Bobby's squint was so tight now I couldn't tell if his eyes were even open. *Clink clink* went the lighter in his hand. He yanked the script out of my grasp and took a passing glance at the cover page.

"TV can go to hell," he said. "You gotta spend half your time figuring out how to *say* this crap so you don't sound special-needs. Show me some razor-sharp dialog in an actual *film,* and I'll show y'all an Oscar nomination."

Then he discarded my script on the counter. He popped another cigarette into his mouth. One scrape of the lighter's starter wheel and an inch-long flame shot upward. I could hear the butane burning.

Of the many forces my best friend Connie feared in his life, close-range fire, especially the sizzling kind, was way up at the top of the list. I'd already pushed him to the point of hyperventilation. He was a slow gas leak, and here was the ignition. At the sight of Bobby's lighter flame, Connie squawked and keeled over fast.

Paige and I sprang for him, but he sagged down past our reach. He dropped to the floor, wedged between two stools, with his arms viced on either side of his head. When Paige knelt beside him, he hunched against her, one hundred and seventy pounds of dead weight.

"Lord almighty!" Sally called from across the counter. "I'm calling an ambulance."

"Well, it's been real," Bobby announced.

Who could blame him? Our meeting had escalated into an *incident,* something the gossip media could spin against him: *Bobby Keene-Parker threatens neurotic Cape Fear boy with lighter.* His best bet was to slip away and deny any knowledge. Even I knew that.

Bobby stepped over the odd pile of people on the floor. Savannah followed him, no big shocker. Her apologetic shrug wrung out my dishrag heart.

I watched the two of them get into the Aston Martin Rapide and speed off with a gut-punching engine roar. Her silken hair fluttered out the open passenger window like exit music before the fade to black.

3:20 P.M.

YOU KNOW THAT trick where a master magician yanks away the red tablecloth from under a fancy five-course meal, disturbing nothing? Well, I was an amateur. I had my Big Day on a silver platter, and I brought the whole damn thing crashing down.

The paramedics strapped Conrad to a gurney and carted him away.

All I wanted was to crack him out of his shell, give him something to boost his self-esteem, an acting gig that would dig down into his psyche. But I shoveled too deep. Worst of all, his nurse mother was on shift at New Hanover Hospital so she'd get the scoop the minute he rolled up. Given my contributions to Connie's nervous breakdown, this was possibly bad enough for a permanent friendship boycott on the likes of Horace Vale.

Paige stormed off with hardly a word and zero footage on her camera. Slouching home by myself, I wished so bad that she would've torn me a new one. Because a lecture on what I did to Connie would mean I was forgivable. Instead, I got Paige's silence. She was giving up on me—and this girl had a life mission to never give up on *anyone*, not even the tragic cases down at the women's shelter where she worked. People who'd trashed their lives, or had their lives trashed for them. Let's face it—everybody Paige met was a fresh chance for her to save her brother, in a sense.

Everybody now except me.

In all the chaos, Connie's backpack got left behind at the diner. I took it home for safe keeping, weighted with books and binders and lost friendships and ruined chances and humiliation by a TV star and a throbbing pain in half my face. Not to mention my flame for Savannah Lark, engulfed in the inferno of Bobby Parker's industrial strength lighter.

In my kitchen, on my mother's white board calendar, a thick red line ran straight through the middle two weeks of April. It was under my name, headed by the big block-letter word: SUSPENDED. The verdict was in. Suspended, splendid. All my efforts to recast Horace Vale as a hero were lost—same little shit I'd always been, as far as friends and family were concerned.

Upstairs in my room, I made a valiant effort *not* to look inside Connie's backpack. But then I did. Clusters of Dr. Who action figures, some Playstation games, folders full of homework and two massive novels by Neal Stephenson.

Then, I found my script. "Take The Leap," the movie I meant to shoot at the Silver Bullet. Connie had gone through it and written in the margins the carefully-considered motivation behind each of his character's lines. Notes about how to say a phrase, accent marks where he meant to emphasize words.

On one page he wrote: *like the last time I said goodbye to Dad at the airport, trying to memorize his face.* I couldn't take it. He'd been willing to use his personal pain for the sake of our dumb movie. His father, who did not die in a motorcycle stunt but even more nobly in a wartime helicopter crash. All of Connie's fears and anxieties rising up from that wreckage.

My own parents were alive and well somewhere in the house. Dad sat wasting away in the attic. He could fill me with facts but teach me nothing about life. He'd never ignored a *no trespassing* sign, never climbed past the safety rails. Mom was the one who tossed me out of the nest—literally, one summer, on a zip-line thirty feet over the canopy of a Costa Rican cloud forest. That green and hazy rush of fear stuck with me ever since, drove me to stupid acts that ruined my mother's trust. If she'd been warming back up to me during the last few months, the cold front had struck again.

So here I was: Dad unable and Mom unwilling.

There was nothing for me now. I wanted to go back to *before*, to kid memories that seemed just out of reach, like those weekends at the Pastime Playhouse theater with Dad. That early enchantment with the magic flicker on the screen.

So I left the house again without telling anyone. Walked down to Front Street, through the old cotton mill section along the river, restaurants and tourist shops now, a gentrified locale specially designed for *Cape Twilight Blues* and other shows to shoot their scenes.

In the midst of TV-land, I was a faceless, unnamed extra.

I came to my destination, an empty gap between two buildings— overgrown grass, broken bottles, and piles of rubble. A missing tooth in an otherwise pristine set of teeth. Five years ago a vintage movie house stood on this spot, the Pastime Playhouse, then burned to the ground.

Movie mogul Marv Parker (aka, Bobby-Daddy) bankrolled the place and kept it in business before it burned. The rumor mill speculated that after he started losing profits on the place, he torched this money pit himself for the insurance. You could still see the char on the walls of neighboring buildings.

Dad and I sometimes came here twice in a weekend, especially summers. This was before they installed the big multiplex farther up Market Street. We'd walk down to this theater, and all the discussions we had, anticipating and then critiquing—let's just say we didn't talk like that much anymore.

For a minute I stood where the ticket booth used to be and looked through the fake camera lens I made with my fingers. The empty lot worked as a perfect industrial wasteland backdrop, or a post-apocalyptic nightmare.

Then I turned and saw the radio tower beacon flash its steady red pulse high above the buildings, and I knew the real reason I trekked out to this part of town, and it was not my distant past. It was my immediate future, and Connie wasn't here to talk me down.

It was still daylight when I reached the headquarters of WCPF, Cape Fear's most popular network station, and Mr. Yes's former employer. The building was just a squat beige box beside the river, but for added flair, a nearby billboard supersized the grinning mugs of the news station's lead anchors and weatherman.

Their steel radio tower loomed three hundred feet tall, tapered at the top. Almost a scale model of the Eiffel Tower. Its upper reaches were fitted with satellite and radar dishes. Below, gray electric boxes with shock danger decals buzzed a constant warning to *keep away*.

For further security a chain-link fence surrounded the tower with razor wire coiled around the top like a badass Slinky. That obstacle might've meant *game over* if the gate were actually padlocked shut like it was supposed to be. But somebody had left the chain and padlock dangling from the fence.

I took out my cell phone, aimed the lens at myself and tapped *record*. "Scaling the WCPF radio tower, because it was there, first and only take. Action." All I had to do was lift the latch, push the gate, and I was in. Then I found the access ladder, and I started to climb.

6:55 P.M.

I CLUTCHED THE rungs of the radio tower high over the Cape Fear River. The red beacon blinked above, urging me to climb. The river below looked calm on the surface, but its undercurrent was known to swallow people stupid enough to take the plunge.

My attempted cell phone video recording was a flop. I needed two hands to climb so I held the phone between my lips, meaning I couldn't run commentary, and my mouth was going numb, and I was probably fogging up the lens with my breath. At least I'd get a good panoramic shot when I reached the top. I'd have my proof.

Anyone watching from the windows of nearby warehouses or apartment buildings could've spotted me. And if they wanted to stop me, they'd call the police or at least yell out. I was prepared for that. Cops gathering around the tower, begging me to climb down—it would make better footage than the climb itself.

Truth is, heights freaked me out, especially when nothing but my balance kept me from a fast and fatal drop. But that's exactly why I climbed, my knack for rushing blind into whatever scared me. It wasn't the ascent. It was the after party, the hours of delicious adrenaline and the conquering spirit I'd be filled with.

Connie would've stopped me but Connie wasn't here. The angel on my shoulder fluttered off. Finally I could hear my own will at work. I had to prove I could take the same crap I was always dishing out to Connie. Had to prove myself apart from everyone else. And if I got arrested, well, it would prove my point, wouldn't it? I was already on the tower that would transmit my news across the Carolinas. I wanted Savannah to hear all about it.

Four stories up, I saw the hazy green outline of the Cape Fear Bridge. So far away, I could make it vanish under my thumb, but when I tried, a wave of vertigo made my palms go slick with sweat. I had to keep wiping them on my jeans, one at a time. Another twenty feet and the winds kicked up. The cars in the lot below were die-cast toys. My jaw ached with the strain of holding that phone, and it was slippery with spit. I'd drop it any second.

When a gull landed on a beam just overhead, I tried to shoo him away. But he claimed his perch and twitched his head as if deciding exactly when he'd drop his milky white crap load.

I chanced another rung upward and the bird flew off.

Then, my cell buzzed in my mouth. It felt like my own shuddering nerves, until I realized what it was: a text message. Could be Savannah, apologizing for ditching me. Or Paige, apologizing for blaming me. But most likely it was Conrad, fishing for an apology.

Even as I thought *not now*, I still had to check, because *who knows? What if?* I hooked a rung by the crook of my elbow, dropped my slimy phone into my palm like a dog giving over a tennis ball. The fact that I'd somehow pressed stop on the recording only barely registered in my mind. Instead, I was focused on the animated envelope icon on the display. And below that, the sender's name: *Horace Vale.* Me.

Never before had I gotten a text from my own phone. I'd seen it happen with email, but always in some virus or spyware switcheroo. My anticipation sank. All that risk for nothing but some stupid piece of spam like *great work study opportunities for high school grads. $$$.*

But that's not what I got when I tapped the icon.

The text was just three words long:

Take the leap.

Somebody was screwing with my head. Had to be.

But that made no sense. No stranger would know my phone number, not to mention how to send a text using *my* ID. The only keyboard cowboys I knew were Conrad and my father. Neither of them had any clue where I was, and neither would callously encourage me to jump to my death. At least I hoped not.

Take the leap.

I kept reading the message. It had to be a coincidence, something like: *Take the leap into a new career with Tucson Online University!* Then it hit me that "Take the Leap" was the title of the short video about the motorcycle daredevil I'd been planning to shoot all day. I'd totally forgotten. Funny how fast priorities can evaporate.

There was a link attached. A gateway to more information.

Click the link, see what a spazz I was being. That's all I had to do. My thumb hovered over the screen. I told myself to resist because I could end up downloading a virus and kill my phone. But I knew what I'd find would be way worse than a virus.

So I did it. I pressed the link. The spiral dot signaled that the system was retrieving the information I sent for, probably using this very radio tower as a booster. The load time was only a couple seconds. What came through was a basic home video. Just a carefully framed headshot of a guy with a blank white wall behind him. The stark light and his darting eyes gave the recording the distinctive look of a hostage recording.

The video star took a hard swallow, faked a smile, and said, "Hi, Russ. It's Russ."

For those first few seconds, I really didn't recognize myself on the screen. Since I *knew* I never made this video, my brain refused to register that I was watching footage of Horace Vale. *Cannot compute.* Not until the *me* in the video actually introduced himself.

Me, down to the shirt I got for Christmas a few months ago.

Except *I did not make this video.* I would've remembered.

I flipped the phone over, looking for what? A false backing to show it was a gag prop? Then I realized Video Russ was talking, and I wasn't listening. I thumbed the volume to maximum, but the small tinny voice still fought to be heard above the wind.

"…to wrap your head around…" he was saying.

I put the phone to my ear "…very little time, so hear me out. You have to trust me—trust *yourself*. Right now, you have no real plans to off yourself, but what's going to happen when you get to the top of that tower? A dark feeling might hit you. We never know what kind of person we're going to be five minutes from now, Russ. Remember last summer, you almost sent that private message confessing your love to Savannah, then you erased it? One minute you're sure, the next, you're not."

Video Russ stared back at me. The dramatic pause, the cinematic *beat.*

"You just told me to take a leap!" I screamed at Video Russ.

The wind drowned him out again so I smacked the phone back against my ear. He was saying, "…a metaphorical leap, a leap of faith. I had to get your attention. The chance you're about to get will seem impossible, but you've seen enough to know I'm legit."

"Wait, hold on," I said, but this was not a two-way dialog. It was just a prerecorded Video Russ psyching me out, even though I never prerecorded anything like this. He knew what I would probably say in response to what he said because he *was* me.

"…at seven o'clock sharp. After one minute, the file will delete itself, and you'll lose your chance. You have to do this, Russ. Your one chance to make things right. This is the *real* leap. Take it."

"What the hell?" I muttered.

Just like that, the video clip was over. A drop-down list gave me options to watch the video again, delete, save, respond. When I considered the strange loop that last choice might set in motion, a fresh nausea washed over me.

My arm ached from hooking the rail for so long, but all my focus was on the *6:59 p.m.* flickering in the bottom right corner of the display. Any second, seven o'clock would hit, and then, according to me, in a video I didn't make, something else was coming. My one chance to make things right.

Seven p.m. The phone shuddered with the acceptance of another text.

After one minute, it will delete itself, and you'll lose your chance.

I didn't see how the video could've been faked. It was me, and I had to trust my own word, because why would I lead myself into a trap, knowingly? But also: I didn't remember making the video, and if I couldn't trust my own memory, I was screwed.

Like one of Dad's game theory scenarios, endlessly judging the probability of what the other guy would do when it was his turn to play. It drove me nuts. I couldn't do the calculations. So, thirty seconds into my countdown, I pressed the text icon.

The digital retrieval pinwheel spun again. There was no actual text with a link to follow or a file to download. It was a one-click maneuver. A logo came up: a clock with backwards-spinning hands and the words *The Pastime Project* in its center.

Then, my phone flashed a light so harsh, all my senses shorted out at once. My vision went white, my eardrums screamed, and every inch of my skin came alive with needle stings. I couldn't feel a thing past the pain.

For all I knew, I was already plunging to the ground.

DAY ONE
(TAKE TWO)

7:00

MY SENSES CAME back. I wasn't dead, wasn't falling, wasn't broken in a heap down below. Both my hands were locked around a rail, and I was still six stories above the earth.

"What the hell, Russ?" I asked aloud, but nobody answered.

Also, something was way wonky with my body. When the prickling faded from my skin, goose bumps sprang up in its place. The chill wind was a factor, but mostly I was cold because I was buck-naked.

I winced, sure my phone had set off a flash bomb that disintegrated my clothes and covered me in third degree burns. But there was no pain. No singed flesh. Just me, just as I usually looked when I toweled off after a shower.

Suddenly, getting caught on the radio tower didn't seem so badass. Outlaw Russ was one thing, but *Naked* Outlaw Russ was way more likely to land me on some permanent pervert list.

So, yeah. I scaled down the tower as fast as I could, hooking the rails with my bare toes. I never felt so exposed, commando on high. Any second, somebody could stop by and snap a photo. Every teenager's literal worst nightmare. And it wasn't like I had a free hand to self-censor my bits.

I dropped into a crouch on the gravelly ground. Pebbles stung my foot soles, but terra firma was sweet relief.

That is, until I realized I was still inside the security fence that boxed in the tower. No biggie, except the chain was wrapped around the gate latch, padlocked shut.

I was trapped.

I rattled the gate with one hand. The other was busy cupping my junk. The chain seemed to wrap even tighter. *Crap, crap, crap, crap.* I was no better off than a zoo animal here.

Scaling the fence wasn't an option. I got queasy just thinking about how that razor wire would greet my most sensitive areas. Hunting for a ground-level breach in the fence also got me nowhere. The chain links were taut as trampoline springs. As a last resort I might've screamed for help, but I couldn't bring myself to draw an audience.

Instead, somebody just showed up without an invitation. I didn't see the truck rumble into the parking lot, but I heard it well enough. I dropped low and pressed myself against an electrical box, hidden from view.

The truck door creaked open, then shut. Rattling keys, clanking chain. Whoever it was, was whistling a tuneless rendition of Taylor Swift's "You Belong With Me." I prayed that this surprise visitor did *not* already realize there was a naked dude nearby. He was an unsuspecting maintenance worker, I told myself. Nothing more.

He gained entry, boots crunching the gravel. I hunkered down as low as I could and tried to guess where he'd go so I could dart in the opposite direction. He grunted as he hoisted himself onto the tower rail. I squeezed my eyes shut and tried to will him away, but all I got for my wishing was the clap of boots on metal. Nowhere for me to hide. He was climbing the ladder, headed for a bird's eye view.

"*What the…*" he said, and that's when I booked it.

Dashed through the open gate, stumbled, scraped my knee on pavement. Found my awkward stride again after more stumbling steps. Didn't dare look back. I just knew he'd be hot on my trail, some track-star-turned-electrician, reaching out to headlock and drop me for a citizen's arrest.

I couldn't exactly make a stark-naked appearance on one of Cape Fear's busiest downtown roads, so I cut south through a stretch of warehouse back lots. Hunched and cupping myself, I couldn't run at peak speed, not while I also had to watch the ground for debris that might slice open my feet.

The sun's position in the sky, the dewiness still spritzing the air, the smell of fresh donuts from the bakery down the street… it all hit me like another disorienting flash.

Morning. It was morning.

The white light from my phone had somehow blacked me out for *hours.* Close to twelve hours. Except it wasn't possible. No way I could've hung unconscious from the tower all night long. Heck, I couldn't have lasted for even a second like that. I should've been a dead guy, a splat on the pavement.

I had to stop my mind-spin and catch my breath. The only choice was to hunker down behind a dumpster. There were probably more fragrant places to gasp for air, but with a few free seconds to think, I quelled the urge to puke and charted my next move.

Two loading docks down, I snagged cardboard from a recycling stack. Sirens down the street, likely meant for me, the Front Street Streaker. I cut across the main road at full trot, knees knocking the stiff toga I fashioned for myself.

Some jerk tapped his car horn at me, but I kept my head in the game. Another back lot, a narrow wooded park, and a cemetery where none of the residents gave a damn how I was dressed.

My last obstacle was a stretch of back yards—uneventful, until I came across a grandma in a housedress, hosing down her lawn. She screeched like I was a scurrying rat. Then she cranked the setting on her nozzle to biting cold Proton Stream and soaked my cardboard clothes into oatmealy goop before I was safely out of her range.

In another few minutes I was heaving for breath out behind Conrad's house. He had to be home from the hospital by now, and Connie's was the closest safe zone I could think of, even if a warm welcome was probably not in store for me. But I was brimming with ready apologies. Funny how a twelve-hour blackout and fifteen minutes of running naked through town could cripple my pride.

I had to talk this through with Connie. I had to count on his forgiveness, but then again I'd never pushed him so far as I did at the diner, at least not since the prank, before we were friends. Under normal conditions it'd take me at least another day to plan exactly how I'd redeem myself. Connie wasn't the type of dude where you could just tell him *chill out, I'm only screwing* and move on. Dealing with him was like constantly making the twentieth move in Jenga.

The trickier part was that his mom was probably also home, probably sewing together a voodoo doll of me so she could torture it in retribution for her son's trip to the hospital. So I decided to be discreet. I snuck around to the side yard and tossed pinecones at his bedroom window. Three tries before he peeked through his blinds at me.

Just as fast, he flicked them shut.

So that was it. After everything I did for him, not even the decency to hear me out. I snatched a rock the size of a golf ball and prepped for a pitch, but breaking glass wouldn't earn me any points. So I dropped the rock and trudged away, shivering. Maybe somewhere in this row of houses I could find a stocked clothesline to borrow from, even if it meant I'd have to dress in drag. Nobody's perfect.

"Russ, what the heck are you doing?" Connie asked from his back doorway. He stepped onto the wraparound porch, still in his bowling shirt from yesterday. Clean freaks like Connie usually didn't wear the same shirt twice before washing, but maybe he'd just been discharged from the hospital, hadn't even had a chance to change.

"I came to apologize," I told him.

"Apologize for what? And why are you wearing a box?"

"For trying to force you to do my movie…"

"You're not forcing me. It's something I have to do."

"Well, it's all in the past now. It's DOA."

Connie's glasses weren't exactly the right prescription so he had to tilt his head back to get a clearer angle. There I was—wet cardboard, teeth chattering. He said, "Uh, okay. You need to come inside?"

"Is your mother awake?"

"She's doing her shift at the hospital. Come on." He turned to head back inside, trusty backpack strapped to him as securely as a parachute, even though it was another hour before we were supposed to leave for school. The backpack was such a Connie fixture that the baffling fact of its being there on his shoulders didn't hit me until we were halfway up the stairs to his bedroom.

It should've been *at my house.* Where I left it.

"Where'd you get this?" I asked, tugging on a dangling nylon strap.

"Target, I think," he said.

"No, I mean—you left it at the Silver Bullet yesterday."

"Didn't go to the Silver Bullet yesterday."

"Jeez—you don't even remember?"

"Huh?" he said.

"Never mind." I didn't want to push too hard about his panic attack and all that, especially if it was so bad he blocked it from memory. Until fifteen minutes ago, I would've thought it was nuts to lose track of time like that.

In Connie's room the blinds were drawn, so the only real light was artificial. His TV airing the WCPF morning news, computer paused on *Dragon Rage 2*, iPad on the bed displaying one of his four alias Facebook profiles. And, of course, the glow-in-the-dark model universe spinning in constant battery-operated orbits along its ceiling tracks.

I grabbed a pair of jeans from the designated cubby and tugged them over my wet legs. When the fabric touched my scraped-up knee, I hissed from the pain. Connie was half a foot taller and a few inches thicker so I was basically in clown pants.

"How about *underwear*?" Connie said.

"Don't have any, and I'm not wearing yours," I told him.

"*Okay*," he said. "So what's going on? Why were you naked, and a half hour early—which you *never* are? What the crap happened to your eye? Did somebody hit you?" The heaviness of his own questions made him flop on the bed, pressing both hands against the sides of his skull.

"I told you already. And it's Saturday," I realized aloud. "No school."

"It's Friday. School," Connie said.

All right, at this point, I had to accept that a huge factor in this equation was missing or wrong, and my gut said it was *me*. Connie's digital clock said it was 7:20 a.m. Lost memory, strange texts and videos, twelve-hour blackouts, public nudity.

I said, "Listen, the freakiest thing happened last night."

"I'm going to go ahead and say it's *still* happening," Connie suggested.

I glanced through the window overlooking the street, unsure what to expect. Police raid? Prank show camera crew? I was the wacko in the spy flick who nobody believed, but whose paranoia *always* turned out to be totally justified.

"Just look at this video I got." I hunched over Connie's computer and minimized the dragon game, brought up Firefox so I could access the online records of my text messages.

Connie said, "Okay, but it's Friday. That's all I'm saying."

Also claiming it was Friday: the computer calendar and the super in the corner of the TV screen.

I entered my login and password. The listing of my texts came up, but the video I supposedly sent myself was deleted. The *take the leap* message was gone, too. So were all the Friday messages from Savannah and Paige and Connie, all the way back to a text from Connie I got on Thursday night, reminding me to set my wakeup alarm to stun.

Like Friday never happened.

"What video?" Connie asked over my shoulder.

"It's gone." And then I remembered what I said to myself in that recorded message—what Video Russ said to me, anyway, just before he sent that app, or whatever it was, the thing called The Pastime Project. He said:

Your one chance to make things right. This is the real leap…

The Pastime Project app had downloaded itself to my phone at seven p.m. Friday night. Judging from the current time, I had been out-of-order for twelve hours exactly. Half a day, but half a day in the *wrong direction*. A leap, like Daylight Saving Time, except it only happened to me.

I was going to have to say it out loud.

"Connie, man, I'm pretty sure I sent myself backwards in time."

7:35 A.M.

"NO WAY," CONNIE said.

"Yes way."

"Not possible."

"But…"

Connie was all about empirical evidence. The video message, twelve hours of skipped-over time, the mysterious traveling backpack, the Saturday-that-was-actually-Friday, the radio tower gate that was locked and then not locked. It took another fifteen minutes to even start to convince him, and he was the perfect uber-geek audience for an idea like this. Time travel via a mobile app.

This was one of those twisted physics scenarios he only ever dreamed of or discussed over endless threads on his sci-fi message boards. I suspected *he* suspected I was rolling out some elaborate Alternate Reality Game, and it was his job to play out my ridiculous scenario through all its logical bends, never once letting on that this was all a joke.

Otherwise, I'd have to accept that he actually *believed* me.

"Okay, let's withhold judgment on this," he told me. "But I have to say, there's an *elegance* to what you're describing," he said. "You don't even understand it. *That's* what makes it maybe kind of work."

"Right," I said. "Wait—what?"

He paced a small stretch of his room, cranked on his Deep Thoughts. His head bumped the dangling model planets and set them on cataclysmic orbits. "*If* something like this could really happen, then *of course* you'd get sent through the warp without any clothes because it could only reconstitute your biological material. Otherwise, you'd end up with fabric woven into your skin, and buttons where your eyes should be, like in *Revenge of the Replicons.*"

"Lovely," I said, feeling pukey again. My whole body suddenly itched.

"If you're making this up, you really thought it through. I'm impressed."

"It happened."

"Okay, *but:* the temporal wormhole, or whatever it was, that kind of tech is total fantasy. It's not logically possible. *Man*, I wish I could've seen that video," Connie said.

I was still working on the logistics myself, and admittedly getting nowhere. If it was really half-past-seven on Friday morning, then the video I watched wouldn't be sent to my phone for another eleven hours and change. It didn't *exist* yet, so there was obviously no way to access it.

"No, no—*wait!*" Connie said. "We're talking information paradox here."

"We are?"

"Info-dox, a time-travel impossibility. You act on information supplied by a future self, who learned the information from a future self, and so on and so on. An endless chain that has no beginning. The information has no actual source, you see?"

I thought about it for a second and realized that Arnold

Schwarzenegger could be used to explain everything. "So it's like how the severed metal arm off the terminator from the future provides the tech that the present-day engineers need to invent SkyNet, which invented the terminator, that went back in time and got its arm cut off."

"*Exactly!*" Connie lunged at me and just about boxed my ears. His manic, magnified eyes darted all over my face. Far as I could remember, he'd never so much as looked straight at me for longer than a second.

"You're creeping me out, dude," I said.

"Actually, your theory works only if you're only counting *T1* and *2* as canon. It falls apart if you account for the temporal modifications in the reboot, but that wasn't really..."

"Connie..."

He cleared his throat and dropped his arms. "*In theory*, I mean."

"So you don't believe me?"

"As a prank, it's a pretty lame one, even if the story weirdly holds together," he said. "Obviously this is just the kind of thing I'd want to believe, so there's that."

"I swear to—" I started, but Connie was already past the part where I promised to tell the truth, the whole truth and nothing but the truth. It was just in his nature to trust me—because why would your best friend screw with your brain like this, right? The way he drifted off in his mind, eyes fixed on spinning plastic Saturn—I could see him thinking time warps and helicopter blades. I saw how his desperate need to believe was drowning out his careful calculations.

"Nothing came through with you? Not even your phone?" he asked.

"Came through what?"

"The theoretical wormhole."

"I don't know. I didn't see a hole. I might've just dropped my phone." All that business with the whistling maintenance man and the fence made me forget to look for the phone on the ground. Even if it was there, it was sure as hell broken from the fall.

Connie scrambled for his own phone, tucked into a side pocket on his backpack. He was so frantic it slipped through his hands like soap. Down on his knees, he huddled over the phone and pressed the speed dial number assigned to me.

Calling Russ on the display.

"What's that going to do?" I asked.

Connie shushed me, then tapped a button. The audio switched to speaker, amping the ringtone loud enough to make us both grit our teeth. We both stared at the Nokia like it was a ticking bomb neither of us knew how to defuse.

It didn't go straight to voicemail.

"Hello?" The voice was groggy, disgruntled—*you just woke me up.*

At the sound of it, Connie recoiled, hands over his mouth.

"Hello? Connie? What do you want?" the voice on the phone said.

It was my dad's voice, slightly distorted by bad speakers, but Dad for sure.

I mouthed to Connie so Dad couldn't hear me: "*just my dad—so what?*"

But Connie gave a slow motion headshake. Uh-uh. Not your dad.

"*It's you,*" Connie whispered.

7:40 A.M.

"WHAT DO YOU mean *it's me*?" the phone voice asked. "Why are you calling so early?"

Connie stuttered, but I didn't butt in. It wasn't like I could take control of the conversation for him. I rolled my hands, signaling him to improvise. He shook his head. I clenched my jaw and glared insistently.

"Um—uh—hey, uh, Russ," Connie finally said to the phone. "I'm just, you know, making sure you set your alarm. We don't want to be late for school."

"Yeah, sure. Thanks for the wakeup call." My patented sarcasm sounded way more bitter when I listened to it from outside my head.

"Oh—uh—okay," Connie said, but the call was already dropped.

We sat on the floor in silence. A fuzzy whiteness was spreading across my mind, like what happens just before you pass out. I kept touching my face to be sure it was still there. All I could think about was the out-of-body dislocation you feel when you stand between two almost-facing mirrors so your reflections curve forever around

66

the double bends.

But *this* was a whole other level of mind-warp. Knowing I existed in two places at once, just a little more than a mile apart. I was in Connie's room, but also half-awake in my own bed, where I was freshly inventing new thoughts that I had already forgot eleven hours ago.

Except I wasn't really that other person at all. I had no access to his mind. His thoughts were already branching off in new directions because I bumped him off the track that I took. I was hit with the panic of being locked inside my own shell. My involuntary reflexes, like breathing, were fighting against me. I had no way to *feel* this situation right, except that it was the most natural thing in the world—me here, and another person there. Two bodies, wholly divided. But how could I be *me* if I wasn't who I was anymore?

"This is phenomenal," Connie finally said.

"But *why* did you tell him to come over here?"

"Because—because that's what we do—we walk to school," he argued. But he wasn't even convincing himself. I could virtually see the multiple bad outcomes springing in his head.

Connie leapt to his computer and spread his fingers across the keys. The guy had a certified superpower for speed typing. In a flash, a website came up full of charts and graphs, with a twinkling star background. He scrolled through it all way too fast for a mental mortal like me.

"Crappity crap," he said. "There's also the grandfather paradox to consider."

"Like 'I'm My Own Grandpa?'" I asked.

"No—well, maybe. I should've considered this before I called the other you, but there's a theory that, if you were to actually travel back in time, then you definitely shouldn't have *any* interaction with yourself."

"What could it do, cause a nuclear explosion?"

"Probably not. Hopefully not. But if you alter events from *your* past, the future *you* come from won't exist anymore. The memories in your head won't be possible. Any little thing can cause a butterfly effect."

"Marty McFly disappears from his own family photo."

"Yes, like *Spaceman from Pluto*, except the divergence you'd cause would be way too complex to fix, and every fix would create more compounded divergences..."

"So I'm screwed already, is what you're telling me."

"You need to lay low, *big time*," he explained. "And I have to act just like I did yesterday. I have to pretend like you didn't show up naked at my house this morning. I mean *your* yesterday."

"Connie, what's going to happen to me?"

He bit his lower lip, dropped his eyes. "I don't know. But listen, tell me everything that happened between us in your yesterday, everything you and I said, and I'll make sure things all turn out exactly the same. And if the Other Russ doesn't know, he won't do anything different, right?"

"Yeah," I said, unconvinced. And I would've rather swallowed tacks than tell Connie the *Chronicle of Russ's Worst Day Ever*. Especially the part where my total assholery gave him a panic attack and put him in an ambulance. I couldn't imagine deliberately shoving him into that blender again. It had to be some kind of international human rights violation.

"You're right," Connie said, even though I hadn't actually said anything. "I'm already compromised. How can I be natural if my whole frame of reference for reality has been changed? *Time travel!* Right here, in my world, my life. I'm never going to be the old me again. I mean, unless this is your craziest April Fool's ever."

"I wish." We were a couple weeks too late for that. I tried to think through what other random chaos butterfly wings I might've set in motion. The people who saw me running in the buff down the street? They'd head off to work and talk about the downtown streaker instead of stock prices or whatever, and somebody would drop the ball and get fired and—and what about that maintenance worker? After catching me inside the fence, would he now remember to lock the gate—and, if so, how was the Other Me going to get in, and would Other Me also receive the *take the leap* text at 6:59?

This was worse than mentally folding those blueprint boxes on aptitude tests.

So I said, "Just, um, do what I tell you. I mean do what *he* tells you. The other one. Russ 2.0. He'll guide you. Don't over-think it."

"Russ 2.0? He's not a software application, Russ."

"You don't know that."

Connie wrenched at his hair so much it styled into an Einstein. Maintaining a sense of control was bad enough for him on a regular day. This could drive him nuts—or maybe, if his obsessive catastrophe-prevention was a coping mechanism, this would be exactly the massive responsibility Connie needed to reach his potential.

He said, "But you have to stay here in my room. Mom won't be home until tonight, so you won't run into anyone. You also can't call anyone. Or post anything on the Internet."

"I won't even eat any of your food," I vowed, meaning it, honestly. My mind was way too blown to think about eating or stepping outside. For the rest of the day, I just wanted to lay back and try my best to understand what was happening.

"All right. This could work."

"But there's a big hole in your plan," I said.

He scrunched his brow for about a nanosecond before it hit him. "Right. Damn it. You can't stay in my room forever."

"Exactly."

Connie put a firm hand on my shoulder, something else he never did before. He said, "It'll work itself out, I think. Yes." Subtext being: *this is a load of crap I'm feeding you, but you'll totally lose your mind if*

I don't offer some lame consolation to get you through the day.

We could've listed concerns for another few hours, but the clock ticked on. A glance through the blinds verified that Russ 2.0 was sauntering down the sidewalk toward Connie's house. Connie had to be down there, ready to go, as always.

"Don't get in any trouble," he said.

"You either."

I took my post at the window again and there he was, down at the foot of Connie's steps, my clone, the first recruit in my storm trooper army. There was no sudden mind-blowing infinite regress, no split consciousness or slow fade of my body to transparency and then nothingness. I watched my hand for five seconds to be sure it stayed solid, and it did.

All the science fiction was wrong, or at least, failed to capture the weird duality. Like imagining my funeral, or what my life would be if I were born to other parents, or if I lived in California in the 1950s, or even something as minor as standing two feet to the left of myself, an out-of-body drift. You are an active mind at an instant in space and time, projecting yourself into another space and time where you are *not*. It is and it isn't. Everything totally comprehensible, perfectly normal, but at the same time impossible. A reality just out of reach. Every dream convinces us of something ridiculous until we wake up.

Watching myself from this angle, I remembered almost exactly what my thoughts had been when I stood down there yesterday— the *other* yesterday. I'd been thinking how Connie's father's death in Afghanistan left this huge house way too empty. But now, in my new, separate self, I stifled a weird urge to leap out the window and pounce onto 2.0 so hard that we'd merge into one body again. It was a wacko idea, but logic had become a lost cause.

Connie actually went out to meet him. I couldn't hear them talk, but all the gestures and movements seemed right—a rerun of the day before. Good continuity. Just like last time, Russ 2.0 offered over the "Take the Leap" script, and Connie accepted it, reluctantly. It almost tore me in half watching them this second time, knowing what torture I'd soon put Connie through, all over again.

But that was how the story played out. Had to be. It was the only way to avoid triggering some paradox that would erase my existence. Or worse, open a black hole in the mid-Atlantic seaboard, sucking the whole galaxy into dark-energy nothingness.

Hypothetically.

As they turned to leave, Connie looked back at his window, at me.

I flinched away from view, thinking he'd just screwed up and created the first major discrepancy. But then I remembered that Connie actually *had* looked back at the house that first time. And when I called him out for it, he claimed it was déjà vu.

My mind was really reeling now. Maybe all of this had already been accounted for. Maybe when I was in Russ 2.0's place, another version of me was here in this bedroom, hoping Connie wouldn't alter a thing. Could be the real reason Connie was so nervous all day.

A strange loop, playing over and over again, always exactly the same.

But, no. There *was* an important change after all. This time, Connie had failed to do his usual last-minute home safety check. He was too distracted by bigger problems. Plus, Connie's clock read 8:01, which meant our wake-up call had gotten Russ 2.0 out the door ahead of schedule. At this rate, he and 2.0 would get to school ten minutes *early*, not ten minutes late. Other Russ would make morning broadcast on time, and that fact alone would tilt his day in a whole new direction.

The paradox was already in motion.

9:00 A.M.

I SPRAWLED ACROSS Connie's bed and considered.

It took ten minutes for me to decide that the worst option was to be left alone with my thoughts like this. The universe zoomed to a tight focus. Stuck in a dark bedroom all day, waiting to blip out of existence or spontaneously evaporate or who knows what. I was a pioneer, but the thrill of discovery was so much weaker than the threat of nonexistence, of death. I kept touching things just be sure my fingers were still there. I couldn't catch my breath or lower my heart rate. Couldn't quiet the existential dread and *just chill out.*

Just to distract myself, I un-paused *Dragon Rage 2* and tried to play, but the controls were wonky. My dragon kept dive-bombing into the same castle turret, over and over. Extra lives depleted. *Game Over.*

I tried to sleep. Staring up at Connie's universe model I wished I'd learned the stars and moons so I could apologize to each of them by name for throwing everything off balance. How could I be so crucial when I was so insignificant?

The house phone rang five times before an answering machine in Connie's mother's bedroom picked it up. Her recorded greeting echoed down the hall—*you've reached the Bower residence*—but nobody left a message.

The quiet was like a hidden intruder. I kept thinking:

One chance to make things right. This is the real leap.

Video Russ was future-me so I had to believe he had reasons for sending me back in time. I had no idea how he did it, but *why* seemed clear enough. He wanted me to fix my mistakes, his mistakes, our mistakes. And his advice had been a warning. It was clear to me now. *Don't sit around in Connie's room and squander this* one *shot. Do something, and screw the paradoxes.*

So I decided to focus on the one change I could make without leaving Connie's house. From his computer, I downloaded the draft of my *Cape Twilight Blues* spec script, gave it a good read-through. I mean, it was fiction, so what could be the harm in messing around with it? Nothing in the real world would be affected. I could escape my universe, fall into make-believe Cape Twilight, and leave my massive worries behind.

The structure was solid, all the major characters got equal screen time, and a single thematic base note echoed across all the plotlines. The sugary life lesson didn't get obvious until the last act. But, all in all, it was a trite little ditty. If I were Bobby Keene-Parker, I would've tossed this chum bucket overboard, too. Even if I had actually read it.

But now I had some critical insight from Keene-Parker himself. I had some ammo. See, I'd been studying broadcasting and media long enough to know that every actor has an emotional scab. If you pick at it just right, you'll get him screaming in no time, but you have to find it first. Five minutes with Bobby and I had found his scab. It was right there on that lighter of his. *The Kindling.*

Daddy issues: Movie Mogul Marv Parker, Bobby's sire, was a certified tyrant.

I switched my episode title from "Daylight Saving" to "Honor Thy Father." The new title was just pretentious enough to make Bobby see Emmy Award angels prancing around his head. And that trigger word, "father," was right there to bait him.

Old version: the boyfriend of Bobby's character gets accepted to Stanford, prompting a *gut-wrenching* decision about their budding relationship—whether to stick it out or break it off. They decide to give transatlantic love a chance. Yawn, I know.

Revision: Reece's (Bobby's character's) deadbeat father comes back into town, and Reece comes out to his dad about being gay. The old man has a bigoted hissy fit, so Bobby gets to pitch a tearjerker speech about tolerance and forgiveness. But get this: the speech is *really* about Bobby needing to forgive Pops for his parental desertion and general douchebaggery. Chewy subtext!

In the last scene there's a small step toward reconciliation, but nothing too final. THE END. <save>

The house phone did three sets of ringing while I wrote, but I ignored it.

Took me two straight hours to edit the Bobby/Reece scenes. Boilerplate dialog, I just had to hit the right dramatic beats and turns. I didn't change a word in the rest of the script. No need. *This* script was designed to please *Bobby*, nobody else. All I needed was to get his attention.

I would've finished faster, but my email system kept chiming new mail every few minutes. I checked them and then re-marked them as "unread" so I wouldn't mess with space-time, though it hardly mattered because the fresh messages were all gibberish, every one. A mash-up of algebra and wingdings, error messages saying the graphics couldn't be displayed.

It got so relentless, I had to log off and close the web browser.

The next time the phone rang I decided it had to be Connie trying to reach me. Any contact between us seemed like it would be against his rules, but he'd know better than me if there were loopholes. I eased open his mother's bedroom door and saw the cordless phone on her dresser. I couldn't resist. I picked up the receiver but didn't say anything, and all I got was garbled pings and whines, like when you dial a fax machine by accident.

Back in Connie's room, his stereo turned itself on and scanned randomly through radio stations. I had to unplug it to make it stop.

After hours of chafing, I finally put on the cleanest pair of Connie's tighty-whities I could find. He owned no boxers. I slipped the jeans back on, belted them to my waist. Flip-flops too big for my feet, and a blue Dr. Who TARDIS t-shirt that draped halfway down to my knees. I plucked a twenty from Connie's R2-D2 piggy bank, fully intending to pay it back.

When I tried to print my *Cape Twilight* script, half the pages slid blank white onto the tray. I ran the print job five more times before I got at least one clean copy of every page. Ate through a whole ream of paper.

The phone kept ringing and ringing. My email logged itself back in and chimed a new message every five seconds. I'd dealt with way too much tech weirdness in the last few hours to dismiss this as coincidence. The video game, the email, the phone, the Pastime Project app…

Somehow, Video Russ was reaching out again. Reminding me, egging me on.

And the message was: *if you don't get out, I'll drive you nuts.*

It was either Video Russ, or whoever convinced him to send that video (because I didn't see myself gleaning any revolutionary time-travel know-how any time soon). It didn't take a huge leap of logic to guess that someone with the tech to warp a live human through time could also disrupt telecommunications, email systems, and video game platforms at will.

Whatever was going to happen was happing now. No point in

pretending I could prevent it. My double existence in this place was somehow not impossible, and bigger changes weren't going to make it any less real.

I had to do it. Step out and take my chances, fix the mistakes I made the first time I lived through this day, without involving Connie or Paige or especially Russ 2.0. It was time to take over my life, just like Video Russ suggested. And for that, I needed to get to school and steal my cell phone from myself.

12:35 P.M.

RUSS 2.0 MAY have beaten the morning bell, but I was more than five hours late for class. I couldn't just waltz past the front office or risk getting nabbed by one of the roving volunteer hall monitors. Couldn't take the chance of being recognized or questioned, either.

The gym was my secret entrance, easy enough, but classes were in session so I had to reach my locker by stealth. I peered around every corner, ducked into bathrooms, hurried down hallways and around stairwells. Connie's oversized flip-flops slowed me down and made an awful *fwap fwap* racket, too.

At this moment, unless events were completely off track, Russ 2.0 would be in English and desperately wondering whether Savannah texted him her decision about the video shoot yet. Not for another twenty-five minutes but, unfortunately, he was about to lose his chance to find that out.

One minute before the period bell, I reached my locker, opened it, and took custody of the cell phone. I knew exactly the anguish 2.0 would go through when he discovered it missing. Robbing myself caused a strange rush of guilt, like I was already being punished for my actions. But it was for a noble cause: helping him/me avoid several of his/my worst blunders ever.

The bell rang, the classroom doors swung open, and students poured into the halls. 2.0 would take about a minute to get here. For cover, I snagged a spare hoodie before I shut my locker door, then rushed down a stairwell I almost never used.

The broadcasting studio was empty and dark. Mr. Yes's office gave off the only light, and he was sitting in there with his lunch, just as I expected. Just as he took a sip from his thermos, I knocked on the open door, and the noise made him swallow his drink down the wrong tube.

"Sorry about that, Mr. Yes," I said with a wince.

He waved it off as he coughed red-faced into his wastepaper basket. A sandwich and a bag of pretzels sat untouched on his desk. He must've already felt crappy, but he didn't look nearly as sick as I knew he soon would.

"I have to do some last minute pick-up shots this afternoon," I explained, "and my camera-person fell through, so I was wondering if I might be able to check out one of the school's cameras, bring it back Monday?"

"*No*," Mr. Yesterly choked.

My gut clenched. Something had gone wrong. I was suddenly sure 2.0's early arrival gave him extra time to screw up any diplomacy with Mr. Yes. I was convinced Yesterly was pissed, and Savannah probably never even got her invitation to the Silver Bullet. I should've listened to Video Russ, locked 2.0 in a closet somewhere, and taken over right from the start.

"No—" Mr. Yesterly repeated, gasping. "No problem."

"Oh," I said. "No *problem*."

"Sorry—water in my throat. Just fill out the release form and recharge the battery when you're done. What happened to you?" He dabbed his own left eye to show what he meant.

My shiner. Dead giveaway I wasn't the other Russ.

"Gym class," I said. "Got shouldered in the face during flag football. That's why I'm wearing my gym clothes. My head was so rattled, I forgot to change."

He could've asked why my gym outfit included oversized jeans and flip-flops, but Yes wasn't in the interrogative mood. "Ouch," he said. "Stay safe, right? You've got a video project due to me first thing Monday. No more extensions, got it?"

"Right," I said.

I would've done a fist-pump if I could've gotten away with it. My time line *had* changed, and it had veered down a positive path. Somehow 2.0 managed to get the Monday extension *without* having to collide with Mr. Yes outside the men's room after school. Probably because the other me showed up, got the morning announcements prepped, and ran a flawless show like he was supposed to. After all that *responsibility*, Mr. Yes couldn't help but give him an extension.

Now it was on me to return the favor.

"Mr. Yes? Sorry for saying this, but you're not looking so great."

"Not myself today, that's for sure."

"You should take an early day—maybe go see your doctor."

"It's that obvious, huh?"

I was wary of saying too much, but I had to convince him. "You should, you know, be careful of your blood sugar."

He cocked his head. "My blood sugar?"

"Watch your insulin or whatever."

"Russ—what makes you think I'm diabetic?"

"You're not?"

"Not that I know of. Did someone give you the impression I was?"

Yeah, you, I wanted to say. But I couldn't accuse him of lying about being a diabetic because he wouldn't actually be telling his lie for another hour and a half. In fact, I pretty much just ensured that he *wouldn't* end up having that conversation with me at all.

"I guess I was thinking of someone else," I said.

"Someone else, huh?"

I could see Mr. Yes didn't buy it, but we were in a standoff.

"All I'm saying is—it looks like it might be worse than just your average flu bug. My Mom's in the pharmaceutical business, so, you know, I hear about these things."

"Okay. Right," Mr. Yes said. "I'll get it checked out."

The mention of my mother, Madeline Belmont, put Mr. Yes on his own dark little cloud. Creepy, but effective, because it gave me a chance to slip away without further questioning. I'm not sure he even registered I was gone until I left the studio, camera case in hand. I had a plan to carry through.

12:50 P.M.

SOMEHOW I HAD to get in contact with Conrad, but there were two Horace Vales wandering the halls of Port City Academy. If no divergences had happened yet, one of me was still in the cafeteria with Connie, so I couldn't exactly make a double showing at my own lunch period, even if, after something like fifteen hours of fasting, I was hungry enough to eat those gray green beans all over again.

Instead, I loitered in the East Hall, a "free zone" just off the cafeteria, where upperclassmen on their lunch break were allowed to mill around and socialize after mealtime. It was mostly just the Future Runway Models of America who refused to eat or even sit within sniffing distance of food.

Ten minutes until 1 p.m., the milestone moment when Savannah sends the text agreeing to meet me at the Silver Bullet Diner for videotaping. Fierce jitters. You'd think the second time around I'd be more confident, but I couldn't be sure 2.0 had laid the groundwork just right. Very possible he blew it with Savannah because of some unforeseen variable, and now I wasn't going to get that text at all.

When my phone buzzed seven minutes early, it was Connie, not Savannah. For privacy, I crouched into an auditorium side-exit alcove and read his text:

testing. r u there?

I considered not answering, but I'd already obliterated Connie's former past. I texted:

yep

who? someone stole russs phone, he wrote.

me, real russ

?

from the future! I wrote. I could erase the texts later if they needed redaction.

ur here? stole his phone???

my phone too. is 2.0 with u?

no. just left, looking for his phone! where r u?

I started to type, but then the implications of Connie's comment sank in.

2.0 was on the loose.

I glanced around the corner and, sure enough, I got walloped by another bout of metaphysical double vision. Because there he was, Russ 2.0, stalking up the hall toward me.

One look at his zombie posture and I could see how stricken with worry he was. I'd probably look like that if my phone went AWOL right before I was destined to get my first text (and maybe *only text ever*) from Savannah Lark.

Even if my day was looking up, *his* was sucking rotten limes.

I popped my head back into the alcove and yanked the hood over it. The phone never buzzed as loudly as it did just then.

Connie: *where r u??* I didn't type back until I was sure 2.0 had walked well past my hiding spot. *free zone, third alcove,* I wrote.

I left the borrowed HD camera in the alcove so Connie wouldn't see it when he came out to meet me. No need to tip him off about what I planned to do. I made sure Russ 2.0 was out of sight and then eased back into the open, cool and collected, hooking a finger through a belt loop on my jeans to keep them from sliding down.

Twenty-odd students filled the hall, arranged in their cliques. None of them looked at me like I was the ghost of the kid that just passed by a few seconds earlier. Nobody noticed me at all. I wasn't part of their circle of friends, so I didn't exist.

But Connie noticed me right off. He stepped out of the cafeteria, glancing up and down from his phone display, like he was following my coordinates by GPS. He rushed over and whispered, "I knew it was you as soon as his phone disappeared. And you're wearing my t-shirt."

The hoodie was unzipped far enough to show off the TARDIS. I decided not to mention the unmentionables I was also forced to borrow and said instead, "You didn't tell me he was gonna mosey right past here."

"Oh God, did he see you?"

"Obviously not."

"There's a really delicate matrix here, Russ…"

"Too late for that. The *past* past is already gone."

"What? How?" He kept squirming, eyes flitting around.

"First of all, you and 2.0 got to school on time. In real life, you were late, and that triggered all sorts of stuff that isn't happening now…"

"But this *is* real life," he whined. "I've been busting my butt to keep things normal here. I tried to call you—"

"Everything in your house was going haywire. I had to get out."

His cheeks went so red I thought they'd start bleeding. "*My house*? What's wrong at my house?"

"Chill, Connie. Your house is fine. I mean mysterious emails and phone calls from fax machines. The video game I tried to play. All of it was these weird tech problems. And it was tech that sent me back in time in the first place. That app or program or whatever it was—the Pastime Project. I'm thinking there might be a screw up in the system."

"Anomalies," he muttered. "Corruptions. Bad code in the program."

"But like you said—"

"A virus…" he went on, ignoring me.

"—*this is real life.*"

"Real life has viruses," he noted. "Did you know our human DNA is actually encoded with residual viral material? Mitochondrial DNA? Endosymbiosis? Look it up. Viruses are part of us. Just like operating systems that gradually draw bad code off the Internet."

"If that's how you want to look at it," I said, "then I'm here to do a virus scan."

"What does that even mean, Russ?" He kept peeking over my shoulder in the direction 2.0 had headed. Probably worried that Other Me would come back and find us chatting in the hall. Good thinking, Connie. I seriously doubted a meeting of Russes would cause a black hole, but it would still be hella awkward.

And was it Russes or Russi?

"I just need you to stay like you've been," I said. "Keep close to 2.0, don't let him run into Paige or Savannah. Got it?"

"Why not?"

"Because it never happened, last time," I lied. "The Other Me wants everybody to get together to make the video, but it didn't happen during the first take, so it shouldn't now, right?"

"No, I guess not, but…"

"Where's your copy of the video script—the one I gave you this morning?"

That wasn't technically right. 2.0 gave him the script, not me. Connie caught the continuity error, and it made him take a step back from me, as if he just realized I was an impostor.

84

"Why do you want it?" he said.

"You were supposed to have a fight this morning, because you didn't really want to do the shoot." My bullshit was piling up, nice and thick, but I had to take Connie out of the equation, for his own sake. "You admitted it, so I got mad, and I didn't give you the script. The shoot never happened. But this time—I guess you didn't say anything to him?"

Connie studied me. I could see belief easing over his face. I had picked the best possible fiction because what I told him was what was in his heart. He reached behind his head and withdrew the rolled-up script from his backpack. But then he hesitated and pressed it against his chest.

"Keep 2.0 away from the Silver Bullet this afternoon, all right?" I said. "Now that things have gone a different way, he might change his mind and show up there."

Connie nodded. "What are you going to do?"

"I'm going back to your house to wait it out." Neither one of us wanted to discuss what that meant—*wait it out*. Seven p.m. would come around again, and there was no way of knowing what the hour would bring.

"Please don't get anything on my Dr. Who shirt, please."

"Don't worry about it," I assured him.

A new text buzzed on my phone, and Connie was too busy wringing the script in his hands to notice. I took a sideways glance at the screen. One p.m., exactly on schedule, the message from Savannah's blocked number. *okay 2:30 Slver bullet gr8 script! —sl*

She was in, just like before, my second chance to get it right. The adrenaline rush, all over again. Except this time it felt a bit like Savannah was praising a script written by some other dude whose chops we both admired. I wasn't the *me* I was before anymore. But I could still make this work. Fixing my mistakes was the whole point of this leap.

"All right, hand over the script," I told Connie.

He sighed, averted his eyes, and made no move to give it to me.

"What's wrong?" I asked.

"We should—we should do an even trade," he finally said.

"What do you mean?"

"The phone, dude. You're not supposed to have it."

I could see his point. As long as I had the phone, Russ 2.0 would keep rampaging around. He'd get more and more erratic. No doubt he'd show up at the Silver Bullet anyway, since he wouldn't know if Savannah texted him or not. And that would ruin my plan.

Still, I needed that phone. It was my only connection to the Pastime Project. My only possible source of answers. After all, Video Russ wouldn't have sent me back here without an escape plan.

"Russ, come on. You're messing with the timeline," Connie said.

"All right, all right," I said, and snatched for the script. Connie resisted, but I couldn't blame him for his lack of trust, especially since my grabbiness was a slight-of-hand trick meant to distract him from seeing me delete Savannah's message with my thumb. When Russ 2.0 got the phone back, there would be no trace of her text.

I offered the cell over, and Connie took it, letting go of the script as he did.

"How are you going to explain having it?" I asked.

"I know your—*his* combo. I'll slip it into the mess of papers at the bottom of his locker. He'll think it just fell down there and he missed it the first five times he checked."

"You think I'm that dumb?"

"It's kinda more believable than the truth," he said.

Connie slid the phone in his pocket. Being without that lifeline was another kind of naked for me, but giving it up would offer a better chance of keeping them off my case. I still had six hours to get it back, and I knew where to find it.

I waited while Connie walked away. At the cafeteria doorway, he took one skeptical glance back at me, and I smiled. As soon as he was out of sight, I ducked back into the alcove, retrieved the camera, and made my escape.

2:15 P.M.

OUTSIDE THE SILVER Bullet, Bobby Keene-Parker's Rapide zoomed up curbside. He stood from his car and posed with one elbow on the roof, as if expecting a team of paparazzi to memorialize the occasion. Too bad for Bobby, he was alone.

Except for me. I was already inside the diner and ahead of schedule, courtesy of Azalea Taxi and a chunk of the twenty bucks on loan from Connie's R2-D2 bank. I was in the middle of rewarding myself with a double-decker cheeseburger and a milkshake. I sat in the same booth where I found Savannah and Bobby last time.

Fifteen minutes till Savannah dropped in. Maybe less, if she showed early.

Everything according to *The Plan*.

Now, if I was Savannah, this was the part where Bobby would scope me out, saddle up beside me and unfurl a killer pick-up line. But I was just a dude in clown jeans and a sweaty nerd shirt. So he sat as far from me as he could, just inside the door, at the lunch counter.

No time now to psyche myself up. I napkined the ketchup off

my mouth and moseyed over to him like some big-time talent agent. "Bobby, hey, it's Rusty, how you doing?" I said. Held up my palm, came close to slapping him on the back.

He raised an eyebrow.

Widening my grin, I rolled right into the pitch. "Your publicist told me you were headed over here, so I said, you know what, I'll just meet him instead of getting all tangled up in the hubbub down at the studio. No biggie."

Bobby gave his stool a slight tilt in my direction. "Who're you, again?"

"Rusty Vale. Writer. Flew in from LA this morning. Phil Cole thought it'd be great if you and me sat down for a spell to go over this spec script I'm polishing up. He thinks this one's a real showcase for you, and I have to admit, that's exactly the reason I wrote it."

Philip Cole was a random producer whose name I remembered from *Cape Twilight*'s opening credits. I could've name-dropped Father Dearest himself, Marv Parker, but I wanted to inflate Bobby's ego, not crush it.

I smacked the script down on the counter. My name and address were on the cover page, according to all the formatting guidelines. I swept my hand over the title, "Honor Thy Father," to direct his attention to those words. My smile came on as a wince.

"Man, I read so many of those things…" Bobby groaned, not even glancing at it.

"Let me pitch it in two words," I said. "*Emmy Award.*"

"Yeah, I hear they just hand those out like sleeping pills."

All right, so I launched into the synopsis. Sold it straight to his soul. All Bobby needed was one juicy episode to prove everybody wrong. His career wasn't just a sham. He had the soul of Marlon Brando, reincarnated. *I just knew it,* I told him.

Picture this, Bobby: your character Reece's estranged father comes back into the picture, gut-wrenching arguments, and then the kicker, the poignant third-act twist: your character realizes his own sexuality *is far from decided*. This shocker opens up a hundred new possibilities for where Reece can go from there. Maybe he'll even get to kiss a girl or two in future episodes, just to shake things up.

When Bobby grabbed my wrist to stop the pitch, I knew I had him.

"Wait," he said. "So he thinks he might not even be gay?"

"You want to give your character room to grow for future episodes, right?"

"I'd rather the bastard got shot in the head, knock me out of my contract." But still he picked up the script, leafed through it as casually as possible. I had taken the liberty of marking his scenes in green highlighter so he wouldn't have to bother with the stuff that didn't pertain to him.

One specific moment snagged his attention. He moved his mouth as he read. At the bottom of page twenty-six, he chuckled, though I couldn't remember writing any funny lines there. From down the counter, my buddy, Sally, the waitress winked at me.

"This is grade A cheese, Rusty Vale," he said. "It's kind of amazing. But one question."

"What's that?" I asked. Five minutes to spare before Savannah, and I had this puppy in the bag. I knew it, Sally knew it, and Bobby was coming around.

"What's with that line of b.s. y'all fed me just now?" he asked.

"Pardon?" Crack in my voice. The burger in my stomach was considering a rerun.

"First off, I didn't tell nobody I was coming here. Second, Phil Cole left the show last season. He's doing telenovelas down in Mexico now. And you? You're a high-school kid with a Carolina drawl and a Cape Fear address. You ain't got one single day of LA sun on your skin."

My accent and my cover page had betrayed me. I tried my best to laugh it off. "Well, ha—you know," I said. "That's my pitch. I make up stories, right? I play a character, just like you. Think how all this will sound next year in *Variety*: 'Keene-Parker discovers high school writing prodigy in Cape Fear greasy spoon.'"

Sally called out in protest: "Sugar, my spoons are spic and span!"

"Just an expression, Sal!"

Bobby flipped though the pages one-handed, musing. In his other hand was that lighter of his, the top scraping open and shut to show his apprehension. He sighed and said, "I don't like bullshit."

"Let's be for real, then," I said, then I sucked in a long breath to keep from passing out. "Your dad is a hack. Rough to admit, but there it is. We both know it. He's been popping out inferior fare since the start. *The Kindling*? The book was a hundred times better. *You're* a hundred times better. Jump out of that nest, man. This is your leap. Bob, you gotta take it."

"Eh," he said, scratching the back of his neck.

Deep in the zone, I didn't hear the jingle bell chime at the entrance door, but I couldn't miss Savannah Lark stepping up behind us, right on cue. "Russ," she said, widening her eyes on Bobby's back. "Is that...?"

"Bobby Keene-Parker," I said, "meet Savannah Lark."

He swiveled around in his seat, and the admiration was instantly mutual. I was a bona fide director, even with the camera still in its bag. Meticulous timing, perfect blocking, my own stable of actors: A-list star and budding ingénue, enacting their meet-cute.

"She's my girlfriend," I added, for good measure. "And another rising star."

The *girlfriend* bit was a risk, but Savannah didn't bat an eye, and Bobby's Alpha Male rivalry hormones kicked right in, as I expected. All I had to do now was stand back and let the chemistry between them react.

I stood there telling myself that the cosmos had literally folded itself around backwards to make this happen. We gathered together in a booth, got to talking about Savannah's guest shot on *Cape Twilight*. Savannah showed Bobby a demo reel clip on her iPhone, a local spot she did for an Italian restaurant, playing hostess and narrator. The host site was called YouView—some new knockoff of YouTube, I figured.

When the moment was ripe, I butted in: "Don't you love when the big stars do those little one-off videos, like on Funny or Die? You know the one with Jay-Z teaching those Korean kindergartners? It really humanizes you, for the fans."

Bobby listened, but his male gaze was zeroed on Savannah, just as I hoped.

I said, "Savannah and I were gonna shoot this short script I wrote. Just a scene about a motorcycle stunt man who wants to…"

My starlet burst into light, finally realizing what I was driving at. "Wouldn't it be *crazy*!" she said. "Bobby Keene-Parker in our movie?"

Man, she was *good*. And she said *our* movie.

"Dunno," Bobby said. "I'm pretty beat. Been at the gun range all morning. Y'all ever been out shooting, Rusty? Across the river in Leland? They'll let you pop off whatever you want. I unloaded a .357 Magnum today. Dirty Harry, the next generation."

"You got a future action franchise on your hands with that," I said. "But listen, if you could take like an hour, hour and a half, *tops*, we can do this thing. You and Savannah. Like I said, your character is the son of a motorcycle stunt man who died in a fiery crash, and you want to eclipse his glory with your own record-breaker. Savannah's your best friend, and you're saying goodbye, just in case you don't make it, but you're both secretly in love with each other, even though she's totally against the risk you're taking. She hates everything your father stood for. It would be a great break from your *Cape Twilight* stuff."

I scooped the video camera from its bag.

"Y'all got a script or am I s'posed to improvise?" Bobby asked.

And that was it—off and running. No science in the world could explain how I got here, reliving a moment I thought I lost, but I didn't care. I wasn't going to sit around brooding on the paradoxes and let a miracle fizzle away.

Action.

Bobby flubbed a few lines but covered it with graceful improv. He played my cocky/vulnerable stunt guy better than he ever played his *Cape Twilight* character, in my humble opinion. And Savannah was perfect, understated, empathetic. Every line she spoke welled up in her throat but never quite gushed forth until the finale.

Between takes, Sally the waitress clapped.

Bobby said, "You gotta write a speaking role for Savannah here in that *Cape* script you showed me."

I mostly kept my wits in check. Just once, I went into the men's room, spiked an imaginary football, did a frantically silent touchdown dance, and collected myself again.

There was a nagging worry in the back of my mind that Russ 2.0 or Connie or Paige would show up and wreck my moment, but I was betting I'd changed circumstances enough to keep them at their distance. Connie sure as heck didn't want to show up, and his only job was to keep Russ at home. Doing this shoot alone meant I was my own cinematographer, but losing Paige's perspective was a small price.

Because, I mean, *Bobby Keene-Parker was in my student video,* people. Guaranteed million hits online, even if I didn't win the internship. Plus, with that spec *Cape Twilight* script in his hands? Who knew, I might even get hired outright at the studio.

Two hours lapsed before I said, "That's a wrap."

Bobby's eyes were damp with emotion. All that father/son soul-search dialog was kicking in. My words, worming into his psyche and breaking him down. In a way it was too easy, having this psychological advantage over him—simply knowing things about him he didn't think I knew. I could glimpse into his soul.

"Some heavy lifting you put in there," he said. Dabbed his eyes with a napkin.

"Thanks, Bobby. I can't tell you how much—"

"Y'all got what you wanted, yeah?" he asked.

"Absolutely," I said.

"Then let's leave it at that?" he suggested, going suddenly stiff.

"Okay, but…"

His clenched jaw muscles told me not to push the issue one more inch.

I'd just coaxed out the best performance of this guy's career, but now it felt more like I whipped his ass in a high-stakes game of *Settlers of Catan*. He slapped down some cash for his meal, stood from the booth, nodded a terse goodbye at Savannah, popped his sunglasses on.

She and I didn't say a word to each other until he was out the door.

"That went… well?" I said.

"Uh, *yeah*. Look under his arm," she said.

Through the diner window I saw him headed to his car. Tucked into his right armpit was a stack of paper. Bobby Keene-Parker, one of the biggest teen-demographic cable TV stars in the world at that precise moment, had taken my *Cape Twilight* spec script with him.

We watched him rev the engine three times and peel off down the street, just like before. Except in this new, alternate take, he didn't have Savannah Lark in the passenger seat of his Rapide. Savannah Lark was still in the booth with me.

"That guy's intense," she said.

"They're supposed to be, I guess. The good actors."

"Can you believe this? I mean, really? *What just happened*?"

"We deserved it," I said. "We've got the talent, right?"

"You know what? We *do* deserve it." She flash-posed for an imaginary glamor shot.

"That's the spirit."

"When can I see the footage?" she asked, pawing me.

"I need to get with my friend to edit it, but soon. Later tonight?"

She wrote her phone number and home address on a napkin, then tucked it into my hoodie pouch pocket. Information I'd been desperate to attain for more than a year, offered with the trustful ease of old friends. The afternoon sun streamed through the window and lit her profile. A professional lighting crew couldn't have made her look more destined for stardom.

Together we laughed—because of serendipity, because we navigated two straight hours of impossible luck, because we just cast a lifelong memory, because the thick social walls between us were crumbled, and we saw each other for real.

"Why'd you say I was your girlfriend before?" she asked.

"*Uh...*" I said. Liar, blundering idiot. No serendipity here at all. I had manufactured and manipulated everything. And Savannah was about to shut down the whole production.

But then she wrapped her arms around me, bands of metal bracelets tingling the back of my neck, and planted a strawberry-and-nirvana kiss on my lips.

4:45 P.M.

A FEW MINUTES later, Savannah and I said our goodbyes at the corner of Market and Front. I wasn't alive, not really, until her kiss. The way she transported me felt even more mind-blowing than my leap through time. *This* was the reason I leaped. Somehow I'd found a way to arrange this for myself. Every day I sat around regretting the chances I didn't take, but here I was, the chance taking me.

I couldn't believe it was true, yet all the buildings around us stood concrete as they ever were. The smell of hot grease from nearby restaurants, the fresh yellow pollen coating all the parked cars. The only oddity was the temp-and-time display on the Carolina Credit Union bank sign, which showed nothing but digital eights, straight across. I wanted to stop time, too. I wanted to get trapped in this instant forever, but Savannah was already walking away from me, glancing back with a smile.

There was no time to lose myself in a mental music video. I needed to edit the footage I captured, and Paige was my only real digital editing contact. She knew the bells and whistles on Final Cut better than anyone, especially me, even though I owned the platform on my home computer.

I'd have to convince Paige to help me cut the movie, and the best plan was to grovel in person. Five bucks left, I hailed another taxi, gave the driver Paige's address. The meter reading clocked a $2.50 base fare and climbed twenty cents every few seconds. We were still a ten minute walk from her place when it hit $4.50, so I ditched the ride, paid the full five bucks, and hoofed it from there.

South of downtown, the front yards were all sand and pine straw, if there were yards at all. Ramshackle bungalows built sixty years ago for dock and farm laborers mostly. The faded paint signs on storefronts hadn't been changed in all that time, either. They still advertised *fresh chitterlings* and such.

I'd never been inside Paige's house, but we'd picked her up from there a few times for little league. No secret she was on full academic scholarship at Port City Academy. Her socio-economics thing, not to mention family tragedy, was part of what drove her to act scrappier than the trust-funders, I guess. Fuel for her inner fire.

Hers was the left half of a duplex across the street from a brick apartment building decked with a dozen window unit air conditioners. I rounded the corner of that building full stride—and fell back when I caught the scene unfolding in front of her place.

Twenty yards away from me, three cop cars sat parked, one of them with its light band spinning. The lack of sirens was not a relief. Nobody was in any hurry to help with whatever went wrong here. A sudden swerve in the road, a derailing on the track, a wicked divergence. In an instant, even before I understood what had happened, I knew I'd been making all the right changes to all the wrong conditions, the trivial things.

An officer stood guard at Paige's front door. Two more occupied the walkway, paired up with civilian passersby. I didn't know the heavy woman with the baby in her arms, probably a neighbor, but the other one I recognized because I saw him every morning in the mirror. Russ 2.0.

Conrad was also there, but he sat alone on the curb with his head in his hands. He didn't seem to notice he was inhaling the exhaust fumes from one of the idling cruisers. The set of bikes lying on the sidewalk explained how 2.0 and Con got here.

But *why?* The question wiped the taste of Savannah's kiss from my lips. I kept my distance, pressed to the corner of the apartment building. I touched my pocket and realized for the hundredth time I didn't have my phone. I couldn't exactly stroll across the street toward Connie, either, not with the Other Russ standing nearby.

Catty-corner from Paige's duplex was a gas station that still had an old public phone stand beside the parking area. Probably a relic without a dial tone, and besides, I had no money left.

Weighing options, I glanced back at Connie just as he lifted his head and matched his eyes to mine. He bolted upright. I sucked in my breath and slid out of view, wishing I could will myself invisible.

I wanted to draw his attention, sure, but not this way, lurking like I'd been here all along, hiding out, guilty of something. The lush spring air was almost too stifling. My head full of particles and cotton. Suddenly, all I wanted was lay down and sleep. Recharge, reboot.

The camera bag slipped from my shoulder and the Canon spilled out. Before I could crouch to pick it up from the dirt, Connie was there with his silhouette ringed by sunlight. I had nowhere to hide and no reason to want to.

"What are you doing here?" I asked him first.

He was gasping for breath, his eyes huge and desperate behind the lenses of his glasses. I'd seen him like this before in another existence. That panic attack all over again.

"Connie, what's going on?" I asked.

"Why didn't... I don't understand. Why didn't you tell me?"

"Didn't tell you *what*? What's going on?" I asked.

"They think she… they think she killed herself."

The idea was so ridiculous I snorted. "Come on," I said. "It was her brother, years ago. She's probably just not answering her phone. I mean, seriously, she's last person in the world…"

But Connie shook his head. "No, she's there. She's in her house."

He didn't have to explain the rest. I understood just then, like the final click of a combination lock, what had happened, or what *didn't*, and why it was my fault.

This was because I told Connie to keep 2.0 away from Paige. And this was because I deleted Savannah's text, because then my other self never had any reason to go find Paige and ask her to be the cinematographer. Which meant Russ 2.0 wasn't at the track to defend Paige against Asshat's bullying.

And without me there to deflect his taunts, Paige took the full impact, and limped away with a fatal wound nobody could see, the kind that grows in your thoughts and kills you from the inside, the kind that runs in the family, no matter how hard you try to fend it off.

"There's—there's a mistake," I said. "A paradox."

"Why didn't you tell me?" he pleaded.

I touched the tenderness below my left eye. It shouldn't have been there anymore because the sucker punch from Asshat never happened. If I never got punched, then the black eye should've disappeared. Even *my memory* of it should've disappeared. The swelling and pain on my face was supposed to be my badge of honor for saving Paige.

"This is total bullshit," I said.

"You're saying you didn't know?"

"This didn't happen before, Connie. I swear. She was fine."

He wouldn't stop looking at me as if I'd murdered her myself. Any second, he'd signal to the cops across the street, and they'd descend with their handcuffs and batons *You did this to her, Horace Vale. It's all your fault.*

All this tampering turned *me* into a paradox. My memory stored events that never were, like Paige chiding me on Connie's front porch. *You really don't get it at all,* she'd said. Somehow, I vividly recalled a past that never existed, a past that could've been but got erased…

I was stranded in a history that wasn't mine.

"There has to be something. Some fix," I said.

Connie slipped the backpack off his shoulders and leaned against the brick exterior wall. Sweat dripped from his bowed head, even as he shivered. He said, "Almost right after school she stared posting these updates on thefacebook. Lashing out at all these people, making threats to hurt herself…"

"I haven't been online," I said.

"I didn't notice right away, but there was this chatter. Other kids linking to her posts, egging her on. Making cruel jokes about her brother. Like one every thirty seconds. She was totally on the ledge. I tried to call her. Russ—" He stopped for a second, realizing the possible confusion. "*He* tried to call her, too. The other… you. She wouldn't answer. We biked over, but we were too late. Her mother found her when she came home from work."

I shook my head. My rage flew in all directions, including at Paige. She shouldn't have been so weak. Should've built thick skin after her family's tragedy, after years of the sexist, classist, homophobic crap she dealt with at school. There was no good reason for her to suddenly cave, after everything.

I snatched up the video camera and pitched it with a furious howl at the brick wall beside me. On impact it burst into a dozen careening plastic bits.

Connie dove to the ground, shielding his head.

"I wasn't aiming at you," I said.

"You… you…"

"What do you want to say, Connie? Spit it out," I insisted.

"It's just… you showing up… and Paige… what happened to

her…"

"You think *I* made her do this?"

"No, not that," he said, unconvincingly. "*Something's* too much of a coincidence. All this happening on the same day. That's all. Something changed that shouldn't have changed."

"I know," I admitted. "She should've been with me down at the diner."

"But you said—"

"I *lied*, Con, because I wanted to fix what went wrong. God, she wasn't even on my radar. Paige was fine—her same unbreakable self. She was the last person… it wasn't *her* I was worried about."

"I think you need to get out of here," he said, "before they see you."

"I have to fix this."

"What can you do? It already happened. You can't—"

"*I know*, damn it! 2.0 should've been there to stop what they did to her. He was supposed to be there. *I* was there. I took a punch for her."

"Who? Where?"

"The other me, does he have a black eye, too? Does he?" I asked.

"I don't understand what you're saying. You *told* me to keep him away from her," Connie said. I was supposed to be the one Connie could talk to without hesitation, his best friend, but he acted like he was confronting a bully. It tortured him just to be honest with me.

"Connie…"

"You shouldn't have changed anything," he said. "You need to get out of here, *completely*. Out of this—this existence. Go back to wherever you came from. You're calling him 2.0, but that's not how it is. He's the first. *You're* the copy."

"He would've put you in the hospital with a panic attack if I hadn't stopped him. That's what I prevented from happening. You know that? I'm not him—not anymore. I'm better."

"All these weird glitches?" he said. "Technical malfunctions? You said how it was like a virus got into the system somehow. Well, I get it now. I see what you mean."

"*Don't...*" I begged him.

"*You're* the virus." Almost silently, eyes on the ground, but he said it.

"Connie, something's not right here."

"You. It's *you.*"

"No, listen. Paige couldn't have..." I watched a third shadow lengthening on the sand, and the sight of it shut my mouth. It was the same shadow that followed or led or trailed beside me all my life.

The other Russ came around the corner.

I was there, out in the open. Nowhere to hide from him, from myself. I'd been easing into the idea of two Russes for hours, but the fact of my sudden existence slugged him out of nowhere. He had no chance to prepare himself. The sudden body horror, the dislocating vertigo, the splicing of consciousness—it all came racing across the ten foot span between us.

"*What the*?" said Russ 2.0.

It was too much. I couldn't face him. I turned and ran, Connie's stupid flip-flops catapulting sand up my back and slowing my escape to the pace of a nightmare. But if I didn't keep moving, my molecules would come apart and disburse in the breeze. I was sure of it.

Because I was the copy. I was the virus.

5:30 P.M.

I STOPPED RUNNING when I hit the part of town that was nothing but empty grass lots and garbage blown against chain link fences. My lungs heaved and my bare toes burned from blisters, and I'd completely failed to outrun the images of Paige in my head. A Paige who wasn't but should've been, who could never have killed herself but supposedly did.

Already I knew it was a mistake to run. I should've faced him, the Other Me. I should've convinced him to let me have the cell phone back. That cell was my only connection to the Pastime Project, and maybe one more chance. My clock was running down. Because seven p.m. was an hour and a half away, and what came then was the Great Unknown.

I hurried the rest of the way downtown and nearly crawled back into the Silver Bullet, aching with thirst. Sally the waitress was kind enough to sport me some ice water and quick use of the vintage yet functioning phone mounted on the wall. My finger was so shaky, I could barely get it into the slots that spun the dial.

Dad answered on the first ring, like I knew he would. The only person left who might be able to wrap his head around what was happening and forgive what I did.

But to explain this to Dad on the phone would've been the quickest way to reserve myself a cot at a drug rehab center. I couldn't go back to that house, either—because Other Russ might show up before I could fully plead my case. It was his house, after all. He was the *true* Russ, not me—at least according to Connie. I needed neutral territory. So I asked Dad to meet at our old headquarters, the Pastime Playhouse.

"Buddy, that place burned down years ago," he pointed out.

"I mean the empty lot, the spot where it used to be."

"I guess you'll tell me why when I show up?" he said.

I was only a couple blocks away, so I got there first. The place was fully marinated in the coulda-been mood of overgrown grass, scorch marks, and rubble. I belonged there, maybe forever, so I took a seat on a sturdy cinderblock and watched the brick wall where once there was a movie screen.

There was a trace memory under the whiff of gasoline: the scent of buttered popcorn and the low bass rattle of the theater's cheap speakers. Of course it was just nostalgia, that quieter kind of time machine.

On my imaginary screen was a shot of a little league game. Mom calls me in to replace Paige on the mound. I won't budge from the bench. "Let her finish," I say.

But that's not how it really happened.

Instead, I jumped in, eagerly, and failed.

Here's another classic blast from the past: Ninth-grade Conrad dials the combo wheel on his school locker. Just before he pulls up the latch I jump in and say, "Don't."

But that's not how it happened, either.

In truth, Connie opened the locker, and out flew a camouflage toy helicopter, piloted by remote from down the hall. The chopper buzzed past his head, and he collapsed with an ear-splitting scream. Everyone doubled over laughing, and I caught it all from a few feet away, play-by-play, on my cell phone video camera.

That sickening prank wasn't my idea. I was an accomplice. I was the one who figured out Connie's combo by watching over his shoulder while he dialed it. Just so some other moron I was trying to impress could startle him with a toy. Harmless fun.

At the time, I didn't know Connie's father was killed in a helicopter crash. I was brand new to Port City Academy. I didn't realize how vicious that prank really was. Did my ignorance matter, or my apology and best-friend repentance every day since?

A few minutes into my mental *Worst Of Russ Vale* clip show, Dad showed up at the former site of the Pastime Playhouse. Sweat pants, shirt stains, and scruff—the perfect getup for an abandoned lot. He eyed the place like he could see my past projected on the wall just as sharply as I could.

I knew Dad could game-theory a solution, just like the time he drove me over to the Bower house and pressed me to apologize to Connie and his mother for the remote helicopter incident. I was gut-twistingly sorry, but Dad made me prove it. And Connie's forgiveness turned out to be the deciding factor that kept me from getting kicked out of yet another school.

When I stood up, Dad hugged me and asked, "What's going on, kiddo?"

"What do you think are the limits to what's possible?" I asked.

A slight grin. Subtext: *you worry me, but you're talking my language.*

"In a shoot-the-breeze kind of way," he asked, "or scientifically?"

"Hard core science."

"*Well*, anything's possible as long as there's no explicit physical law against it. That's the uncertainty principal, the basis of quantum theory. An electron can exist in several places at once until it's observed. Wave-particle duality, and all that. Even things that are against the rules could happen, theoretically, in another dimension, if there is such a thing."

"This is going to sound nuts, but what about a person?" I asked. "Is it theoretically possible for a person to be in two places at once, like an atom?"

"A person's neither a particle nor wave, so things are a bit more complex—"

"What about time travel?" I asked.

Dad's hesitant smile dropped. He glanced at the street behind him like he just realized we were far too public for a top-secret chat. "Wh—why would you ask me something like that, Russ? Have you been talking to anyone?"

"About time travel?" I asked.

"I just mean… it's a strange question." Dad grasped my forearm and led me further away from the bustle of the street. He was twitchy, watchful. He made us look like a pair of downtown junkies waiting on our dealer. Somebody was bound to call the cops any minute. "Why are you asking me about time travel?" he whispered, leaning so close his breath was on my neck.

"It's hard to explain…"

"My God, Russ. Has there been a temporal anomaly?"

So there it was. No need to convince a man who'd already convinced himself. He was baited. It was as if he'd been confined in his attic for weeks waiting for this moment, just jonesing for a *temporal anomaly* the way other folks look forward to packages from Amazon.

So I told him what happened—fast and plain, everything except for Paige because I couldn't bring myself to admit just yet how catastrophically I messed up. There was no delicate way to couch such information, but he listened with such laser-eyed intensity that

I almost stopped talking, afraid I'd given him an aneurysm. He didn't say a word until I was done.

"The other me is probably back at the house right now," I said. "If you called the house, chances are, I'd answer."

He scratched his facial scruff and paced in the grass. "It's not impossible, but also not technically possible. You'd need to have cylinder technology, for one, but that itself is only theoretical. You'd also need a massive quantity of negative energy, which is far too rare to harvest, unless you could somehow produce your own miniature black hole. *Then* you might be able to generate an infinitesimally brief wormhole..."

"Dad," I said.

"...but sending a human subject through it? Without total cellular disintegration? And with any degree of temporal accuracy or continuity—no, it's just not—"

"*Dad!*"

The way he blinked at me, it was obvious he'd forgotten I was there.

"I'm clueless about quantum mechanics," I said.

"The concept's ultimately rather simple because—"

"I know. You tried to teach me, but the truth is, I'm stumped. All I can tell you is the tech *exists*, and it's been developed into a program. Because I received it on my phone. Some future-me sent it to present-me with a video explanation, starring *me*, which I know *I never made*."

"You said the name of the company was The Pastime Project?"

"Yeah. Like the theater that used to be here. Pastime Playhouse."

"Curious," he said. "But no one else could be working with these developments, not so soon at any rate. Not unless it was stolen. But even then, nobody else could've worked out all the variables so quickly. It would require a radical discovery, or a genius greater than Einstein."

I couldn't believe how lightly he seemed to handle the emotional weight of what I was telling him. "So you're not slightly floored by the part where I said it was sent *to me, by me*?"

For a second, he seemed stumped, but then he waved off my buggy question. "That part makes perfect sense," he said.

"*Really?* Why's that?"

"Well, because I'm your father, and I'm the one who invented the program."

6:10 P.M.

FIFTY MINUTES TO spare before seven o'clock, *zero hour*, but Dad did not take me home to confront Russ 2.0. "That's not the strongest angle," he said. "I've got a better plan." His certainty hit like the waft of air conditioning from the dashboard vents. Off we rushed to Rush Fiberoptics, the software firm where my father, it turns out, invented a time machine. Or designed a prototype, at least.

It was breaking news to Dad that his former employer had obviously taken some steps beyond the blueprint in the two months since he left. Like, massive, reality-altering breakthroughs. Dad's aim now was to see what the hell happened inside that development lab, and why the program was leaked, or *would be*, to me. Back to the source, and hopefully a solution.

I couldn't process what was happening. The forefathers of science had led the way to the necessary quantum theories, but time travel was a greater breakthrough than anything Newton or Einstein or Bohr or Heisenberg or Schrödinger could've dreamed. And *my own father* was the mastermind.

In his driver's seat Dad was still himself—scruffy, pot-bellied. Not some alternate-reality avatar of Kasper Vale with a massive cerebral cortex swelling his head to twice its size.

He explained as he drove, how the spark for his invention happened fifteen years ago, back when I was still learning how not to crap myself. He was working on probability algorithms meant to render player choices in video role-playing games more naturalistic and intuitive. Like, thirty options for how to use your shrapnel bomb instead of just three, and level bosses that adjusted their attacks to your personal playing style—innovative stuff at the time. But the US government saw military uses, so Rush Fiberoptics chased the money, moved out of gaming and into artificial intelligence for drone warfare. Real-life remote control missiles that could think for themselves so you don't have to.

Then, more research and development with MIT, involving theoretical non-silicone computing at the atomic level, stuff that was poised to make binary coding as obsolete as horse carts. Like, your whole computer could be a dollop of jelly, and similar weirdness. But Rush kept it under wraps until the ideas could be applied in real life. All the theory in the world meant squat if the bulb stayed dark when you flicked on the switch.

In the meantime, Dad retooled his breakthroughs for a computer program that simulated quantum computing. In a virtual sense, he could vibrate subatomic strings at precise frequencies without collapsing the wave functions of electrons. *Virtual* negative energy could be harnessed from those vibrations, enough to fuel a *virtual* wormhole. But all it did in actual practice was *look* kinda cool, like a fractal screen saver that dances to the music.

All the specifics were lost on me, but not the gist. Dad's computer program could make a virtual black hole that stayed stable for almost a whole second (a seriously long time in quantum terms, apparently). Rush had almost all the ingredients for folding up time. All they needed, he said, was the mixer: a Tipler Cylinder that could spin fast enough to drag the fabric of space-time into a vortex. A time machine.

They don't sell Tipler Cylinders at Target. In fact, the device didn't even *exist* until serious advances in nanotechnology (another division of Rush) put the tech within Dad's microscopic reach. A Tipler Cylinder the size of a rice grain, and suddenly, the possibility of time travel wasn't sci-fi anymore, it wasn't just theoretical math, and Dad freaked out. He refused to take the project any further.

"Never a good idea to steal fire from the gods," he said.

"Can I ask you something?"

"Shoot."

"Why did they fire you?"

"I resigned, actually," he said. "For ethical reasons."

I didn't need to ask about the ethical dilemma. I was experiencing it first hand. But what I didn't get was why Dad let everybody think he was fired, especially Mom. Fewer questions he didn't want to answer, I supposed. Better to look like a loser than expose a dangerous company secret.

Dad told me how he didn't lose much sleep worrying that the eggheads at Rush would crack their code without him. They'd have to actually harness enough negative energy to keep the vortex stable, for one. Stability is what keeps a guy intact when he warps through. Stability is what drops him at the right space-point coordinates instead of, say, into dead space on the far side of Pluto. I was a big fan of this stability thing.

At red lights, Dad uncapped his green erasable marker and plotted equations on the windshield. New variables based on my account of the last eleven hours. How he converted my nightmare into numbers, I had no clue. It was all *The Social Network* to my eyes, but I was desperate to know the outcome.

"Wait," he said. "Your consciousness is singular, correct?"

"Huh?"

"Do you experience the other's Russ's perceptions, like double-vision?"

"No, he's separate. Another person. So was the one who sent me the video."

Dad slapped himself in the forehead and thumb-erased a few numbers. "I forgot about that one," he said. "But he could be you in the future, yes?"

"He didn't have a black eye."

Dad did a double take. Apparently he hadn't noticed my shiner until I mentioned it.

"Fight at school," I explained. "Well, not this time. The other me never got into the fight, so he doesn't have any battle scars."

I still hadn't told him about Paige. I couldn't find the words—and *suicide* wasn't one of them. I refused to believe it. Plus, that level of problem would've been too much added pressure for Dad, so I kept it filed away, a draft I could open later and revise. Her fate didn't have to be permanent or real anymore.

"Temporal paradoxes resolving themselves," he said. "Strange. In fact, impossible—except…"

"Except what?" I said.

He studied the numbers cluttering the windshield glass, but the marker just ticked in his hand.

"Everything keeps dissolving into irrationals," he said.

"Tell me about it."

The light turned green and Dad moved forward with the traffic, peering through his own chicken scratch.

"Maybe erase it so you can see the road?" I suggested.

"Right. We don't want anyone to spot these formulas. In the wrong hands—"

"I don't think we need to worry about that, Dad."

"Of course. Duh, me. It's backwards from their point of view!"

Rush Fiberoptics was in a sterile compound of plate-glass office buildings with manicured lawns and precisely spaced trees. Product development divisions for dozens of tech and medical companies.

Deep in the corporate zone, we were surrounded by reflective glass walls. Mirror images of our car and its riders kept flitting in and out of our view. Dad swerved into a nearly empty lot, one of the few that wasn't gated and manned with a booth, probably because its matching building was still under construction.

Rush was across the street. Ten stories, evening sunlight shimmering orange on the glass. The grounds were fortified with a tall fence and concertina wire. For a company supposedly hiding the biggest tech secret in human history, it probably should've sported military choppers, searchlights and turret guns mounted on towers.

"Now what?" I asked.

"Don't know. They won't be happy to see me." Dad glared at the edifice of his former employer's headquarters. I'd never seen him look so fierce, so determined, and all for my sake.

We got out and crossed the street. An hour past the workday commute, the whole compound felt evacuated. The only noise was the slow echoing clang of metal on metal somewhere high above. Like a bird in flight mode, I wanted to soar up to a safe and surrounding view of the threats down below.

The guard who manned Rush's security booth was retirement age, more like a Wal-Mart greeter than a first line of defense. *Chip*, his nametag read. "Mr. Vale," he said to Dad. "Long time, no see. Who's the young fella?"

Dad slung his arm across my back and grasped my shoulder. "This is my son, Russ. I know it's late in the day, but I was hoping the two of us might see Ed Corrigan in R&D. Or even Mr. Proust if he's available."

"Sorry, Mr. Vale. Both of them's gone for the night."

Dad grinned at me as if to apologize. It seemed that the sum total of his plan was simply to pretend he was way late for a board meeting on bring-your-son-to-work day.

Chip was assessing Dad's unemployment outfit. "Anything else I can do for you?"

"Actually, yes," Dad said. "I stopped by because I realized I left some important personal effects…"

"Sorry again," Chip said, dropping the customer-service charade. "Building's shut up for the night. Not to mention, y'all been put on the no-fly list, if you catch my drift. Can't let you in under no circumstances." Chip raised a clipboard and tapped his gnarled finger on a blacklist of names. Quite a few names, in fact.

"I see," Dad said.

"Happy to pass along a message Monday morning if you like."

"That's okay, Chip. Thanks." Dad put his hands in his pockets, slumped his shoulders, and headed back toward the car.

I couldn't bring myself to follow him. I just stood there by the guard post, huge imaginary question mark over my head. My resistance gave Chip the jitters. He reached under a shelf. Alarm or gun, I didn't know.

"Russ," Dad said. "Let's go fix that clock."

Back across the street, I leaned against the car while Dad ducked into the driver's side and rummaged through the opened center console. After a second he popped out and held the prize between his thumb and index finger.

"Jackpot," he said.

"Flash drive?"

"Working prototype. This baby's got five petabytes of storage."

"I guess that's a lot?"

"*Yeah,*" Dad said, with a snort-laugh. "More than any lone consumer could need. Unless he's uploading and running a time travel program. The plan is, I'll get in there, download the program from their servers. If it exists, of course."

"What do you mean *if it exists*? I told you I used it."

"Yes, but *when* was it sent from? That's the question."

He had a point, and it poked a hole in all my inflated hope. We were a couple of burglars on the biggest heist in human history, but there was a damn good chance we'd find the vault completely empty. If the app was sent to me from the future, a working version might not even have been developed yet, here in the present.

"Could somebody else in there have finished your work?" I asked.

Dad sat down sideways in the driver's seat, shoes still on the pavement. "Nobody I worked with had the brains, frankly. I would've bet we were decades, maybe even *centuries* away from harnessing the exotic energy we'd need to make time travel work. I would've said it was impossible, ever. Still, the computer simulations assured us it was all right there for the picking, inside our electrons. And to think, whoever finally developed a working application for this thing even figured out how to *transmit* the wormhole by satellite to your phone."

He sprang up, an instant mood shift, and grabbed both of my shoulders.

"Russ, what you're telling me, the means of time travel is spinning inside our every atom."

"I know. If you'll recall, *it already happened to me*."

"Yes! You're a pioneer, son, a freaking chrononaut."

"Uh, couldn't have done it without you?"

Dad frowned at my sarcasm. I could understand his thrill, but the clock was ticking, and he didn't know the horrors I unleashed with my ridiculous *pioneering*.

"What was it like, going through?" he asked me.

"Kind of like getting shocked, punched in the stomach, the giant whirlpool at Six Flags, all at once, compressed into less than a second."

"Right, all right, excellent," he muttered. "I'm going in."

"What are we doing?"

He pressed the car keys into my hand. "Keep the car running."

"So I'm the wheelman?"

A slight grin sneaked back onto his face. "That you are. Wish me luck."

I kept the driver's seat warm, started the ignition. Watching Dad head back toward Chip at the security gate, not knowing what he planned to do, frayed every last one of my nerves.

I begged Paige, wherever she was, to wait just a little longer. Reel the film in reverse, the train goes backward and the damsel is in one piece again, sprawled across the tracks, desperate to be untied from the ropes. I scanned the radio, looking for something calm, but none of the available music kept rhythm with my heartbeat. I tapped the radio off, resumed my surveillance.

Dad was nowhere to be seen, and Chip's security booth was also empty.

Time sticks when you're in a panic. I don't know how long I waited for some sign of life, but what I got instead was the wail of far-off sirens ricocheting off the echo chamber of glass buildings around me.

Then, over at Rush headquarters, about six floors up, an office window burst outward from the force of a human-sized projectile. My body jolted at the sight of it. Both my hands pressed the horn. No idea why.

When the object bounced onto the courtyard lawn in a rain of glass, I saw that it was just an empty office chair and not, say, my father falling to his death. Six stories above, nobody appeared in the jagged opening formerly known as the office window. No movement at all.

Still, this didn't look like part of a plan.

I could've imploded from helplessness. No matter what Dad said, I should've gone in there with him. I should've insisted he take me home instead of here. He was a desk jockey, not a Navy SEAL. For the extent of his physical prowess and stealth, he might as well have been a brain floating in a jar.

Another few seconds, and police cruisers blared down the road in both directions. They screeched to a halt in formation outside the gate, as if this siege was all choreographed ahead of time. Cops deployed from their vehicles and breached the "security checkpoint" no problem. All they did was duck under the lowered toll bar, or hurdle it, in the case of one showoff.

There was still a chance, if I timed it exactly, that Dad might sprint out of the gate with that flash drive raised triumphantly in his hand, leap over the hood of a parked cruiser, and dive into the car just as I pulled up to grab him.

So it was on me now.

I had maybe a few seconds to recall everything I knew about driving a car from the three or four training sessions I had with Mom. I held my breath and eased the car out backwards, shifted into drive. At the main road, I flicked the left turn signal and waited, counting the seconds.

Behind the gate, blue uniforms converged in the courtyard like a whole football team in a pile-on tackle. A glimpse of my father's gray sweatpants in the center of it all. The crowd broke and there was Kasper Vale with his hands cuffed behind his back.

That's when I knew for sure that Dad's plan was no plan at all. He'd totally winged it, and he failed. The guy could invent a time travel device, but he couldn't figure out how to break into a building without instantly attracting the attention of the entire Cape Fear Police Department.

As much as I wanted to, I didn't cry out. I didn't ram the gate with the car or throw myself at the mercy of the lawmen. Nothing but my own arrest would come of it. So I played a random passer-by rubbernecking for a glimpse of the ruckus at the Rush building. *Don't mind me, just taking a shortcut home.*

What else could I have done? I left my father to his fate. Took that turn and drove.

6:50 P.M.

I CLIPPED AN SUV at an intersection and scraped a long thread of paint off its passenger door. I wouldn't have realized if not for the chorus of horns. Without a backward glance I left the scene of the accident, because why did it matter now? Dad was arrested and Paige was dead.

Nearing twenty-four hours with no sleep. So exhausted, I could hardly climb the main staircase in my house. Up ahead in my room the lights were on, the doorway open. Russ 2.0 lay sprawled on my mattress, hands behind his head, thinking, while Connie manned the keyboard and monitor at my desk.

I stood there for a few seconds before anyone noticed.

"*You*," 2.0 said, bolting upright. "What are you doing here?"

When Connie turned, his glazed eyes cleared fast. He glanced back and forth between the twin Russ replicas as if he forgot which was which.

The computer monitor displayed a familiar video: Bobby Parker and Savannah Lark seated in a booth at the Silver Bullet, playing

119

characters who weren't themselves. The footage I recorded just a few hours earlier.

I didn't have to ask where Connie got the video. He must've salvaged the memory stick from the camera I smashed against that brick wall across the street from Paige's.

2.0 rolled off his bed and came at me with an open hand. I flinched, but all he did was press his palm against the side of my face, probed my skin with his fingers, staring. Nothing happened to correct the paradox. No sick mutant melding together of our flesh, no body molecules suddenly unsure which Russ to cling to.

His own face was so slack with idiotic wonder, I was embarrassed for us.

"I still can't believe it," he said.

"Believe it," I said. This had to be exactly how schizophrenics experienced their lives. Like me, Russ 2.0 was also wearing a hoodie. I noted the sliver glint of our cell phone, peeking out from the belly pouch.

"Time warp? I'd never do anything so stupid," he claimed.

"Hindsight, Monday Morning Quarterback, and all that, brother."

I swung a fist at his stomach. His abs clenched and my sudden sneak attack put him off balance. He stumbled backward into the dresser, toppled a pile of clean laundry we had both forgot to put away.

I had the cell phone in my hand, neatly pickpocketed.

"Guess I should've expected that," 2.0 complained.

"You of all people," I said.

Connie stayed out of it. He returned to the keyboard, minimized the video display to uncover the WCPF local news station site, and dialed up the volume so we could all hear. It was aerial shots from a helicopter. Cruisers on a roadside somewhere.

For a second, I thought he was showing late breaking news of Dad's arrest.

He wouldn't look at me, but I saw his tortured expression reflected in the screen clear enough.

"You're the outsider here," 2.0 told me. "And you're a disaster. Look."

The news clip wasn't about my father after all. Chopper footage showed a single-vehicle accident, a car crushed against a telephone pole. The front end was a squeezed accordion, but the back was all I needed to guess the make and model. Only one guy in town had an Aston Martin Rapide.

The voice-over reporter solemnly intoned Bobby Keene-Parker's name. A high-speed wreck, emergency airlift to New Hanover Hospital, critical condition. Then, they cut to a live shot of movie mogul Marv Parker outside one of the Silver Screen sound stages. He was a thick man with a trimmed beard and sunglasses to keep his dead eyes from view. Couldn't be bothered to rush to his son's hospital bedside, apparently.

Marv Parker told the press, deadpan, "Kid's been on a self-destruction streak for a long time now, so frankly I'm not surprised. Ruined a beautiful car. Eventually a parent's got to let go. The boy's responsible for his own screw-ups, you know? He's got to realize there's a lot of people in this business depending on him."

The minions crowded behind Marv Parker tried their best not to grimace.

I'd thought those hours at the Silver Bullet were the only stretch of perfection I managed during this disastrous second pass. But I was drunk on my own glory. Didn't pay enough attention to the way Bobby got up and sped off as soon as the torture of recording his scenes was over.

He left distracted, his emotions scraped hollow from the inside out. All that daddy subtext must've wormed into his thoughts, took his mind off the road...

"This happened after you finished shooting your video," 2.0

121

said. "This, and Paige. I don't know what you did. What I know is you're *not me*—because I'd never go around hurting people like this, knowing what would happen."

"But I *didn't*… I wouldn't…" I tried to say. He didn't even know about Dad's arrest yet.

The movie posters on my walls, the close-up faces of Batman and Tyler Durden and Walter White and Imperator Furiosa and Dr. Manhattan all glared at me. My jury, just waiting to have their unanimous guilty verdict read aloud by the court.

My alarm clock read 6:58. Less than two minutes to go.

"Look," I pleaded. "The message told me I had one shot and I had to take it. The message was from *me*, from the future, so why wouldn't I?"

"I don't know… common sense?" 2.0 said.

"We suck at common sense and you know it," I said.

The phone buzzed in my hand just as the clock flipped to 6:59. Right on schedule, the text from the future coming through. *Take the leap*, it would offer, just like last time.

2.0 leaped for the phone, caught me off guard, and a tangled mess of Horace Vales bounced onto the bed. Lookalike pairs of hands grabbing for the phone. I clutched his arm. We put me in a headlock. He elbowed his face.

The phone spun out of our hands and dropped to the floor at Connie's feet. He leaned forward in his chair, hands squeezing both armrests. The phone was Connie's for the taking.

We froze and looked at him, but he hesitated.

"*Connie*," 2.0 said.

Connie picked up the phone. "You're my best friend," he said. "You're *both* my best friend. I didn't know which one of you to trust, except that you… *you're* the one causing all of this."

The phone buzzed a second time. Seven p.m. The Pastime Project had arrived.

"Connie," I said. "Please be careful. You could mess up everything."

2.0 squirmed out from underneath me, shoved me into the headboard, and slid off the bed. I thought he'd take the phone from his accomplice, but instead he backed away from both of us, toward the open closet. He crouched in there, enveloped by the hanging clothes.

Then he shut himself inside.

"Do it, Connie," he called out from behind the door. "Like we decided."

My attention snapped back to the guy with the phone, my best friend, just as he pressed the icon. An arm's length out of reach, I couldn't stop him in time.

Too late I realized: 2.0 had ducked into the closet so he wouldn't get caught in the wormhole.

I screamed, "*Stop!*"

But it wasn't what I expected, as usual. Connie didn't take the leap for himself. Instead, he turned the display against me, and I was bathed once again in a blast of bright white light.

DAY ONE
(TAKE THREE)

WH**ΛM, I WΛS** awake. Just like that.

But I didn't know where I was or how long I was gone, not until total recall smacked me across the skull. Then I realized I'd lost barely a second of time. A nanosecond. My hands were still clutching at nothing. If I was screaming before, I was screaming still.

Naked on my bed. Pins and needles head to toe.

This time I knew exactly what happened to me: a program created by my father sent a localized black hole cycloning out from my phone, and it spun me in its vortex at such an absurd speed that my molecules stretched like sugar in a cotton candy machine.

Like, instant death. Except now I was reconstituted and deposited on a precise point in the space-time continuum. Born again, the new Horace Vale, same as the old Horace Vale.

My alarm clock *bleep bleep bleeped*. I whacked snooze but the racket kept going. No actual time was displayed—just random digital dashes. Glitches. I found the cord, pulled the plug. The clock went blank.

Over on my desk, my computer clicked away at a frantic round of internal processing and spit the results onto the monitor in a running trail of alpha-numeric *Matrix*-style nonsense. The toy lightsaber in my closet was firing off the electronic sizzle it was only supposed to do when it hit something. And when it sported batteries that hadn't been dead for at least four years.

I knew 2.0 was not inside that closet. Connie was gone, too. Empty desk chair. Or it was me who left *them* behind. Or maybe their time line was completely deleted. Or the fabric of the universe was so twisted now, I didn't know when or where the hell I was.

Footsteps pounded in the hall. I got my bearings enough to sit upright before my surprise visitor arrived. It turned out to be Dad, out of breath, gripping both sides of my doorframe. He was home and safe and sound, not locked away in a city holding tank for breaking and entering. He was still wearing his morning bathrobe over the sweats.

I laughed aloud to see him here, pardoned of his crime because he never actually committed it. His presence in my doorway had to mean the whole day was reset, back to seven a.m.

Bobby Keene-Parker would soon be cruising around in his pristine Rapide.

Paige Davis would be *alive.*

Everything could be fixed or rigged never to happen in the first place.

"Um…" Dad said, and averted his eyes.

Because, you know, I was naked. I made a fast sleeping bag out of my comforter and then waved my hands at him, insisting, "no, no, no, I wasn't…"

"No, no," Dad parroted, urgently agreeing with whatever it was I was going to say. He pulled the door almost shut to give me privacy, then spoke through the crack. "Don't be embarrassed, son. I was a teenage boy once—"

"Dad—no! It wasn't that. Come in here."

He eased back into the room, but it took him a couple tries to actually look at me. By then I'd pulled on a pair of shamefully old *Despicable Me* boxer shorts. All this awkwardness was Dad's fault, actually. He was the one who invented a time-space transport that rejected all carry-on items, including clothes.

"I heard you screaming," he explained. "Are you home sick today?"

"Sick? No. Maybe? But something is definitely wrong."

"What happened to your eye?" Dad asked.

Before I could answer, the barrage of meaningless script on my Mac smash-cut to a video feed, even though I didn't touch the computer. The speakers filled will the hissing white noise of an open mic, demanding our attention.

Once again, the talking head news anchor for today's webcast was your host, Horace Vale. There he was on my monitor, without my distinctive black eye.

Video Russ leaned in and said, "Dad—Russ? God, I hope you get this recording. We tried to time it for right after your leap." Static interference crackled through his voice. The video feed digitized and wobbled like a roving weather update from the worst stretch of a hurricane.

Dad crouched into the desk chair and slipped on his reading glasses.

"Hello?" he said to the screen.

"It's not a Skype session, Dad," I said. "It's pre-recorded."

"I can barely see it. Is that you on there?" Dad said.

Video Russ went on, "We're transmitting this back, but we can only do it once, so—" Most of what he said next was garbled by ear-splitting static, laced with snippets of random music beats accidentally borrowed from some other frequency:

"...warning... pay attention... no matter what..." Not a great time for bad reception. I slapped the screen as if violence would solve something, but of course it didn't. This was a transmission through time, not a jammed jukebox.

"Is this a school project of yours?" Dad asked.

I shushed him. This recording wasn't the same Video Russ who spammed me the original pitch for the Pastime Project. At least, it didn't seem to be the same video shoot. The first one used a steady camera and professional framing. This one was slapped together stat, totally amateurish. This Video Russ used the jittery selfie-cam method, the final victim's desperate plea for rescue in a found footage horror flick.

"…someone else… not just you…" Video Russ went on. The image flipped to negative, went to black, stabilized, pixelated, froze. The static inhaled and exhaled. I couldn't make any sense of it, except when Video Russ said, "*You have to stop the leaps.*" I caught that message with sky-blue clarity.

"Stop the leaps?" Dad asked.

"*Shhhh!*"

"…every time you leap… messing with the space-time fabric… *holes*… through the wormholes… glitches… someone else besides you…"

At that, the video cut off for good. Just a blinking cursor on a black screen, and then the random characters tumbling merrily along again. Dad leaned back in the chair, took off his glasses, scratched his scruffy cheek with an earpiece. He stared at the screen like he could actually read that gibberish—and who knows? Maybe he could.

"Did you catch much of that?" I asked him.

"Space-time fabric?" he asked. "Wormholes?"

"Exactly," I said, squeezing between him and the computer to grab his full attention. His eyes drifted up to mine. "To be clear, you never told me about the time travel program you developed for Rush Fiberoptics, right? You never said squat about mini-black holes and algorithms and tiny tilt-a-whirls fueled by cosmic energy—"

"Negative energy," Dad said. Even flabbergasted, he had to correct me.

"Whatever. The point is, as far as you know, you never breathed a word about your top-secret experiments to me because this shit was way too dangerous to leak into the world, right? Stuff you couldn't even trust your teenage son with. Am I right?"

"But—then—how?" he asked.

"Because *we've had this conversation already*, Dad."

His face went slack with the weight of understanding.

"Or we will, later today," I said. "Listen, your theoretical time-travel device has been developed, and I used it. Twice. Just now. That's why I showed up naked out of thin air, and why we just watched a video of me from the future."

"Russ, hold on a second—"

"No time, Dad. I already had to waste time convincing you once before—or actually *later*—and we ran the clock down. So now you have to just listen. We've got twelve hours to figure this thing out. You heard the guy: I can't use the program again. I'm screwing with reality here and making it worse every time."

"Twelve hours?" Dad said.

"Half a day, seven a.m. to seven p.m.—that's the span of the leap."

"But, no, this can't… there were so many insurmountable technical problems and inconsistencies at the prototype stage. Not just negative energy, but radioactive decay, safety concerns. I never really got this thing out of the brainstorming stage."

"Here and now you didn't. But something changes, eventually."

"Yes… *yes*, I see," he said. But then his face soured. "No."

"What's the matter?"

"A time machine couldn't be used to change the past. The slightest change creates a paradox, because now the world is no longer the world in which the time machine was invented. Do you see? Paradoxes can't happen. Schrödinger's cat can't be both dead and alive in the box, unless…"

I planted my hands on both sides of his face and brought our eyes just a few inches apart. "I don't know about a cat, Dad, but *I'm here,* in my own past. This is the *third time* I've lived through this morning."

"My God, Hugh Everett was right all along."

"Who's Hugh Everett?"

"That band you like, the Eels? They did the songs for that ogre thing—"

"*Shrek* soundtrack, and it's *you* who likes the Eels, but what's your point?"

"The main guy," Dad said, "Mark Everett, well, his *father* was Hugh Everett the Third, a quantum physicist with honestly almost zero clout in the field because he developed the Many-Worlds Interpretation to solve the Schrödinger problem, and everyone thought he was a fool.

"Everett said the only way to avoid paradoxes is parallel universes, discrete from one another. Nearly infinite multiple realities branching off like grape clusters, each just slightly different from the other. What happens in one doesn't affect the others. If it were possible to jump between them…"

Parallel worlds. So that was it. I wasn't warping back into my own time line after all. *That* was a logical impossibility. Instead, those patented Pastime Project wormholes were sucking me into the near past of *another universe*, one almost identical to mine, but still different.

There I was, proof of a concept that physicists would only take seriously in mathematical theory. Consider our known universe, Dad explained. You know, the one that's still in mid-explosion after the Big Bang fourteen billion years ago? The one with three dimensions and particles of matter floating inside a vast shell of empty space? Well, *this* universe is only one of an infinite series of them, trillions upon trillions born and dying at every millisecond.

There is a new universe for every possible thing that could happen, an endlessly branching tree of options. So let's say you erase a word you wrote down in your TV script: *boom*, a new universe where you *didn't* erase the word. A guy in Moscow decides not to pick his nose: *boom*, a new, nose-picker universe. An alien protozoa-type-thing on Alpha Beta 516 decides to wriggle its cilia backward instead of forward—*boom*, new universe.

Consider a reality where Hitler won World War Two or the Cuban Missile Crisis ended in Nuclear Winter. Heck, in a zillion other variations, life on earth never even started, or, if it did, the dinos never died out.

All these possibilities were *absolute reality* somewhere.

Everything possible, happened, and was happening still.

In the reality I came from, a boy named Horace Vale went out for a walk downtown and disappeared forever. There would be search parties, milk carton photos. His parents would deplete their bank accounts looking for him, but they'd never get any closure, because *that* Horace Vale simply slipped through the cracks…

…and found himself deposited into a new universe not his own. Russ 2.0 wasn't *me* me, but an alternate me, a living entity completely separate from me, the same as me, but not exactly…

"I'm an inter-dimensional alien invader," I realized aloud. And another insight, another glitch, suddenly became glaringly obvious. I was sent back to my own bedroom at seven a.m., a point in time when my *original* self should've been fast asleep on his pillow. I should've materialized right on top of him, but he wasn't here. Just me and my father.

"Where's the other me?" I wondered aloud.

"Other you?" Dad knotted his eyebrows. Smart guy, but I was asking him to jump into a scenario that was already moving at approximately light speed. Confusing to anyone, even the guy who would set this crazy stuff in motion.

"When I go back in time," I told him, "there are two of me. The me I *was* and the me I *am*. So where is the Was-Me me?"

Dad nodded, checked his watch. "I guess he's at school," he said.

"What's he doing there this early?"

He shook his wrist, put the watch face against his ear. "Ticker on the fritz," he said, "but in my office, just before I heard you scream, the clock on my computer said it was exactly one in the afternoon."

The shock of misplaced time. It wasn't seven a.m. It was one p.m. A six-hour leap instead of twelve. My time sliced clean in half.

And almost half an hour had already passed since I came through the wormhole. At this moment, Paige was out by the high school track being bullied by Asshat. Soon she'd be headed home, headed toward a death I refused to believe was self-inflicted. And here I was, wasting time across town, debating physics with my father.

2:OO P.M.

THE LOSS OF six hours stumped my father. A few hasty recalculations gave him a fresh hypothesis involving half-life atomic energy decay. It seemed the device might only be able to recapture half its energy after every use. Twelve hours becomes six becomes three and so on. If I did it again, I'd leap to four o'clock, then five-thirty, or so he figured.

But I'd received my own stern warning (from myself) *not* to do it again.

After I vetoed Dad's predictable idea to drop by Rush Fiberoptics, he returned to his attic office, cracked his knuckles, and set off to solve the problem I presented him with. We needed a new approach—one that involved gaining *remote* access to Rush's database to see what they knew about a time machine. Even if he had zero hope of replicating the program, there was still a chance he could find a way to stop this perpetual spin cycle.

He was a much better hacker than chauffeur, so I biked to school alone.

No answer when I called Paige on the cell phone I borrowed

from Dad. She was still in class. I couldn't bring myself to leave a message. How do you explain to a friend that you're calling to thwart a suicide she hasn't even contemplated yet? How do you tell her when you know, and she knows, that she'd never do such a thing to herself in the first place? I'd just have to intercept in the flesh.

I felt optimistic with fifty bucks in my pocket and my own clothes on again, especially a pair of firm running shoes. I had a mess of stinging blisters from Connie's flip-flops. My stupid bicycle was another story—rusty from disuse, chain jerking between gears.

Though the sky had been clear in the last two variations, in *this* universe it was gray, almost buzzing electronically like TV static. The shaded windows on cars seemed to almost glow. But when I looked head-on, just a regular window. Usually, you'd need Photoshop or CGI to get these unsettling effects, these glitches in the space-time fabric that could be my fault.

I hit the school grounds during the end-of-day rush, later than I hoped. Solid lines of buses, cars, and walkers streaming out of every exit, diesel clogging the air. As I coasted along the access road, some wiseass yelled from an open bus window, "Hey, Vale! Y'all're going the wrong way! Escape! Escape!"

He was right, though. I was too late. Paige would already be on her bus headed home, and I didn't know which one was hers.

I cut across the sloping eastern grounds and pushed the bike behind a cluster of bushes. Right away I spotted them: Connie and 2.0 exiting through their usual side door, headed toward a backwoods trail that cut a few minutes from their afternoon commute.

I couldn't hear them, but 2.0 was broadcasting his agitation obviously enough: blabber-mouthing, throwing off wild gestures, walking backwards in front of Connie when he wanted to emphasize a particular point he was making. General obnoxiousness.

Connie was just about sleepwalking compared to his sidekick. He was weighted with too many secrets and plans, more than I could guess. For now, I had to keep my cover, had to restrain myself from leaping out and confronting them, setting off some fresh chain of butterfly effects.

But, believe me, I'd been doing some calculating, and I had a few accusations to level at my *closest friend,* Connie. For starters: there was the issue of how fast he initially bought into my time-travel story when I showed up at his house in a soggy cardboard box, or how easily he formulated theories about how it could've happened, even though nothing like this had *ever* occurred in the history of humankind. How easily he betrayed me in the end, even if a second leap was my only choice. He zapped me out of his life with the press of his thumb. All I knew for sure was Connie knew more than he knew he knew.

For now, I had the facts I needed. Russ 2.0 was leaving school on time, uninjured, instead of nursing a wound in the assistant principal's conference room. Which meant he never went out and confronted Paige's bully. Which meant he got distracted because somebody stole his cell phone. *Which meant* there had to be *three* of us now, not just two.

The Horace Vale who was born and raised in this universe.

The Horace Vale who leaped to seven a.m. and was now at the Silver Bullet.

And me.

Me on a rescue mission, 2.0 headed home with Connie, and 3.0 (really, what else would I call him?) plotting to tinker mercilessly with Bobby Parker's brain. Three Horace Vales fumbling around, screwing up the universe.

Back on the banana seat, I tried to dial Paige's cell again as my bike jostled down the hillside, but my fingers hit all the wrong digits. I called her when I reached smooth sidewalk. Straight to voicemail. Left a message this time, begged her to call me back on my Dad's cell *a-sap,* then I cut as straight a path toward her house as I could.

In twenty minutes I skidded up to her duplex. My dismount was more like ramming the front steps and tumbling over the handlebars. I slapped her screen door two-handed instead of knocking, wheezing for breath. "Paige!"

Nobody was in the living room when I shielded my eyes and squinted.

The doorbell buzzer didn't work.

"Paige!" I yelled again, and opened the screen door a crack.

Still no answer, so I stepped in. A cat leapt off the back of her couch and skittered past, scaring the crap out of me. I went into the kitchen. Tried to prep myself for what I might see—down on the floor, slumped over the table.

Nothing but a slow drip from the faucet. Dishes piled up for cleaning. Then, a toilet flush, water running in the bathroom sink. Paige came out still buttoning her pants. The moment was awkward for both of us, as she noted aloud, using her spiciest language.

Paige could curse me for hours for all I cared because *she was alive.*

"I was worried," I explained. "You weren't answering your phone."

"So you break into my house?"

"I didn't break—the door was open. And I called your name twice."

She swiped her cell phone off the kitchen table and checked. "No missed calls," she said. She wasn't wearing her hat for once. I couldn't remember the last time I saw her hair unfurled. She looked almost—soft.

"There's been some—technical difficulties," I said. To prove it, I nodded at the digital display on her microwave. 8:88 o'clock.

Paige didn't seem concerned. "What were you *worried* about, that you'd have to come all the way down to the ghetto to check on me?"

"It's not… I heard you had a run-in with some douche in gym class. I thought maybe you might be upset about it."

"I'm legit impressed that you care," she said, "but I'm also fine. Same old b.s. I get all the time at school. Nothing new. I learned a long time not to get worked up. Who even told you?"

I couldn't think fast enough to be sure my answers would gel with the rest of the facts, but I also couldn't exactly ask her to believe I was an inter-dimensional visitor with time-travel foresight.

"I, uh—people were saying you wrote some stuff on Facebook."

"I don't even have a profile on thefacebook."

There is was again, *thefacebook.*

"Why are you saying it all foreign-exchange like that—*thefacebook*?"

"Because that's what it's called," she said.

"Is it?"

"Anyway, who cares? I have like zero interest in 'social media.'"

Of course Paige was right—she *didn't* have a profile, at least not in the universe I came from, where the site was plain old Facebook, minus the *the*, and YouView was called YouTube. All these dizzying little variations.

She said, "Somebody's messing with y'alls head, Christopher Nolan."

Then she chuckled at me, broke out a six-pack of Coke from the fridge and popped one open for each of us. When I took a sip, it wasn't my universe's delicious and refreshing Coke. It tasted like a Xerox machine smelled after too much duplication.

"What happened with Savannah?" she asked, leaning against the counter. She'd taken off her trademarked flannel, and her white tank top was rather form fitting. She'd... *developed* since last time I noticed, which was probably back in little league.

"Oh, uh, the whole thing fell through," I said after too long a pause.

"Bummer. Listen, I'm sorry for busting your balls about the project deadline. Sometimes I think things are funny that aren't. So, uh, thank you for checking up on me, even if it's a false alarm and—"

"Do you mind if we look?" I blurted.

"At what?"

"Facebook. *The*. Just to see. Maybe there's an impostor or something."

Paige shrugged and said, "Knock yourself out. Laptop's upstairs."

Carpeted steps led to a narrow landing with Paige's room straight ahead. The only other bedroom was her mom's, I guessed. She and her mom moved here about a year back after what happened with her brother and her parents' separation. Trying to get out from under the shadow of *things that should never have happened.*

Her room was a sports hall of fame where she was the only inductee. Mounted baseball bats, field hockey sticks, soccer trophies. Not a teddy bear or scrap of pink in sight. She tossed herself onto the bed and flipped open the laptop lying there. While it booted up, I admired a shelf loaded with baseballs and a procession of Paige's snide grins on the yearly baseball cards our little league association made for us.

Comforting to see mementos from a past I actually remembered.

Freakily, she had a 2004 Curt Schilling baseball card, faded and scarred with creases. It was a duplicate of the lucky card I used to keep under my cap. The one I dumped in the trash after my disastrous last pitch.

"Did I ever tell you about my Curt Schilling card?" I asked her.

"Um, yeah," she said. "That *is* your Curt Schilling card, genius."

For a second I thought maybe in *this* reality, our past actions were different. Maybe here Mom *did* let Paige pitch the rest of the game. Maybe in this world, we won, and I gave Paige the card as a gift for bringing home the trophy.

Maybe, but no.

"I fished it from the garbage after you chucked it," she said, "which I thought was pretty asinine. I wanted to keep it as a reminder of how y'all screwed up my big shot on the mound and ruined my major league dreams. Grudges inspire me, sometimes."

"Glad I could be of help," I grumbled.

She got the Internet running and logged into thefacebook with my account. Same password, even in this reality. I got a hit on Paige's name and called up the profile. The pic was definitely of her, standing in the woods, wearing an Aussie bush hat instead of her trademarked baseball cap.

"That's you, yeah?" I said.

"Uh-huh, but I did *not* set up this profile. That picture's on the Cape Fear Wilderness Trail website, from when I did volunteer work last summer. Anyone could've grabbed it off the site."

I agreed. The profile was little more than her name and her school. Only three friends, all of them dickheads from the academy that Paige wouldn't in a million years want to be associated with.

"One of those assholes must've set this up," I said, but I wasn't so sure.

There was a stream of posts, dozens of them, stretching back for an hour (but none earlier). Paige Davis had supposedly written a full menu of emo clichés about feeling dead inside and just wanting to end it all, nobody understands me, my sex life is private, gay pride forever, etc. Generic filler that seemed lifted straight from song lyrics or It Gets Better campaign slogans.

None of it was anything that Paige would ever say in *any* universe.

Every few posts, one of her three "friends" would jump in with a callous *just do it* or *I dare you* or *come over to my house and I'll make you feel better*. I wouldn't have been at all surprised to see someone write: *take the leap.*

"They're not even trying," Paige said with a snort.

"This doesn't bother you?"

"Anyone with half a brain could tell this is fake," she said. "No offense. And, again, thank you for caring enough to check on me, but as you can see, I'm fine. People depend on me, and I don't forget that."

"I can't believe you aren't furious that somebody's aping you. I'd be—" I shut up because I was making Paige's point exactly. It was just as I suspected. She wasn't the sort to get so desperate, and certainly not anyone you'd believe was a suicide risk, *especially* because of her brother.

"Just a bunch of pampered junior ku klux sheet-heads," she said, clicking to refresh her false friends list.

But another profile appeared. One more person had accepted a friend request she didn't actually make, a guy named Rob Davis. For a second, the name didn't register with me, that is until I saw Paige bite down hard on one of her knuckles.

"How did they..." she asked.

Rob Davis was Paige's brother. I'd seen his Facebook account before, actually, after it became a spontaneous memorial site, with hundreds of goodbyes and fond memories, heartfelt and clunky alike. I assumed the account had been taken down after a while, so I didn't expect to see it again like this.

Plus, the profile pic was different—used to be Rob's kindergarten graduation pic but now it was just a .gif of a prescription pill bottle, a heartless joke about his suicide method. Whoever created Paige's profile had also hacked into Rob's dormant account.

"Paige, the person who did this is a serious asshole," I said, not knowing whether I should touch her, if she'd want that kind of comfort. "They all are. You really don't have to be ashamed about who you are. Your love life is your own business and there's nothing wrong with—"

She nodded half-heartedly and leaned her head against my chest. I wished our first hug could've been for better reasons than this.

"I don't understand," she muttered.

"We'll find out who did this. They should be arrested at least..."

Her breath warmed the hollow of my neck. "Thank you for

coming over here," she said. Her voice was raw, completely stripped of its usual tough protective shell. It made me want to tell her the entire ridiculous truth.

But before I could, she sat upright and steadied my head between her hands and pressed a forceful kiss on my lips. A long, deep inhale through her nose, like she was breathing me in. My eyes went wide and my mouth wouldn't quite shut from the surprise.

This was how Paige Davis dealt with her pain? Even when she broke away, I didn't have time to say a thing, because one last post had just blurted onto Paige's fake wall. It said:

That's it. It's done. All I have to do now is bleed.

Her supposed final post.

The culprit had to be the same sicko who'd been taunting me with mysterious phone calls and garbled email messages, who had the power to make the whole local grid go haywire with malfunctions. The *same person*, period. Someone targeting both of us, maybe even luring us together into one room. Here, now.

Paige put her fingers to her open mouth. Suddenly, that kiss was probably the last thing on her mind. And suddenly the fake profile wasn't a lame prank anymore. Because now I understood how it could possibly be that a brave heart like Paige Davis would wind up dead.

It wasn't suicide. It was murder.

Just as the insight hit me, an electric shock jolted through my spine, far too painful to be another time warp. A brilliant blinding light flashed from every direction, but my body stayed solid. The recorded warning on my home computer from Video Russ blared in my memory:

Someone else... can get through the holes... you understand?

A deafening static screech, and something burst into Paige's room.

2:50 P.M.

PAIGE DIDN'T HESITATE. In one sleek motion, she rolled off her mattress and swiped an aluminum bat from where it stood in the corner of her room. She wasn't going to die a passive death.

But the intruder wasn't a person. It had no real shape at all. More of an unfolding web of radiance, it seemed to be on the stairs and in the hall and bulging through the bedroom door, all at once. It was a digitized angelic glow—light dancing midair like slow-mo paint from a sprayer, full of crackling static electricity—except there was nothing heavenly about it.

The whole room was charged with its power. The currents cramped the muscles in my throat. I couldn't speak. Wisps of Paige's hair lifted upward as she crouched to take a swipe at anything that might happen to turn solid inside all that ambient light.

But the glow pooled in the doorway and darkened bluish. Another kind of doorway was opening.

And whatever came though would be hell-bent on killing Paige.

I knew, because it had succeeded once already in another world. Took her life and made it look like suicide. I couldn't understand why, but it had to be my fault, clear enough. For starters, I tore the rifts in time-space that would help Paige's killer step through, but it was even more than that. She was bait. Her "suicide" was a setup to lure me back here. *Save her.* Step right into the trap.

With the doorway blocked, our one escape hatch was Paige's bedroom window. I pointed to it, and she nodded. We were one floor up from the ground, but the risk of a sprained ankle and bruises seemed more pleasant than staying to see what would happen in her room once the radiance engulfed us.

Paige sidestepped and took a line-drive swing, shattering the window glass. Efficient, but she might as well have popped an airplane hatch thirty thousand feet above ground. An instant suction wrenched almost everything toward the opening that wasn't hammered to the floor.

A spinning baseball clocked my shoulder. Notebooks and commemorative cards and pendants and stray socks all smacked the window frame and coughed through the broken glass. Paige's bat snapped from her grip and was gone. Even the air in my lungs was expelled with one painful hiccup.

Despite the airborne chaos, we weren't affected. Our clothes rippled and our hair was tossed around, but our feet stuck as firmly on the ground as ever. It didn't make any physical sense. Not the pressurized vacuum, and not our resistance to its suction.

The pulsing electric light bled along the walls and surged toward us with an ambient roar. Paige's room was disappearing in a solid wall of static, like jumbo-tron screens set to dead channels on full volume. We were being enveloped. Even the window was swallowed up in its reach, painted over by an electric film.

Our only exit route was gone. And no more air to breathe. So much pressure, my head would implode if this lasted much longer.

I had to look at this situation backwards by using some serious Alice in Wonderland upside-down logic, like *no way out except through*, like the spaceship in all those sci-fi movies that rushes deep into the black hole in order to escape its event horizon.

I was fairly sure, at least, that this radiance was some kind of wormhole, or similar in principle, and I knew from two prior experiences that you could leap through the center of one and live to brag about it. That's what we had to do: dive into the dark blue core of what used to be Paige's bedroom doorway. I decided.

I grabbed her by the wrist. Wherever we were headed, we'd go together.

At least, that was the plan. But when I stepped toward the door, Paige fixed her sock feet to the floor and refused to move.

The noise was so loud we couldn't hear each other, but her wide eyes and frantically shaking head told me her opinion well enough. All I could think to do was put my hand against my chest, a silent vow—*we'll be all right.*

She studied me for a beat, snapped her eyes at the live electric meshing that closed in on us.

Then she let me do it, take her into the eye of the storm. The closer we got, the more that blue nucleus seemed to repel us. When I reached into the static, I didn't know if I'd be burned or electrified or sucked through a space-time vortex onto the bottom of the deepest part of the Atlantic Ocean.

Turned out to be none of the above. What happened was my arm went numb, but I felt the edge of the doorframe, just like you'd expect. I held fast and pulled us both through to the other side, into the hall.

Instant silence, except for our gasping breath.

Everything was perfectly ordinary, except behind us, where the doorway to Paige's room was still the butt end of the electrical field we just escaped. It filled the space, flat as a television screen, but it emitted no light, no sound.

Paige touched it, flinched back her finger after a bug-light *zap*.

"What the f—" she started to ask.

And something lunged out of the crackling blue gel and grabbed her wrist. It yanked her back toward the static wall from where it came. It was the shape of a human hand, but more like the gray fractal *image* of a hand, what you'd see if you stared at a Magic Eye picture for long enough. And its contact with Paige's skin gave off a feedback screech.

It was hell-bent to drag her back through, or kill her trying. All I could think to do was anchor both my arms around her waist. She leaned against me and planted her feet on either side of the door. When she grabbed for the virtual hand, her fingers passed straight through the illusion.

Except it was still pulling at her, real enough. We growled and howled. Neither of us used real words. A second virtual hand emerged from the static, but this one wasn't empty. It clutched a weapon, long and sharp. A knife.

And it swiped the blade toward Paige's captured and vulnerable wrist.

All I have do to now is bleed, that thefacebook message said.

I tossed my own hands into the pile of real and unreal fingers on Paige's arm. Slapped my grip across her wrist, superimposed over the virtual hand, just in time for the knife to strike.

The blade sliced just below my knuckles, sprouted instant blood.

For a second it didn't hurt. For a second.

I pressed my face against the back of Paige's neck and stifled a scream.

The mindless hands seemed to think they accomplished their mission, so the grip relaxed, and we took our chance. Together, we heaved ourselves away from the static wall.

Good news: the virtual hands disintegrated in a shower of pixels.

Bad news: the sudden momentum sent us backward over the landing. We tumbled down the stairs, arms and legs smacking the wall and banister and each other as we took the fast route down.

EXTR/ LIFE

Without the plush stairwell carpeting, we probably would've broken our necks. Still, the grand finale was a tile floor—not quite so soft. I was splayed out snow angel-style, head ringing from the impact, but at least I served as a cushion for Paige when she landed stomach-first.

For a second, we breathed into each other's faces, astonished. To be slammed together like this. To be attacked out of nowhere by a virtual assassin or whatever. To still be alive, pressed together, both of us heaving and alive.

Then she rolled away and dropped to the floor beside me.

A few more minutes' recovery time would've been nice, but nope. Relentless tendrils of sparking, sputtering electronic ooze leaked down the stairwell walls toward us. More a force than a physical thing, though whatever-it-was had a clear enough purpose—a *program*:

Slice Paige's wrist and make it look like suicide.

And now it was coming at us for another shot. The pulsing, mesmerizing light froze us into easy targets. We just stared at it, coming at us. Until, from the center of the vortex, something flung out, swished past my ear, and sank into the wall behind me. It shuddered into place.

A chef's knife. Real metal, a blade you'd find in any normal kitchen. It was thrust to the hilt into the wall, dead center between our two heads.

After that, the ooze of light in the stairwell flashed, sputtered, and faded away. As if, with its knife-throwing sideshow act complete, it had finally exhausted itself. Nothing left but a burnt plastic smell.

We both kept our attention fixed on the empty stairs, just to be sure. I couldn't say how long it was before Paige sprang up and went toward the kitchen. She came back with a dishtowel and wrapped it a few times around my wounded hand. Blood all over the carpeted stairs and the tile, smeared across the front of my shirt. Just looking at it made me woozy.

"All right, Russ, please explain what the hell just happened."

"Something tried to kill us," I said.

"*Something*?" She wrenched the chef's knife out of the wall and brandished it at me. "This is *mine*, from my kitchen. I don't know what that pyrotechnics show was all about, but a pair of pin-art hands just tried to cut me with my own knife, and now my mom's apartment looks like it got hit by Katrina."

I had zilch for answers. Sure, I'd been warned. The Future Russ who sent me the video knew loads more than he ever wanted to know, but he was no help to me now. I wasn't working with the information he had.

Paige was still studying the knife, testing its sharpness with her fingertip. I could see my distorted reflection in the metal when she asked, "Could it—that wasn't a ghost, was it? I know it's crazy of me to even ask. I'm the most rational person I know, but after that stuff on thefacebook... I... wait." She narrowed her eyes and grabbed my shirt collar, twisting it in her fist. "How'd you know?"

"Know what?" I croaked.

"About *this*. That I was in danger."

"I saw the online posts."

"Any idiot could've seen it was a fake profile."

"I wasn't one hundred percent sure."

"You're lying. How did you get here almost right on time?"

Paige's cat meowed questioningly at us from the top of the stairs. I could empathize.

"*Russ*," Paige insisted.

"Listen to me, please. I have no clue what just happened or why it stopped happening or what to do if it happens again. All I know is we both need to get out of here. And you have to contact your mom and let her know not to come home."

I was kind of hoping she'd be spooked enough to just go with it. Nope. "*Why*?" she demanded.

149

"Whatever just attacked us—you need to keep away from it," I tried to explain. "Go someplace unexpected, and don't even tell *me* where. I think it's following me, or it knows what I'll do next. We'll have a better chance if we fool it with unexpected moves."

She clenched her jaw at me, glared down at that knife in her hand. My blood was on her tank top and her hair was an alluring mess. Right then probably wouldn't have been a good time to ask her more about that surprise kiss. "Tell me why you know these things," she said.

"What if I said it was way too much for you to deal with?"

"I'd say *try me*, or I'll kick your ass."

Her cell phone jingled. She gave me a *don't move* scowl and shimmied it out of her pocket. I was so focused on escape, I never even thought to wonder who might be calling.

But then she answered, and listened to her caller, and the impact of this bizarro scenario corrugated her forehead. She said to the caller, "Shut up. Who is this really?"

My own voice came faintly through the receiver: "…just make sure you were all right." Russ 2.0 was calling, just like he did in the last reality I visited. Only this time, Paige wasn't dead, so she answered.

"What kind of sick prank is this?" she asked.

In that moment of uncertainty, I took my chance, pulled open her screen door and made a break for it. No time for goodbyes. I leaped off her front stoop, tripped over my bike in a lame attempt to mount it. My shoes couldn't find the pedals fast enough. The tires wobbled through the sandy lot before they reached the sidewalk.

Paige grunted as she pounced on me. The bike flopped over, trapped my left leg against the ground. I rolled onto my back to scramble away, but she squatted onto my stomach and jammed an elbow under my chin to keep me docile. Her knee braced on my sternum thrust away my breath.

Gritty pavement bit through the towel wrapped around my hand.

"You just—called me," she said. "That was you on the phone. I don't know how—but it was."

"...wasn't me... not exactly..." I choked out.

"Talk, Russ." She lifted her knee to let me breathe.

There wasn't much left to hide so I did talk. I told her everything in a rush, from the first leap and my solitary confinement at Conrad's house and then the escape and the news of her supposed suicide, to the second half-leap that landed me in my bedroom at one o'clock in the afternoon.

And I told her fast—because I was running out of time to stop Bobby Keene-Parker from crashing his car.

3:00 P.M.

PAIGE WAS A born myth-buster, so she wasn't going to let me off after some rant that totally sounded like I'd taken a major dose of Molly. I was lucky she even released me from her death grip.

"We should call the cops," she said.

"And tell them what?"

"I don't know, but it'll be interesting to hear their opinion."

I said, "They'll think we're both nuts, and they won't be any help."

"You don't seem to have much of a handle, either, coming at me with this story."

"I haven't had tons of free time to Sherlock through everything."

At least the nightmare in her bedroom got her to vacate her apartment. One small victory. Another plus was getting her to agree not to let anyone else in there. She volleyed quick phone calls between her mom and grandma, convincing them they needed to have dinner at Grandma's straight after her mom got out of work because the landlord just up and had their duplex fumigated for roaches without any notice.

As for Paige herself, she refused to go into hiding like I asked. Instead, she bummed a standing ride on the back pegs of my bike. Gripped her fingers on my shoulders as I pumped us back uptown toward the Silver Bullet Diner. She wasn't going to let me out of her sight.

Bobby's Rapide was still parked outside. I leaned my bike against the diner's siding—nowhere to lock it and bigger things to worry about. When I pushed through the entrance, the bell hailed my arrival. No time to form a plan or consider how the other version of me would react.

There he was, standing beside the far-end booth, the Russ Vale who'd taken a leap through the wormhole only once and was still under the impression he had his universe under control. I had to think of him as Russ 3.0, even if his existence in this universe technically started six hours before mine. Those were hours I already lived.

He glanced up at me from his camera, put his attention back to the screen. Then he did a double take. *Yes, it's you, Russ Vale. And by you I mean me.* I don't know why, but I kind of expected 3.0 to raise his hands in surrender.

In the booth, Savannah and Bobby were still acting the scene, unaware that the camera eye was tilting to the floor and their director had totally quit paying attention to their performance.

But then Savannah spotted me—a mirror image of the guy standing beside her—and she bolted upright. At the soda machine, Sally the waitress also saw double and sprayed Coke all over her hand instead of into a cup.

Behind me Paige muttered, "Y'all were really *serious* with this," as if the phone call from another me, and the inexplicable techno-vortex that almost killed her, weren't enough evidence already.

Russ 3.0 rushed at me, bug-eyed, waddling in Connie's flip-flops and oversized jeans. Savannah followed close behind him. With Paige at my hip—and her kiss still fresh on my mind—this was the weirdest double date in history.

"Aw, don't look so surprised," I told 3.0, even if I had to admit that when I was still him, I never would've anticipated *this*.

"What're you doing here—what is this?" he asked. His lips were stiff as a ventriloquist's, so nobody else could read them, I guess.

"I'm not who you think I am," I said, voice dialed down to private mode.

"Who do you think I think you are?" 3.0 asked.

"You think I'm the blissfully unaware Russ who lives in this reality…"

He jolted back as he realized. "You're…"

"From the future," I said. "Already ahead of you."

"But… I'm supposed to be…"

I mean, he'd already taken one leap, so he knew exactly what wacko physics we were dealing with. He should've been able to process the concept of another Russ showing up, further down the time line. Seriously, just a few hours ago, I *was* this guy. I remembered the triumph of standing behind that camera, the sense of invincibility. I remembered everything except this part, where another, future me shows up.

"I'm here to stop you from making a huge mistake," I said.

"What mistake?" he asked. "And, Paige—how did you—"

"Not the right place to explain," I said, nodding at the bystanders.

Sally leaned over the counter, drying her hands with a towel. "Care to introduce me to your look-alike, sugar?" she said to neither one of us in particular. Savannah was also pondering the existence of two of us like we were matching statues in a museum. *See if you can spot the fake.*

"This is my—my twin brother, Seth," 3.0 explained.

"Nice save," Paige snarked behind me.

I tried not to wince at 3.0's improv. Not that I could've done better, even considering my time-space advantage. And since we had the same brain, I caught on to his little inside joke: Seth (or Set, if you like) was the Egyptian god of chaos and destruction. The brother and polar opposite of the good god Horus, who, not so incidentally, was the deity of time, source of the word *hour*.

Horus. Horace. Clever.

"How come I never knew you had a twin?" Sally asked. "Lemme guess—y'all been playing me, coming in here pretending to be the same kid but I don't know the difference, right?"

I shrugged and said, "You caught us."

"You boys," she said, wagging her finger.

Easy enough, until Savannah stepped forward and studied us in that heart-melting wistful way of hers. "You both have black eyes," she noted.

"Mine's painted on, stage makeup," I blurted. "It's part of what we do, pretending to be each other, so Horace Vale can be in two different places at once. We've got to keep it authentic."

"Why?" Savannah asked.

"Well, uh, it's a kind of performance art. We're prepping for a mockumentary where we fool people with our twin antics. A punking-people-out kind of thing, like *Bad Grandpa*."

Paige snorted.

"Wait a minute," Savannah said. "So this whole thing... why aren't both of you going to Port City Academy? There's no way you could get away with pretending to be the same guy if you're both..."

This wasn't going well. I'd hoped to just barge in, fix everything in a few seconds, then run off without all the pesky explaining. But I hadn't even gotten to Bobby yet.

"You're right," I told Savannah. "I'm the home-schooled one. Don't like crowds, plus the 'rents can only afford tuition for one kid in private school. Free online education. Wave of the future."

While I talked, 3.0 gave me looks like he was holding off explosive diarrhea. Luckily, Savannah was enough of a go-with-the-flow kind of girl that she'd accept just about any cockamamie answer I gave. Already she was on to other things.

"*Ouch*," she said. She raised my wounded hand by lifting my fingers gingerly with her own. Even a gentle touch made the pain throb up my arm. Paige's towel wrapping was soaked through with blood, some of it drying brownish. Not exactly the ambiance you want in a diner.

3.0 went pale when he saw it. Imagine knowing you were fated for a painful injury in the next few hours, thinking it was unavoidable. The anticipation could be worse than the aftermath. "What happened?" he asked.

"Yeah, we didn't coordinate so good on this," I said. "It looks worse than it is. Listen, Savannah, I know this is a lot to take in at once, and I'm sorry for the gotcha here, but would you mind if me and my brother have a chat in private for a second? Bobby's getting lonely over there."

"Oh! Sure." Ms. Lark jaunted back to the major TV star she'd somehow neglected for at least a full minute. Down at the booth, Bobby had lost interest in the twin brother routine and had instead taken to flicking his lighter in agitation again. Not a good sign. Why couldn't he have a harmless text-checking compulsion like everyone else?

I kept tabs on Paige every few seconds, trying to assess her mood, how long she'd let me play out this scenario. She was over by the newspaper rack, leafing through a local *Star-News*, as if in search of a splashier headline than multi-reality clones.

"Why're you here?" 3.0 demanded.

"To stop you," I said.

"Stop me *what*?" He hugged the digital camera against his chest like I meant to knock it out of his hands. I was here to crush his big-time dream, and he knew it. I felt sorry for him—the deepest kind of empathy you could feel because *I had been here.*

I said, "What you're doing to Bobby, you can't. You're tapping into some wicked daddy psychology stuff. You—*we* arranged it that way. It was our plan, but it's gonna backfire *big*. This guy, he has the fragile psyche of a lab test animal."

"What will happen?" asked 3.0.

"He's fixing to crash his car," I said, pointing outside to the Rapide.

Just then, Paige ducked under my elbow and popped up between the two of us. "Wait a second," she said. "We rushed down here so you could prevent some spoiled brat actor from *crashing his car*? Seriously?" At least she was keeping her voice down.

She smacked the local section of the newspaper against my chest and said, "Take a look. Here you'll find reports of *important* things, like children with smoke inhalation from a house fire and men arrested for assaulting their girlfriends. Y'all could've looked up some of the more heinous stuff and, you know, tried to stop *that* from happening. If you cared."

"You're right," I said. "I can only do so much. The main thing was to *save you*. I'm sorry for being so *selfish*."

3.0 took a step back from Paige, in case she needed some space to swing her fist. She said to me, "Cleaning up after yourself, is more like it. I think you know more about what happened back at my place than you're letting on."

"*What* happened?" 3.0 begged. He was bubbling over, and not just because I took control from him. Before I walked into the diner, he believed he was the definitive Russ, the oldest if only by hours, no matter how many leaps he took. Now he had to accept that he lagged behind at least one leap. There was a more experienced version of himself in the house.

While we argued, Bobby Parker was getting up, ready to leave. The first time this scene played out, Bobby didn't stop for more than a smoke break until we were finished with the shoot, but this time the interruption and commotion must've dispelled the magic he was under. The vibe in the place wasn't all about Bobby Parker anymore, so it was time for him to split.

Headed right for us, Bobby didn't look quite as keyed up as last time. Probably because I just prevented 3.0 from prodding around in his subconscious for another full hour. Chances are, Bobby wasn't going to drive off and play chicken with a phone pole this time around, but I still had to be absolutely sure he was in the clear.

"Bobby, Bobby, we're just getting started," 3.0 complained.

A cigarette sagged in the corner of Bobby's mouth, James Dean-style. His lighter went *clink clink clink.* He said, "Twins are cool and all, but if y'all're gonna have a family reunion, I gotta get back to the studio."

3.0 said, "No, no. Everything's fine. We're ready to roll."

My body double couldn't see he'd lost his lead, so I had to step in.

I cleared my throat. "I'm Seth Vale. I co-wrote the script. Did Russ tell you that?"

"Oh yeah?" Bobby said. "Y'all a creative duo, like the Coens?"

"Exactly," I said. "And speaking of relatives, I personally feel the 'father' stuff in the dialog could be taken too serious, you know? The old dad-as-the-punishing-god routine? It could—*should*—be played a lot more casually, like the dad is not the real motive behind your stunt. He's just an excuse for something deeper, you know. It's really about realizing you're in love with the girl, that you're doing this stunt all for her."

Bobby did his hundred-thousand-dollar-per-episode eyebrow arch.

"Deeper?" he said.

"Deeper, yeah," I said. "The father's a red herring."

He gave a slow nod, mulling it over.

"You know," I said to everybody else. "Maybe Bobby should wind down a bit, and we can pick this whole thing up later if Bobby feels like it. I mean, this is a lot to ask of a big star—doing a short student film for free and all?"

"Wait—" 3.0 said.

"I might could use a break," Bobby said.

Savannah's serene grin finally dropped. I was ruining her big moment, too. Her leading man was about to make his exit. She said, "Bobby, you're not leaving, are you? Just a few more minutes. We're really putting together something special here."

Bobby drew my *Cape Twilight Blues* script from under his armpit and flapped it a few times. "Been real, folks. This right here is some excellent stuff. I'm going to take a closer look when I get a chance…"

"Maybe show it to your father?" I suggested. "I think if you really sat down with him and talked it out, man to man, he'll see where you want to go with the show."

Bobby hitched his lip. "And what makes you so sure of that?"

"Because I know if you go in there with a clear head, you'll convince him to let you start making creative decisions. It's just a matter of talking through it. Never good to keep it bottled up. You're the star of the show, you know?"

Star was a stretch. There were three other actors billed higher than him.

Bobby looked to my co-writer, my twin, who was forced into giving an approving nod. Here I was, this third wheel just rolling in off the street, messing with everyone's alignment. But I couldn't let Bobby go without planting a goal in his head, something to keep his focus.

Finally our TV star said, "Tell you what. How about y'all come down to the studio and I'll introduce you to my pops? I'll make a personal recommendation that he look at this script, right then and there."

"Me?" Savannah said, inching in.

"Why not? All y'all. Savannah, the Wachowskis here, even that redhead you came in with, wherever she went."

I took a long, dry swallow. The idea of getting into that Rapide wasn't stellar, but with a carload of people, there was no way Bobby'd pop a fuse and plow into a phone pole. All he'd do was take us to the studio, show us around, talk to his father in a constructive way for once.

"That's okay, right? We can do that?" 3.0 whispered to me.

3:30 P.M.

OUTSIDE, PAIGE LEANED against the diner's aluminum siding and slapped an unsteady beat against her thigh. She watched the others head toward Bobby's car, but I paused beside her for a second.

"We've been invited to the studio," I said.

"Good for you." She looked at her shoes instead of me.

"No, all of us. You too."

"Didn't you tell me that car is going to *crash*?"

"Not anymore."

"Should probably get your hand cleaned and stitched up," she said. "So you don't get sepsis, yeah?"

"It's fine. I'll take care of it."

"Blood on your shirt."

I didn't know if she realized my blood was on her clothes, too.

"Just a little," I said. "No big deal."

"Well, I guess y'all got this under control. I'm out."

"Wait. Not home, right?" I said. "It's not safe to go back there."

I tried to touch her shoulder but she ducked away.

"I know," she said. "I got the message."

"Then where?"

"Um, you told me not to tell you, right? So: none of your business."

"Paige," I said, but she was already trudging down the sidewalk. She wasn't going to turn around. An hour ago, Paige Davis blindsided me with a passionate kiss. But now she was back to the Paige who fished my Schilling baseball card out of the trash and kept it, just because it reminded her what a crap example of humanity I was. Even after I *saved her life*. If she couldn't see the good I was doing...

"Hey," Bobby called out. "You coming or what?"

Yes, of course I was.

The back seat of Bobby's car was for dwarfs, so 3.0 and I crammed our shins against the blank video screens on the stitched leather seat backs. There was a console between us, twin drink cups sporting identical unopened cans of Red Bull, as if Bobby was contracted to do product placement inside his car.

Bobby slipped his weird jump-drive key into a compartment in the center of the dash. Turned on, the car revved like the MGM lion. Savannah did a little excitement dance in the shotgun seat. Tweeter speakers rose out of the dash sci-fi style. I expected hip-hop but got a full orchestra instead.

"Beethoven," he yelled. "Ninth symphony. Beethoven's all I listen to. He's that good."

"Okay," 3.0 and I said.

Bobby roared out onto the road, pressing us all against our seats.

We passed Paige on the sidewalk but she didn't so much as glance.

Savannah stuck her head between our seats, gave 3.0 a delicate high-five, and mouthed "*wow*." I could tell how her attention jacked poor 3.0's brain. Better that he didn't know she would've kissed him if I hadn't screwed up their date.

"Wait a minute," Savannah said. "Are we like in your twin mockumentary right now? Is this part of it?"

I didn't have to say a word because 3.0 ran with it. "We're still in the conceptual phase," he said. "Testing ideas."

"Like dating the same girl, see if she notices, that sort of thing?"

"Exactly," 3.0 told her.

"So, Seth, have I met you before, really, at school?" Savannah asked.

For a second, it didn't even register that she was talking to me. My attention was on Bobby, watching his speed, how often he flexed his hands on the steering wheel. I wanted to be sure he stayed on an even emotional keel.

So 3.0 answered for me. He said, "He's never been. I'm the only one you ever talked to before today."

What 3.0 didn't realize was that Savannah's interest in the "Vale Twins" was totally in proportion to Bobby's interest in us. If Bobby cared, so did she. And if not? I learned that truth the first time through, when she ditched me for the TV star at her first possible opportunity. Maybe the second run-though ended with a kiss and a phone number, but that was because I choreographed her every move, even her thoughts, really. She'd just been acting her part. And who could blame her? She didn't want me—she just wanted what I wanted, the Hollywood life.

All these insights, all these variables, kept taking my mind off the moment at hand, so I didn't instantly realize what I was seeing out the Rapide's back window. But then, a quarter block away from the Pastime Playhouse marquee, I bolted to attention.

The Pastime Playhouse marquee, advertising new movies. *Not* an empty lot filled with debris, not just a memory up in flames. In this reality, it appeared that the Pastime Playhouse was not destroyed years ago. It was still intact.

"Did you see that?" I asked 3.0. "The movie theater. It wasn't burned down."

"Was it supposed to be? Is someone going to burn it down?" he whispered.

I leaned away from him, disturbed, as if he'd turned into someone else. Because, in a way, he had. If *this* 3.0 came from a reality where the Pastime Playhouse never burned down, then he was not exactly the *me* who leaped back to seven a.m. He was another me, one who must've gone to the movies with Dad way more times than I ever did, for starters. To what degree could something like that change who I was, fundamentally? I couldn't know how different his path was from mine, but here and now it took us both to the exact same place:

Silver Screen Studios. Straight North from the city and just a jot from our dinky regional airport. I was riding in style with the prince of the kingdom, and all I could think was how much the entrance to Silver Screens reminded me of Rush Fiberoptics: the high fence, the booth, and the tollgate. Except here the guard was a college girl who swooned as soon as Bobby pulled up. After a light round of flirting, she raised the tollgate bar and we were in.

The surging Beethoven gave everything an air of triumph. Sacred ground. No cops, no padlocks—just free and clear. Okay, one police car: property of the Cape Twilight Police Department. A TV prop, a fictional cruiser. A glimpse of the fantasy world behind the curtain.

The lot was mainly pavement dappled with a few tree islands, palmettos and sea pines. The tin-sided sound stages stood in two rows of five, all painted beige. There were no wide open doors revealing all the treasures of movie making. For the outside view, the place might as well have been one of those depressing self-storage compounds.

Stage Six had the *Cape Twilight Blues* logo on its door. Under that, a paper taped up that read: *Crew Only! Shooting in Progress!* Bobby stopped his car just outside. He watched the building, taking long drags on his cigarette. Savannah took the opportunity to pull a compact out of her purse and touch up some blemishes only she could see.

Finally, Bobby said, "Funny, I don't know you folks, but I feel like

I do, like I met y'all in another life or something. You believe in that? Past life experiences?"

"*Absolutely*," Savannah said, tucking her shoulders bashfully.

"*This*," Bobby said, stabbing a finger at my script on the dashboard. "Y'all really opened something in my soul with this. You know, I ain't really talked to my father in forever. We say crap to each other every day, but never really *talk*, know what I mean? He thinks I'm some kind of sissy, which is why he did what he did to my character."

"Hey, there's no shame—" 3.0 chimed in.

"Shut up," Bobby snapped. "That's not what this is about."

Bobby shook off his nerves, took a few boxing jabs at the steering wheel. His sudden mood change was like a bad fart with the windows up. It made all of us squirm. Savannah, his muse, stroked his arm two-handed. "That's a good thing, Bobby," she told him. "You should have more creative control. My agent says that's important."

"Right," he said. "I deserve some recognition from that bastard. Y'all heard he left my ma when she was still pregnant with me? How sick is that? Pop the glove box a sec." Bobby motioned to where Savannah's knees touched the dash.

She opened it, and a black pistol practically dropped into her cupped hands. Before she could even let out a gasp, Bobby snatched the gun and slipped it into an inside pocket of his jacket.

"That's a prop gun, right?" 3.0 said, a second before I would've.

"From the shooting range this morning, remember?" Bobby said. "I told you. Can't keep the damn thing in the car where somebody could steal it. It ain't actually loaded, so don't freak."

We chuckled nervously. Bobby had it in him to crash his car against a phone pole, so I didn't much like the idea of his waltzing around with a concealed weapon. Suddenly the movie magic had gone a little stale.

Bobby pushed his swan door open and up, and got out.

Savannah checked her makeup in the mirror one more time

while Bobby went around to open her door. I touched her shoulder and said, "He's making me a little nervous. Maybe it's better if you stay—"

"Are you *kidding* me?" she said. "Once in a lifetime."

And then Bobby had her door open, and she was getting out. When it was just the two of us in the car, 3.0 barked at me through his teeth, "Tell me what's going to happen in there. This is all a rerun for you, but I'm winging it here, so clue me in quick."

Bobby rapped on my window. Show time.

"We'll be fine," I told my clone.

"You're lying. You think I don't know when *I'm* lying?"

"I'm two steps ahead of Bobby, literally," I said, which was not exactly the truth, either. I'd never been in this moment before. But I had insights, I understood motivations, and ninety percent of getting into trouble was the surprise factor.

Bobby Parker wasn't going to surprise me. I was on full alert.

"I just don't think—" 3.0 started.

"Then stay in the car."

"Hell, no. Once in a lifetime, like Savannah said? Or twice, for you."

I looked at my double but didn't see myself. He was a separate person with a different history. We were nothing more than twins after all, two different minds. I mean, what happens when a worm, chopped in half, becomes two fresh worms and they meet each other in the mulch, months later?

Do they recognize themselves?

3:50 P.M.

BOBBY LED US into the sound stage. And there on the set was *Cape Twilight* star Morgana Avalon's television bedroom with its four-poster bed wrapped in frilly lace, an impossible stack of childhood teddy bears on top of the dresser. And on the edge of the bed was Morgana herself, long bronzed legs stretching out from her silk pajama shorts, one pink slipper dangling from her upturned toes. She was chatting away on her cell phone.

I couldn't quite enjoy the spectacle. I was too on guard.

Three cameras set up, but all of them were currently unmanned. The studio lights were dim, some of them fluttering, some dark. It looked like a break in the taping schedule. A few crew members muttered to each other through headphone mics, but nobody paid any attention to Morgana. Or us, for that matter.

Bobby headed for a metal staircase along one sidewall and we followed. At the top was a narrow platform and a door marked *Production Office*. Russ 3.0 and I waited a few steps down while Bobby pressed a buzzer. Savannah was eager at his side, raising her heels up and down. A canned voice spoke through a speaker: "Yeah?"

I'd heard the infamous Marv Parker enough times on DVD extras to recognize his voice. He sounded, as usual, like he'd just swallowed a cocktail of tacks and BB pellets. As soon as he spoke, Bobby morphed into his TV character. He was all stutters and stoop shouldered, timid as a lap dog.

"Mr. Parker—Dad—it's me, Bobby."

The door lock disengaged automatically and we all piled into a room that was hardly bigger than Mr. Yesterly's office in the broadcasting room back at school. Same dented aluminum desk, too. I expected Movie Marv to have three levels of waiting rooms, secretaries, security guards, a mahogany desk, and one of those giant old-world globes that's actually a secret liquor cabinet.

The only nod to his empire was the array of movie posters on the wall, all Parker Productions, blockbusters and turkeys alike. Kind of like my room, except these posters were in nice gold frames, not tacked up with pushpins.

When Marv stood up behind his desk, his head nearly broke through the drop-down ceiling panels. With his full beard, thick black arm hair, and tan vest, he looked exactly like a bear who had eaten a fisherman and then put on his clothes. "What's the problem?" Marv asked.

Bobby said, "Just wanted to introduce some folks."

"No time," Marv said. "Full shooting schedule, and everything's backed up because of all the glitches."

"Glitches?" I blurted. Couldn't help it.

"Power outages," Marv explained. "Whole Eastern Seaboard's on the fritz. Probably a covert terrorist attack or the government making us think there's one. So who're you, Mr. Glitches?" Marv's question was aimed at me. He was staring me down, waiting. 3.0 and I had been in the room for at least a minute and Marv apparently hadn't noticed, or cared, that we were the same person twice.

Before I could answer, Bobby whipped something out of his jacket and aimed it at his father. Savannah gasped. Too fast for me to react, and all my plans about keeping a step ahead of Bobby were exposed as complete delusions.

But what he drew wasn't his gun. It was my script, and he tossed it across the room. It fluttered in the air and landed in a pile of other papers on Marv's desk. Bobby said, "There's *Cape Twilight*'s first Emmy Award, right there." There was a quiver in his voice. Trying his damndest to act the part of the Bobby Keene-Parker we knew from the diner and *Access Hollywood* red carpet interviews.

"Oh, yeah? Where'd you scrounge this up?" his dad asked.

"These guys right here, the Vale Brothers. Russ and Sith."

Apparently, Bobby mistook me for Darth Vader.

Marv Parker finally took a gander at us.

"Twins?" he asked. "And what are you guys, twelve years old?"

"Doesn't matter," Bobby said. "They're gold, and you—" (his voice cracked on *you*) "—are gonna want to produce that script, early next season."

"Am I?" Marv said.

"You are. I figure it's time for me to be giving creative input," Bobby said, rolling his shoulders back a bit for effect.

"And who's the broad?" Marv asked with a creepy smirk.

"Savannah," Bobby said. He put his arm around her waist and lashed her to his side so roughly that she cried out in surprise.

This whole charade was getting way too personal—family stuff we didn't need to witness. Even if I was in the middle of a pitch meeting for my script, I wanted so bad to tip my proverbial hat and exit stage left, let them work it out between themselves. But I wasn't about to leave without Savannah. It appeared I'd have to un-knot her from Bobby's arm if I was going to get her away from here.

The look on Marv Parker's face as he studied his son, it was the expression a kid gets when he fries ants with a magnifying glass.

"Tell you what," Marv said. "You obviously got a real package deal here, Bobby Boy. You take your twin scriptwriters and you prove your collective chops by racking up a coupla million bucks in foreign and domestic profits on some cheap thriller pictures, build your own studio, score three hit dramas on one network, and *then* we'll talk about your *creative input*. Till then, *read your lines* like every other pretty face around here."

It was too small a room for this much pent-up aggression. If Bobby's brain was a corn kernel, we would've heard it pop. But all he said was, "That's not fair."

"*Fair?*" Marv said. One of the veins in his forehead got red and round and fat.

I slipped my dad's cell from my pocket. 3:56, more than three full minutes till four o'clock, which was the next half-life point, according to my dad's theory. If something drastic happened here, if I dissed every warning Video Russ sent me, if I warped through space-time yet again, the leap might only take me back three hours. And if that was the case, anything that happened before four p.m., anything I hadn't already fixed in this time line, would be out of my reach forever.

Bobby inhaled a deep, defiant breath.

His grizzly bear father sat back down, lifted my script off his desk, and tossed it in a nearby wastebasket. All I could think was Bobby, over and over, always crashing in the same car.

"You're right, Mr. Parker," I jumped in. "That script is trash. It's a first draft, really. We—my brother and me—we banged it out in like ten minutes. I'm deeply sorry for bringing it to your attention before it was really ready."

"What the hell?" Bobby asked me, clenching his jaw. Those smoldering eyes that girls *so* loved looked more like three-alarm fires from my perspective. He wasn't even bothering to fuss with his lighter, which worried me more than anything.

170

"We could stand to do some more work on it," I admitted.

Marv snorted and said to his son, "Where'd you pick these twins up, anyway? Boyz R Us?"

"*What the hell?*" Bobby said again, this time to his father.

"It's the girl!" 3.0 jumped in. He kept glancing at me for guidance. "She's why. My friend Savannah here. She's beautiful, don't you think, Mr. Parker? See, she asked Bobby to talk up our script and he just couldn't resist her. You know how it is. She's got a lot of charm."

What a save. Wished I'd thought of it, though, in a way, I did. Savannah had both her arms wrapped around Bobby's left bicep. He was her hero, her protector, and Bobby was the biggest Alpha Male in the room, if you didn't count his pops. Never mind the useless Vale Brothers.

"Her *charm*, huh?" Marv said. "Is that what they call it these days? Back when I scooped Bobby's old lady straight off the bar top—"

Two minutes to go. Might as well have been a decade.

"Damn you, old man," Bobby snarled. He jerked out of Savannah's grasp, shoved his hand inside his jacket. If his life went a different way, he might've been the next Hollywood gunslinger—cop dramas, westerns, spy flicks, you name it. But instead, all that gun range practice led up to this moment, drawing his weapon and aiming straight for his father. In that instant, I was almost positive Bobby had also been lying about the gun being empty.

"Oh, please," Marv said. "Save the theatrics for the camera."

"Shut up," Bobby whispered with his eyes squinted shut, like Marv's voice wasn't real, just an unending rumble in his head.

"Put the gun away," Marv said.

"Shut up."

"I bought you that thing, and everything else."

"*Shut up!*" Bobby's psyche had been shattered to bits. I knew, or at least I had anticipated, but in all my hurry to get past the gate, I couldn't accept that we were walking into death's chamber with the reaper himself.

Marv stood again, curled his hands into thick fists, and pressed his knuckles into the desk. He was purple-faced and shallow-breathed, working desperately to keep from raging through the room. Between the gun and Marv Parker, I don't know which scared me more. He started to say, "You little shit, you don't have the—"

But then he stopped, clutched one hand to his chest, and flopped back down in his seat so fast that the feathery hairs of his toupee lifted fully from his skull and settled back. He was grunting, ripping at the folds of his vest like he was shot, but the gun had not gone off. Something on the inside attacked him instead. And it was not yet four o'clock.

Bobby turned his eyes to Savannah, wild black eyes that seemed to accuse her of causing this chaos. Her seductive charm, like 3.0 suggested. When his gun tilted in her direction, more from momentum than malice, she backed against the door and screamed. I wrapped her in my arms and turned her away from Bobby's half-raised aim.

3.0 had the same protective impulse, but the slight difference between us made this other Russ Vale choose a different tack. He dove straight for Bobby, shoulder to chest. The impact was point-guard perfect. The two of them hit the wall so hard they shattered the protective glass on a promo poster for *Summer Camp Slaughter 2.* The back of Bobby's head dented the wood paneling.

3.0 wrapped his hand over the gun and steered Bobby's aim toward the wall. But Bobby took a cheap shot. Elbowed Three's tender eye, sent him reeling into the aluminum desk. The desk scraped backward and heimliched Marv Parker's gut, forcing an even deeper groan from his lungs.

Back in control of the gun, Bobby leveled it at my stunt double. I must've yelled "*no!*" but it did no good. The gunshot put an angry

172

hornet in each of my ears, and the question crossed my mind—what might happen if one of me…?—just as 3.0 took a bullet in his chest.

I reached out, as if I could meld this other version into myself and rescue him, but we were several feet apart, and it was already too late. My double sat down on the floor and his startled eyes turned to me, pleading.

To him, it didn't make any sense that he should die, if I was standing here alive. It was a paradox. Because he had no clue about the parallel universes. Because I didn't tell him.

A chaos of fluttering papers, stench of smoke. Time wound down to a sluggish tick. Russ 3.0 slumped over and should've hit the floor, but he never reached it. Instead, he disintegrated. He *blurred*. He turned into coronas of color, then gray tone static, shrinking into nothingness. All in the span of a second or two. Connie's empty jeans and Dr. Who t-shirt flopped to the ground. And 3.0 was gone, like he never existed.

All the lights in the ceiling panels brightened in unison. Air conditioners and generators inside the building chugged back into action. I didn't have to be a theoretical physicist to get it. *Of course* 3.0 disappeared—because he wasn't *from here*. He was a projection from another dimension, a glitch, a virus.

Savannah buried her face against my chest. Her fear was an awful thing to share with her, but we were both still alive, at least for now. Bobby staggered. He pressed his fingers into his eyes. If he spoke, I couldn't hear through the wall of cotton the gunshot had put into my ears.

I braced myself on the door and lifted Savannah upright. This moment, while Bobby was disoriented, was our window of escape. At least I thought it was, but I was wrong yet again. Bobby slipped his hand away from his face, like tearing off a mask. He would've won an Oscar for that lunatic look, if only he were acting.

"You made me do this," he said, and he lifted the gun at us.

Now it was exactly four o'clock. I knew this not because I checked the time. I knew it because of the leap.

4:00 P.M.

BUT NOT *MY* leap.

Instead, a person materialized in the space between us and Bobby's gun muzzle. It started as distorted air, heat waves off the grill, until it took a human shape outlined in a dark blue aura. It lingered for a second, there but not there.

Then the shape emitted a single flash pulse that knocked Bobby back a step. My first thought was of the murderous techno-vortex that attacked me in Paige's room—and *not again*. But then the gray shape turned real. A human male solidified directly in Bobby's line of fire. Someone had just leaped in from some other space-time, and all I saw from my angle was his bare ass.

The lights dimmed again, live machinery shut back down. Marv Parker was still too bowled over by the pain in his chest to notice. Bobby was too baffled by this crazy magic to shoot. So the naked dude took the opportunity to strike. A swift karate chop at Bobby's gun hand and the pistol dropped into the pile of Connie's clothes on the floor.

The naked dude pivoted and howled *"Run!"* at us. I had a split-second to catch his face before Bobby's fist smacked him sideways. Our rescuer reeled in such a way that all his flopping private-part glory was offered for Savannah's scrutiny. And big *whopping* surprise: the naked dude from another dimension was another copy of *me*.

Savannah turned away from the unexpected crotch shot just as I wrenched the office door open. The two of us hit the rickety landing so fast we almost went over the rail. I urged her down the stairs ahead of me, fast as we could, straight into a gauntlet of set-crew people clustered below.

They'd heard the commotion, of course. The gunshot, the screaming.

"He's got a gun!" I yelled at them. It was a stock line, but it worked. The crowd recoiled, bumbling into each other, either because of my warning or because of whoever was behind us, rattling the stairs twice as hard with his stomping feet.

I shouldn't have looked back. Didn't really need to get a good look at the other me coming down after us with the Dr. Who shirt balled up against his most vulnerable bits. The sight of him mucked up my stride so bad I slammed against the rail and lost my grip on Savannah. She went flying and was caught by some burly crewman at the base of the steps. Her purse took a wide swing on its strap and slapped some other dude in the face.

I found my equilibrium, snatched her wrist again, and made for the exit. With the door wide open, our escape was a blindingly clear rectangle of sunlight. One last glance at the *Cape Twilight Blues* set where Morgana Avalon was still propped on the edge of her TV bed, wearing her sexy TV pajamas, talking on her real-life cell phone, completely oblivious to what was going on.

A voice from above: "Stop them!" Bobby's voice.

Out in the lot, hand in hand, Savannah and I froze, both of us panting. We were free and clear of the sound stage, but we were still inside an arena surrounded by high fences. If we took the wrong turn, we'd be trapped.

Behind us, my naked twin slammed the sound stage door shut on his way out. Still with the shirt pressed to his crotch. Two security cars sped at us from the far end of the warehouse row, sirens blaring. Not prop vehicles this time. They'd be up our butts in seconds, and even if we were innocent of any crime (besides indecent exposure), they'd still detain us long enough for Bobby to get outside. Bobby was the heir to the throne of this gated little kingdom, and we were the invaders. If we got caught, he'd shoot first, and the studio security people would ask questions later.

"Get in," my new twin said, and aimed a black device at Bobby's parked Rapide. Bobby's car key. In the struggle upstairs, it seemed he'd managed to get a hold of it. The car chirped and the door locks disengaged. So this was our getaway.

Go ahead and add grand theft auto to the list of crimes. Why not?

I yanked open the back passenger door. Savannah dove in, rolled over the center console, knocked Red Bull all over the place, and flopped into the seat that 3.0 had formerly occupied. The video camera with the Silver Bullet footage of her and Bobby fell to the floor at her feet.

I slid in behind her. Naked twin took the driver's seat. He slid the key-thing into its port and pressed the R button. With his bare foot on the gas, we rocketed reverse in a roaring gush of engine noise.

"You all right?" I asked Savannah, jostling her shoulder.

"I'm—no—what—who—"

Naked Russ looked back at us and repeated my question:

"Savannah, tell me you're all right? Are you hurt?"

"No…" she whimpered.

The relief buoyed him, and I realized circumstances must've gone another way in whatever reality he just leaped here from. That had to be why he leaped into our universe—because Savannah hadn't made it out safely in his.

"Hold on," Naked Russ said. He put the car into a spin while Bobby's Beethoven blared a rousing crescendo to urge him on. When the tire squealing stopped, the oncoming security cars were suddenly behind us, and the front gate with its closed traffic bar was straight ahead.

He slammed the Rapide through the toll bar at thirty miles per hour. At that speed, the bar snapped and tumbled over the car roof. Savannah screamed, planted her shoes on the seat in front of her. Naked Me jerked the wheel, fishtailed southward onto 23rd Street.

We ripped through roadside gravel and decorative bushes, but the car righted back onto the road fast enough. I'd like to say I had faith in our rescuer's stunt driving, but I knew better. He was totally improvising movie stunts. Unless he was from a *very* different universe, the guy could barely drive. I would know.

We gained speed with a straight shot back to the city through an industrial park. The security cars peeled onto the road behind us with less enthusiasm than the Aston Martin. I kind of hoped they'd screech to a stop at the edge of their jurisdiction, but nope.

"They're after us!" I yelled. Every muscle in my body was locked in place.

The needle passed ninety. The limit on this road was forty-five.

Naked Russ smacked buttons to turn off the orchestra. The stereo went silent, but the screens in front of us turned on, playing the opening credits of *Cape Twilight Blues,* feel-good theme song and all. And there was Bobby Keene-Parker, arching his eyebrows at us from TV land.

Savannah kept her hands clasped over her ears. I could only imagine. All the mind-blowing I had gone through came in increments, but for her it all happened in one big blast.

"We need to stop!" I yelled to Naked Russ.

"Fat chance! You want to get arrested for killing Marv Parker?"

"But we didn't... he wasn't..."

"His kid's a psycho—and who are they going to believe? Us?"

I grasped him by the shoulder, just to be sure. He was real, and he was *me*, though not the *me* in the back seat having these thoughts. He wasn't 3.0 either—because that version of us died and disappeared in Marv Parker's office. I watched it happen. I was the Real Russ, the *oldest* by several hours, the original. That's what I told myself, anyway. Until this guy.

"Where did you come from?" I asked him, just as we lurched across some railroad tracks. The car hit air and my teeth cracked together.

"From the future," he said. Blunt, because there was no better way to deliver the news. I had to assume he was a variation of me who'd just leaped a third time into the alternate past, the leap that took him to four o'clock exactly. I wasn't the first or the last—just one in a long line stretching off in two directions to who knows when.

"You're the original Russ," I said aloud.

"You got it backwards," he yelled over the engine noise. "It's the one who's from here. Wherever you are in time and space, there's always one Russ who never took the leap. The Virgin Russ. He's the one."

He could've picked a better title for the guy, but I knew what he meant. *Virgin* as in never-took-the-leap, still native to this reality. I tried to tell myself it didn't matter which of us was first because each of us was as real as the next. I could feel my own heartbeat. Hear my own thoughts. You think, therefore you are, and all that philosophy crap.

But in this car was a Russ who'd gone deeper into the labyrinth than me. A Russ who somehow escaped the shooting in Marv Parker's office, a shooting in which Savannah apparently *died*, and then somehow managed to sneak his way *back* into that office by 7 p.m. in order to leap back to four o'clock and save us.

"Listen," Naked Russ said. "Virgin Russ has to be protected. What happens to him, happens to us because we're just his shadows in this world, you understand?"

"How do you know this?"

"Trust me, I've seen more than you."

Where did I hear that before? Me, telling the same thing to 3.0, is where.

Nothing seemed solid. The outskirts of Cape Fear rushed past, but it might as well have been a simulation. A cop car sped at us from a side road, then, with a cough of smoky grit from its spinning tires, took chase at the head of the pursuing posse.

Video games antics. Just hit the power button and it all goes away, including your extra lives. I was 4.0. A copy, a projection, a ghost. But my lizard survival brain kicked in anyhow, reminded me we were topping one hundred mph and plowing back into a downtown sprawl full of stop signs and side roads. This death-defying chase was real enough.

"You gotta slow down!" I screamed at the driver.

I wrenched the seatbelt over my chest and latched it into place. Savannah had hers on already. She sat clutching her purse like it was a life preserver. "Let me out of here," she insisted. "Stop the car. This is *not* cool."

I touched her arm and said, "We're going to be all right. Just stick with us."

"I don't have anything to do with this!" she screamed. "Let me out!"

Naked Russ wasn't listening. We blew through a stop sign and barely missed getting jack-knifed in the crossroad. Cars from both directions came to a rubber-burning stop.

The cruiser on our tail got nailed into a sudden half spin by an SUV. The sickening pitch of that crunch wormed deep into my spine. Even further back, the Silver Screen security cars were blocked by the sudden chaos of traffic surrounding the SUV/cruiser wreck.

We were in a residential neighborhood, speed limit thirty. Thick live oaks made a natural tunnel arch over the road. Sirens from every direction. Maybe even the rhythmic thump of a helicopter overhead? We zipped under a green light, but there were three more stoplights until—

"Market Street!" I said. Our road would end there at a T-intersection.

"*I know!*" Naked Russ said. He stomped the brake and made a hard left aimed at a cluster of trees. My seatbelt locked me in place. I cried out and ducked, but we missed the trees by at least half an inch.

Instead, we skidded onto a blind side-road. On the broken-up asphalt, the car leaped and lunged wherever it pleased. We might as well have been off-roading. Naked Russ worked to keep the wheel straight.

"*Let me out!*" Savannah screamed, clutching the chair-back in front of her.

"Where are we *going*?" I asked Naked Russ.

"Listen to me very carefully," he said. "Are you listening?"

"Yes!"

"Keep her safe…"

In the rear view mirror, I saw his eyes (one of them swollen and bruised) flit over to Savannah. I didn't need to hear him say that Bobby would've shot her if Future Russ didn't materialize and stop him.

But what happened there did not happen here. This was a different universe. Savannah *didn't* die. She escaped because he came back to rescue us. It *already happened*, and because it happened, my time line was forever separated from the one that brought our driver back to us.

We were different Russes. Different, but almost identical. Naked Russ had no bloody towel on his right hand. His hand wasn't even bleeding, though the knife cut was there, gaping open, tender and ugly. A trace of stitch marks, but no actual stitches.

He yelled to me, "You have to be careful not to trust—"

Just ahead, a rusty pickup truck backed out of a dirt driveway. Out of nowhere, from behind a fence. Future Russ was watching me in the rear view, so he didn't see, not until it was too late.

He cried out, jerked the wheel. The pickup's back bumper scraped along the side of the Rapide with a metallic scream. Then, my skull was shaken like a Magic Eight Ball. A few seconds of hazy dreaming, and—

We were still in the car, but it wasn't moving. A hissing noise, leaking liquids. Smoke or dust stung my eyes. The sun seemed a hundred times brighter than it did a few seconds before. Air bags went limp in each of the front seats. Savannah sobbed beside me.

The contents of her purse were all over the back seat: mascara brushes and lipsticks and little snap cases of I don't even know. She was scooping it all back into her lap as if everything would be better if she could just retrieve her makeup.

There was my camera, next to her foot, and I couldn't care less.

"Are you all right?" I asked her again.

She didn't answer, but she was upright, breathing, alive.

Sirens. It wouldn't be long before the police got to us. Only when I unlatched my belt did I feel the impact pain lashed across my chest. My door was already wrenched out of whack. It groaned when I pushed it up and away. I got it open just far enough for me to tumble out, and I pressed my hands and knees into the crumbled asphalt.

Time out, please. Just need a couple seconds. I tried to chart which Russ I was, which world I was in. What just happened and what was bound to happen any second.

The car, once a feat of modern engineering, was now abstract art. The front end was crunched into black metal waves against a sturdy telephone pole. The hood was littered with glass.

The driver whose truck we hit eased his boots onto the road. Overalls, straw hat, a hundred years old. He yelled, "Hey, you folks all right?" but neither of us answered.

Through the Rapide's missing windshield I saw two empty front seats. Our driver, the future incarnation of me, was completely gone. No sign of him in the road ahead. No blood. No remnants at all.

Future Horace Vale must have died on impact. He'd come on like an explosion and just like 3.0, he vanished from existence. Deleted, because he wasn't of this world. *Be careful not to trust...* he warned. But he never got a chance to tell me who.

4:15 P.M.

"**OH MY GOD** oh my god oh my god," Savannah chanted.

She skittered across a grassy lot away from the accident, away from me. Hands on her head, like she was under arrest, though no cops were actually on scene just yet.

"Savannah, wait," I called out.

"No. *Nope.* Leave me alone. None of this happened."

I tried to catch up, but she jacked her pace up to a jog almost. She was aiming for a row of houses on the next street over. A backyard pathway toward downtown and away from me.

"Savannah, please."

She stopped and spun on me with a full-toothed wince, "Please don't say my name again. I don't know you, and I don't know what's happening, so please leave me alone."

"I'm Russ—your friend. Did you hit your head?"

"Which Russ? You're here and then not and then back again and people get shot and a car wreck and I didn't ask for this. All I wanted was to hang out with Bobby Parker, and then he—you—I'm just going to go home and sleep it off and when I wake up, it'll be a dream, okay?"

The old man kept guard over his busted taillight and dented bumper. He watched us flatly, a reality TV show aimed for some demographic totally not him.

"I'm sorry, but it's not a dream," I told Savannah.

She stiffened her arms at her sides, took a breath, and stormed off without me. For a second, I thought maybe she was the person Future Russ warned me not to trust. But that theory didn't fly. He was talking way worse than Savannah ditching me at the scene of an accident.

He couldn't have meant Bobby Parker, either, because Bobby was a no-shit-Sherlock on the threat level scale. I didn't have to be told not to trust him. No, my worst enemy had to be the one who sent the techno-vortex that attacked Paige in her room, the one who psyched out my moves like he knew them all ahead of time, like my every choice was furthering somebody else's plot against me. Even when I thought I was winning.

If only I could play the game over from the start. If only I could stop thinking like this was some elaborate upgrade of *Grand Theft Auto: Cape Fear*, where all I had to do was start back at the last save point.

The *whomp whomp whomp* of helicopter blades kicked me back into gear. No time to ponder existence. The authorities had taken to the sky to track me down, so I had to hustle on out. I cut across a yard and strolled down a few sidewalks, easy pickings, right out in the open. But that was my strategy. Cruisers zipped by, sirens blaring, while my chill stride must've fooled them into thinking I wasn't the fugitive they were looking for. Just out on a stroll, even if underneath I was massively overdosed on panic hormones.

I fished Dad's phone from my pocket and found the touchscreen black and shattered. Ruined in the crash. The case broke open in my hand, battery and microchip clattering to the sidewalk. I didn't even bother to pick up the pieces.

I had probably two and a half hours until seven. My only options were the hope of a breakthrough solution from Dad, or another leap from the Pastime Project. The second choice was a risk I didn't want to take, but if there was no other way, I'd have to get my phone back again.

Here again on Market Street, I was only a block away from Connie's house, ten minutes away from my own. If the universes aligned the way I thought, then this world's Connie would not be over at Paige's house getting the news of her death. Instead, he'd be at his house with so-called Virgin Russ, still trying to keep Virgin from finding out about me, for fear that our meeting would cause a meltdown in existence.

If the cause-and-effect stayed steady, and *if* I could trust Conrad Bower.

Because I knew from experience that my best friend could be convinced to turn against me.

I crept around the back of Connie's house and quietly let myself in through the kitchen. The downstairs was abandoned as expected. They'd be in Connie's room, his safety zone, so I slipped off my shoes and took the stairs in my sock feet, trying not to make the old wood creak. Upstairs was the low mutter of a television or radio or both. If Connie or Virgin Russ opened the bedroom door, I'd be spotted instantly, but there was no other way to get closer.

I had no plan other than to eavesdrop on their conversation and see if Connie had spilled the big secret, especially after Virgin's weird phone call with Paige. I had to gather some info I could use, convince them to let me have the cell phone. Tackle Virgin Russ and take it from him, if necessary. As long as I caught them before they cooked up a plan to zap me out of their lives again. Whatever way I needed to play it would be justified.

Connie's bedroom door was open a crack. Three steps from the landing, I finally heard a hushed voice that was neither Virgin Russ nor Connie. A girl's voice was saying "…should force him to explain what's happening here because…" It was Paige Davis.

I took the rest of the stairs in one stride, shoved through the door, and there was Connie hunched over his keyboard as always, and Paige seated at the foot of the bed, watching him type.

Paige flinched at the sound of my entrance and cut off her sales pitch.

"Russ," she said, squinting at me, like it'd help her figure *which* Russ.

"It's me—the one who saved your life. Why are you here?"

Connie turned in his seat, gripped his armrests, and wheeled backward against his wall. Even the planets dangling from his ceiling seemed to be spinning out of control.

She stood, hitched her hands to her hips and said, "So you're the same Russ who ditched me at the Silver Bullet, *after* assuring me I was in serious danger? *That* Russ? And why I'm here is none of y'alls business, but I'll tell you anyway. I wanted Connie's side of the story. Since he's an actual trustworthy person and all."

"*Trust*?" I asked. "Do trustworthy people hold secret meetings against me?"

"Whatever," Paige said.

"Nice job keeping this quiet, by the way, Connie."

"No, no—she already knew," he protested, which was true.

Paige said, "Remember, Russ? *You* told me?"

"With your elbow in my throat, yeah." I had one small advantage here. Unless it was already on Twitter or whatever, neither of them had heard the latest developments over at Silver Screen Studios. I had at least a few more minutes until news of heart attacks and shootings and car chases got broadcast to every social network and news program in the world.

"I wouldn't have said anything to her—" Connie started.

"Thanks for your vote of confidence," Paige snarled at him.

"See, you can't trust anybody," I told her. "This is the guy—*my best friend*—who at the end of the day ends up mugging me for my cell phone, and then uses it to zap me into particles, him and Virgin Russ, conspiring against me."

The stereo turned itself on, then off again. Two seconds of Foster the People, a taunt: *better run, better run, faster than my bullet...* The glitches were leaking back into the system again.

"I didn't take your phone," Connie said.

"Not this time, not yet. But you have it in you to do it," I said.

"You're deluded, Russ," Paige said. "Seriously."

"Who's Virgin Russ?" Connie asked.

"Me—the other me. I call him that—it's not what you think. And this morning, Connie, you told me not to interfere because of paradoxes, but that was bull. You wanted me to hide so you could be in control."

As I said it aloud, the details fell into place like expert Tetris. Connie was honors across the board, so loopy about math and science he'd spend more time hanging out with my dad than with me on sleepover nights. Software design, game theory, physics. They'd sit in front of the computer and fire off into mental space while I twiddled the Playstation controller.

Connie was the only dude I knew who could theoretically wrap his head around my father's time-travel invention. Somewhere in a million alternate realities, he could've convinced some other Russ Vale to give it a test drive. Maybe even helped him make the infomercial pitch video to go along with it: *your one chance to make things right—call now while supplies last!*

Paige stepped between me and Connie, like she expected me to take a swing at him. Instead, I pointed an accusing finger, straight over the top of her head. "I figured you out, Connie. You been soaking up my dad's time-travel intel for months," I told him. "So you probably knew the lowdown on this program long before it ever popped up on my phone. In fact, I think you *put it there*. Like, the most elaborate prank of all time, just to get back at me for the helicopter thing."

He clenched his fists against his stomach, trying not to freak. "I don't even care about the helicopter," he said. "I forgave—I forgave you for that, like you asked. And I can't—I can't answer for things I never even did, or things you think I'm going to do."

"Convenient," I said. "You're going to tell me you weren't the one who made up that fake account for Paige on Facebook or thefacebook or whatever? You make up weird aliases on there all the time. It's your modus operandi."

"Russ, *no*—" Paige tried to interrupt.

"For fun, not because—" Connie pleaded.

"Did you have anything to do with this?" I asked. I showed him the bloody mess wrapped around my hand wound. I couldn't imagine him taking a slice out of me or Paige, but people can surprise you.

He went pale and slumped back into his desk chair.

"Are you serious?" Paige asked me.

"I don't know," I said, confidently.

"You know what I know?" she said. "The only way I can tell Russes apart is by who's the biggest asshole."

"You kissed me!"

"My mistake," Paige snapped. "And by the way, where is everybody else? Where's the Russ we met at the Silver Bullet, the one you left with. How do I know you're not him?"

They really hadn't heard. Paige didn't know that Russ 3.0 was dead—if that was the right word for his sudden nonexistence. She didn't know about the brief and wild flame that was Future Russ, now vanished in the crash. Russes everywhere, multiplying. Even as I opened my mouth to lie or explain, I realized who was missing from this debate—yet another Russ. The original, Virgin.

"Woah, wait a minute," I said. "Where's *your* other Russ? Virgin Russ?"

Silence. Paige looked to Connie for guidance, the two of them still conspiring.

"Tell me, damn it," I said.

"He went home almost an hour ago," Connie volunteered. "His— your dad called. He said he had a huge breakthrough."

5:00 P.M.

DAD BROUGHT THE wrong me home. It could've happened a dozen different ways—dropped calls, broken cell phones, phones in the wrong hands. Lost in his calculations, Dad could've easily gotten confused about which Russ he was calling. Didn't really matter now how it happened, and there was no time to question Connie and Paige about it. I had to get back to my father. I had to find out what he discovered.

I'm sure Connie would've let me borrow his bike if I asked, but I didn't ask. When I coasted out from under the canopy of live oaks on Market, the sun made me wish I had shades. Big switch from the artificial static gray that covered the sky a few hours earlier, too fast to be the result of natural shift in the cloud cover.

Was it possible—glitches in the Grand Design on the scale of weather patterns? Video Russ warned me that my leaps were wreaking havoc on communications networks, and Marv Parker said the whole eastern seaboard was struck with electrical outages, but this was way bigger. The natural world itself, the laws of the physical world recalibrated, and it was all my fault. Nobody wants to screw up that badly.

I got home in a record three minutes, dumped the bike in my yard, and rushed inside. Upstairs, the collapsible attic ladder was lowered to the hallway floor as usual. Dad never remembered to retract it, no matter how many times Mom sternly reminded him. I climbed with some stealth, just until my eyes cleared floor level.

Up in the attic, Virgin Russ was in a fold-out chair holding a camera at arm's length aimed back at himself while my father slouched above his work station. Dad had designed the computer setup, stacking four Mac shells to hold all the hardware he used. Cables and wires webbed the floor, a large-scale model of a motherboard. Or, as Mom liked to call it, the world's worst fire hazard.

"Action," Dad said, tapping a keyboard key. His triptych of monitors captured a single screen shot repeated in triplicate: the camera-eye view of Virgin Russ, ready to deliver his selfie video pitch.

Virgin cleared his throat and squirmed in his seat. He said into the camera, "Hi, Russ. It's me—you—from the future. This is all pretty strange for me, but I guess you're getting used to the idea by now…"

I'd seen this setup before. Same Russ, same clothes, same plain white backdrop. Virgin Russ was the one I saw in the video recording on my bedroom computer. He was not the Video Russ who sent me the Pastime Project and encouraged me to take the leap. He was Danger Russ, who sent the warning message back in time so Dad and I would received it at 1 p.m. Dad was closing the loop here, creating the very same video he had watched four hours earlier.

"Wait—cut. That's not right," Dad said. He smacked a key, scratched his cheek, carefully considered the setup. He stood hunched in his bathrobe like Igor the mad scientist's assistant.

"It didn't work?" Virgin Russ asked him.

"You're not saying exactly what you said. What the *you* in the video said. It was a warning about something else coming through…"

Dad's voice trailed off as he noticed me climbing the rest of the way up the ladder.

"Holy Crap," Virgin said, bolting upright at the sight of me.

"Surreal, yes. It's a huge deal, but you'll get used to it," I said.

Dad pounced across the room and grasped me by both shoulders. "Which one are you?" he asked. His heavy breath smelled like an espresso machine after a full day's work.

"I'm One O'clock Russ. The one you watched this video with."

"Good—good. Maybe you'll remember…" Dad was in full DEFCON 3 mode. He fumbled back to his desk and sifted through notepads and empty coffee mugs. He said, "The grid's been haywire all afternoon, so the firewall at Rush Fiberoptics was a mess. Hacking in went considerably smoother than I expected."

He bumped his head on the ceiling, stopped talking. He seemed to have forgotten which Russ he was addressing. No matter: he flipped through the pages of a yellow notepad, then showed us both the shower of hieroglyphs he'd scratched across one sheet. "Once I got access to the prototype in Rush's network," he explained. "I figured out what big breakthrough they made after I left the company."

"And?" I asked.

"And nothing. There *was* no breakthrough," Dad said.

Somewhere was a breakthrough, but not here, not this world. I felt like a guy waking up in a buried casket. You know you're still alive and the world you left is only a few feet away, but you're doomed. There's no way to get back.

"*But…*" Dad said. "I pulled some info off your Mac."

He nodded toward the junk leftovers of my computer dumped in one corner. It looked unsalvageable, but I couldn't be mad, considering. My hard drive was probably swallowed into his monster mainframe already.

Dad went on, bug-eyed, "I couldn't fully recover the actual video that was sent to you from the future, but some residual code was left behind. Enough to cross reference with the prototype and activate a real, working inter-temporal signal."

"You reinvented the program? Is that what you're saying?"

"Ha, not hardly," Dad said. "You couldn't send a whole teenager through. But information? Binary code? That's conceivable. It got me thinking that maybe that's what happened. We, us, here and now, *we* were the ones, or *would be* the ones, who sent, or *would send*, the warning video we saw this afternoon. We made the video and sent it back through time. So I decided I better fulfill the prophecy, so to speak. See if it could be done, at least."

"Which is why I'm here," Virgin said.

Now it made sense why Virgin Russ would be the video star instead of me. He had the wardrobe and the non-black eye, while us other Russes were running around with identical shiners, dead giveaways that we weren't the real deal. Dad had it all figured out.

"Except… I was wrong about the video, too," Dad admitted.

"Huh?" Virgin and I said, in unison.

"There's no way we can replicate what we received."

He was right. In the clip I saw, Video Russ was frantic, worried, and he used an entirely different script. This wasn't the same scenario. There would be no way to purposefully record the version we saw earlier in the afternoon, even if we could remember exactly what Video Russ said.

Not to mention, Virgin and Dad didn't yet know *why* the leaps were bad news. They hadn't witnessed half the malfunctions and screwy anomalies and the murderous techno-vortex I'd lived through. *This* Russ had no cause to be genuinely horrified the way Danger Russ clearly was when he made his video.

Dad watched me, like he could *hear* me realizing. He said, "If our multiverse theory is right, then just think of all the universes where a Horace Vale received a working version of the time travel program. And somewhere in all those universes, different versions of *me* have figured out how to transmit messages through time and space. So the video we saw could be from *anywhere*. Trillions of possibilities and more."

"But not this reality," I said.

"Exactly. And somewhere there is a reality where the physics are skewed *just enough* that some other Kasper Vale could make a time travel program actually work. The tech would be rare indeed—but once it was discovered, it could cut across universes and paradoxically appear in realities where it was a long way from ever being invented, like here."

"I'm surprised this doesn't happen all the time," I said.

"In 99.999999 percent of all possible realities, it doesn't. But keep adding nines until you lose your voice or die of old age. The chances are thinner than anything you could imagine happening to you in this or any other life. Except quantum physics tells us there is a chance, no matter how slight, so it *has* to happen somewhere."

"Lucky us," Virgin Russ quipped.

"Right," Dad said, and he meant it. "The chances of this happening are infinitesimally small, and yet even that tiny number is infinite. So in a sense, this is happening so often, we can't even imagine, yet it is more rare than we could imagine."

We were the discoverers of the most shattering find in galactic history, right here, but also in endless elsewheres, too. Because .0000001 percent of infinity is still infinity. Endless Russes making endless leaps between dimensions, threading an imaginary needle, tying realities together, making a knotted mess of things. That kind of realization can wring out your mind with a good, hard twist.

Maybe there were infinite Russes, but my consciousness only lived in this one. And this one, the one I called *me*, he was adrift from his home port, lost from his reality. I was on the verge of a panic attack. I turned and hustled down the retractable ladder, hyperventilating and hoping I wouldn't pass out before my feet touched the landing.

Down the main staircase. The view through the decorative front door glass showed me that a car was parked out front where there was no car five minutes before. Typical make and colors of a police cruiser.

My gut clutched so hard I almost somersaulted down the steps. They found me, tracked me down at home, though nobody had yet rung the bell. Probably they were positioned around the yard, waiting on backup before they stormed the place and collared me for nabbing Bobby's car. If Marv Parker was dead from a heart attack, I was probably somehow wanted for that supposed crime as well.

I slipped into the den where the windows were wide and clear, planted my knees on the couch to get a look. No doubt it was a cruiser, but just one, parked, lights off, nobody in the driver's seat. The decal along the body didn't quite make sense—not at first.

It didn't say *Cape Fear Police Department*. No, it said *Cape Twilight Police Department*. Either fictional police were here to arrest me or—

I turned around. My speculative script for *Cape Twilight Blues* was right there on the coffee table with my home address typed on the cover page. It had been left in Marv's office, but here it was, returned to me, special delivery.

Clear across the room in Dad's recliner, with a drop-dead scowl, was the delivery boy himself, teen TV sensation Bobby Keene-Parker. He stood, wiped sweat off his glistening red brow. "*Where's my car?*" he asked.

The question struck me as weirdly off topic but, regardless, you can't tell a guy you crashed his quarter-million-dollar wheels. Even if it wasn't *you*, per se. I showed him both my palms. "Your car isn't here, but it's safe."

Bobby let loose an ugly, throaty groan. Bloodshot eyes and wet streaks across his cheeks meant he'd recently had a fierce crying jag. He said, "They're all over, hunting for me, because I pulled my gun, but it was you, wasn't it? You ruined my life."

"No," I said.

Bobby couldn't see from my vantage, so he didn't know Virgin Russ was taking tentative steps down the main stairs. Any second there'd be a creak and Bobby'd hear him, and the surprise would probably be just the kind of freak-out shock that would trigger Bobby's full-on crazy.

I shot a warning glance at Virgin on the stairs. Virgin Russ, who I had to keep safe at all cost. *What happens to him, happens to us,* Future Russ told me. *We're just his shadows in this world.*

Bobby stepped toward me. "You said everything would be fixed."

"I'm sure I didn't tell you to give your father a heart attack."

He cracked a hairline fracture of a smile as he swiped an iron poker from the fireplace stand. The poker, with its curved black claw, was only a decoration, but it could still puncture a hole in my head if he swung it hard enough. He said, "Been telling me a lot of things, all right. But I got notions of my own. Like, if I get rid of y'all, everything will go back to before. No more crazy shit slipping through."

He took another step closer and turned, glaring straight at Virgin. "You, too," Bobby said. So much for Virgin sneaking up and saving the day.

If I get rid of y'all, everything will go back to before. It was another way of saying *you are the virus.*

Bobby had seen enough to break a feeble mind—multiple Russ Vales, dead ones pixelating into nothing and fresh reserves teleporting into place. But he seemed immune to surprise, like he expected all this craziness, like he *knew.*

"Which of y'all is fake?" Bobby asked. He toggled the poker between Virgin and me.

Without warning, our mounted flat screen television flipped on, though nobody pressed the power button. Stereo surround burst out with a cheesy synth score at max volume. *Cape Twilight Blues* soundtrack music again.

And there was Bobby-Keene Parker on screen and in character, embracing his boyfriend inside the local park bandstand, both of them sobbing about some emotional catastrophe.

The real Bobby screeched and hurled the fire poker like a javelin. I ducked, but he wasn't aiming for me. The poker smacked the TV screen and dropped to the floor, leaving a gouge of distorted color in the image. But *Cape Twilight* played on, amping up the drama with a slow zoom into close-up.

Outside, an actual Cape Fear cruiser veered into our driveway. Another slammed its brakes just behind Bobby's dummy car. The sight of them flooded me with relief. They had to be here to nab Bobby, not me.

On the stairs, Dad brushed past Virgin Russ, arms loaded with notebooks. The hem of his bathrobe billowing behind him. I don't know what Dad was thinking. He must've heard the sirens and thought they were coming for him. Maybe it was some inter-dimensional trace memory of his arrest in another life. Or maybe he was just paranoid. Either way, Dad was oblivious to the real and present threat right there in his living room.

Bobby reached around to the back of his waistband. Brought out his gun one-handed, cupped it into his opposite palm, and shot a hole straight through his own televised face. The screen died for real this time, and so did my ears, again.

The gunshot got Dad's attention. He stumbled into the foyer, dropped all his notebooks on the floor and stood defenseless in his house slippers.

Blue uniforms rushed across our yard, sidearms drawn.

Bobby winked at me and said, "Down with tyrant fathers, right?" I couldn't quite hear him, but I read his lips loud and clear. Then he shot my dad square in the chest.

6:45 P.M.

THE TWO OF us occupied a second floor waiting room at New Hanover County Hospital. Virgin Russ and me, seated directly across from each other on the benches. We were twin brothers named Russ and Seth, so far as the police and the hospital staff knew. That was what we told them. Soon enough our lies would get riddled with holes, but neither of us was in the frame of mind to construct a more solid cover story.

I squeezed my cell phone in my hand. Fifteen minutes till seven. After the shooting, Virgin had given it over to me willingly, no questions asked, because he had to believe he could trust me, trust himself.

The back of my right hand was cleaned and stitched, courtesy of a triage nurse. I refused pain meds, so the hurt was wafting up my arm, stiffening all the muscles along the way. Virgin Russ glanced at it, every time my fingers moved, as if he could feel the pain.

Behind him, a glass wall overlooked the parking lot and a baseball diamond on the back edge of the city park. Little league game in progress. A kid pitcher wound up and tossed a wild ball that hit the fence three feet to the left of the catcher. Way off target.

Sneakers squeaks in the hallway, doctors paged on the intercom, the hum of the vending machine in the corner. The muted TV mounted in the corner showed WCPF's coverage of the evening's top story: a "bizarre incident" at Silver Screen Studios, no casualties reported, Marv Parker in intensive care right here at NHCH, a crashed Aston Martin, suspects fled the scene, Bobby Keene-Parker arrested at a local residence, shooting victim also rushed to the hospital... a wild convergence of events that the station had not yet pieced together.

I couldn't read Virgin Russ's thoughts, but I could guess the filmstrip playing on repeat in his head. Same as mine, captured from a different angle. Dad catching the bullet, collapsing backward into the banister as police swarmed through the front door. Bobby dropping the gun like it was all a misunderstanding, just a prop weapon, a misfired blank, no harm intended.

Last we saw Dad, he was strapped to a stretcher gliding through the hospital entrance, and then we were ushered into this room, buffeted with an hour of questions from two police detectives while awaiting contact with Mom, who could not be reached by phone. Police were supposed to be on their way to alert and collect her. All I wanted was Mom with us, even if it meant she had to see her son cloned and hear the crazy story. I tried my best not to be pissed that she couldn't even be reached in an emergency.

Dad was in surgery now. Our last update from the nurse was more than a half hour earlier: the bullet missed our father's heart, but nicked an artery and punctured a lung. Surgeons hard at work, no guarantees, the usual. It all seemed so tentative. A new shape could still be molded in the clay.

Virgin said, "So you're going to do it, then?"

"What?"

"You got the phone, your eject button. That's how it works, right?

You just teleport away and leave this mess for the rest of us?"

"The mess you jump into is worse, believe me," I said.

"It's my choice as much as yours," Virgin said. "I could leave instead."

"Listen, I've been through it. I know what happens. Dad told you about the warning video, but you haven't seen the crazy holes that rip open between reality and virtual reality, or what seems virtual to us. It's like we're putting the universe through a shredder every time we do this."

"If Dad dies…"

"He's not going to die."

"How do you know? Did you see the future?"

"No," I admitted. But our dad could recover, and then the extra leap wouldn't be worth the risk. Even if the worst happened, even if Bobby Parker won his eye-for-an-eye out of some twisted idea that I tried to make him kill *his* father, the program couldn't save Dad in this world. If one of us pressed the button, the other would be left behind to grieve. The worlds I ruined still limped on without me, real as ever.

I couldn't stop thinking of all those other realities where tragedies struck people I loved over and over again… some of those worlds I visited, breathed the air, and the awfulness that happened there still weighed on me. It was all too much for one person.

"There can't be two of us," Virgin said. "One has to leave."

"Wherever you go, there will be at least one more of you."

"But not here. Here, if you leave, I get my own identity back."

I couldn't take his accusing glare anymore. It was confronting the mirror when your self-esteem is in the toilet. When I stood, he asked me where I was going, and I told the truth: to get a drink from the fountain. And I took the phone with me.

This wing of the hospital was mainly empty. Just the uniformed police officer assigned to guard us until such time as the detectives were satisfied with our account of the *incidents*.

We told them what we could, minus the sci-fi stuff, and we even admitted to stealing the car in desperation, out of fear of Bobby Parker's gun spree. They told us that Marv Parker was in stable condition just a few doors down from my father, who was critical. Bobby was in custody—that was all we knew about him.

I nodded at my guard and dribbled water all over my shirtfront at the fountain. Down the hall, the elevator doors slid open, and I stood upright in anticipation. Two people stepped out, neither of them my mother, although I knew them both. It was Connie and his mother Sara, an on-shift nurse at this hospital, in her blue scrubs. Sara held her arm around her son like he'd keel over if she let him go. She regarded me with pity instead of the usual suspicious pucker of her lips.

Twenty feet off, the cop guard got antsy, but he let my two visitors approach. Must've decided a nurse and a chubby kid in glasses posed no threat.

"Russ, I heard what happened," Sara said.

I nodded, wiped the water off my chin. Connie's mom looked a little pale and spaced out herself. She was probably freaked by how narrowly her son escaped the horror that seemed to follow at my heels. But she put her hand on my shoulder and said, "I just checked in downstairs. They're still working on your dad, doing everything they can. It's going to be all right."

I nodded again. For all I knew, my father could be dead already, and the staff were just postponing the news until my mother showed up. If they delayed their worst-case scenario until after seven, I'd be stuck in this world without a father for the rest of my life.

Connie said, "Russ, I'm so sorry."

"This isn't your fault," I said.

Sara lifted my free hand and examined the clean dressing. She must've thought I got hurt when Bobby attacked us in my living room.

"Mrs. Bower, could Conrad and I have a minute?" I asked.

She flinched a little, flared her nostrils. Here she was, finally treating me like a human instead of a nuisance, and I was asking her to scram. "That's fine. Conrad, you know where I'll be, all right?" She hesitated, glanced at the cop, and then made her way back toward the elevator.

"Here," I said, and offered Connie my cell phone.

He looked at the phone but didn't take it.

"I'm sorry I didn't trust you," I said. "I was being paranoid."

He pressed himself against wall, shying away from me like I was a drug dealer insisting he try a sample.

"I've done this twice now," I said. "And every time I've just made bigger and bigger mistakes. You gotta do it this time. Go back to four o'clock, call the cops and tell them that Bobby Parker is fixing to show up at my house. You're not going to screw it up like I would."

I didn't tell him such a change would mean nothing in this world. If Connie took the bait, he'd find himself twinned in another dimension, and I'd be left here to grieve the disaster I caused. It was a desperate offer, it made no sense, but I had to be sure I could trust him.

"I can't," Connie said. "I'm not like you, I can't just—"

"Exactly—you're better," I said. "I knew you'd be too smart to try it." We kept our voices too low for the guard's liking. He was coming toward us to break up the conspiracy.

My voice shuddered. "If my father dies... you know how it is to lose..."

Years ago, it was my dad who forced me to apologize to Connie after that helicopter-in-the-locker prank. It was Dad who convinced me Connie would be a good ally to have in my corner.

Connie swallowed hard. He spoke clear and calm, looking straight into my eyes. "No, Russ. I wouldn't wish that on anyone."

And I believed him. Connie couldn't lie to your face like that. If I saw any kind of hesitation, I might've kept going with the test. I might've even suggested another leap could change something drastic—maybe even reverse the death of *his* father. But I didn't have to play that mind game.

Connie couldn't be the one who Future Russ warned me not to trust. I mean, if my best friend commanded time-space tech like this, why would he decide to use it just to screw with me? He wasn't a vindictive asshole.

"Everything all right here?" the guard cop asked. He studied us, grinding his jaw.

"Fine," I said.

"Mm-hmm," the cop said. "Where's y'alls brother?"

"Where you left him, in the waiting room."

The cop said, "Then why don't you go *wait* along with him?"

My cell chimed in my hand. 6:59. The video message from Future Russ had arrived. Yet another chance to set things right, except the real chance had already passed me by a million miles ago. When Connie and I stepped back into the waiting room, Virgin Russ raised his face expectantly from the mask he'd made of his hands.

I met his eyes—and tossed the cell into the covered trash bin. It landed softly inside, the plastic hatch swinging back into place. No more leaps.

Except Virgin Russ didn't seem to appreciate my grand gesture. He stood up, far more concerned about whatever was happening in the waiting room doorway behind me. I heard the squawk of several police radios at once, then my mother's voice, close by: "Russ?"

I'd never seen her eyes so glossy before. Even in her steely executive suit, she never looked more vulnerable. She blinked and staggered against the wall and Connie reached out to steady her. I couldn't tell if newly terrible news about my father was what made her swoon, or if it was the unnerving sight of her doubled son. She must've thought she lost her mind.

"Mom…" I said.

"Your father…" she answered.

Inside the trash bin, the cell phone chimed. It sounded miles away.

And Virgin Russ made his move. He shoved the bin over with a rubbery thump. The cap fell off and clattered across the tile floor with empty paper cups and balled-up diapers in its trail. He dropped to his knees and scooped hungrily through used napkins and candy bar wrappers.

I was frozen in place, watching him. Any second he would have the phone in hand, and all I could imagine was a flat line on the heart rate monitor in my father's operating room, the relentless single note keening forever.

A device in Virgin's grip. Thumb seeking the touchscreen.

You have to stop the leaps, said Danger Russ, deep in my brain.

And then another burst of clarity reminded me that if Virgin Russ took a leap away from his own reality, then there would be no original in this universe. No original, no copy—and the logic of it could wipe me out completely. I was a thumb-tap away from death.

Damn it. I jumped Virgin Russ, and he folded backward to the floor, stretching his arms to keep the phone from my reach. But I clutched for it, clawing. "No, no, no!" he screamed, pushing me away with one knee. Two pairs of the same hands wrapped around each other until the phone was swallowed whole inside our twenty desperate fingers.

One of us found the icon, didn't matter which. And then, again, the white light.

DAY ONE
(TAKE FOUR)

5:30 P.M.

I COULDN'T BREATHE. A dead weight pressed on my lungs, flattened my naked back against an ice cold floor. I gasped like a deep-space astronaut coming out of cryogenic sleep. There is an instant of nothingness mid-leap. I had to rise from it, find my bearings, even though I was in the same place I left—the hospital waiting room.

The trash bin stood upright and capped, as if a custodian had come in and tidied up while I blinked. Lights out, vending machine and TV dark and still.

The mass on top of me came alive. It was human and groaning and sweaty and now fumbling to get away. It was Virgin Russ in his birthday suit, crab walking backward into a bench. "No, no, no," he was still saying.

"Oh, crap," I said.

We shared a simultaneous physical shudder. I might've thought it would feel familiar, being tangled with my own nudity, but body horror is never natural.

Virgin Russ cupped himself, whimpering. Well, *Virgin* Russ no more—and the first time's a real bummer—because now he was an alien to this reality as much as I was. The two of us had sneaked through, while somewhere else in this world another Russ inherited the title of Virgin. *Twin* Russ would have to be this one's nickname from now onward.

There was nothing in the room for Twin Russ and me to cover ourselves with. Even the bench cushions were the stiff kind, bolted to their frames. We were alone at least, but shouts and sneakers in the hall meant we could get visitors any second.

Somebody out there was calling for flashlights. The hospital power supply was freshly dead, and I could guess why. Me and my twin were mucking up the system again.

"What just happened?" Twin Russ asked.

"We leaped."

"But—it was—it wasn't anything. Just… everything tingles."

"Yeah, that's how it goes," I said. The stitches on my hand were gone, lost in transit. What was left was a nearly bloodless wound split open like the lips of a rubber coin pouch.

"Why are we naked?" Virgin demanded.

"Why'd you press the icon?"

"You pressed the icon."

"I was trying to stop you."

"So you could take the leap yourself," he insisted.

"That was *your* world. You actually *existed* there. Now—"

Twin Russ slapped his bare chest to show he was made of solid stuff. He said, "I exist here, too. I had to get out of the mess you made of my life." He didn't have to say what he meant. The mess was our father's fate, whether or not he'd died.

"You had no qualms about leaving me behind?" I asked him.

"Who are you?" he snapped. "A copy. Like an old videotape."

I shook my head at him and said, "You're rough footage now, bro, same as me."

Just then, the fluorescent lights flickered back on and the deep continuous rumble of the hospital resumed itself. Hospitals had dependable generators on site for the life support machines, defibrillators, CAT scans, and these had just kicked in. Somewhere, somebody clapped.

The embedded electrical clock on the wall got ticking again. But the time was not what it should've been. It said 5:30, and, judging from the baseball game outside, it was evening. An hour and a half too late. The four o'clock half-point had been skipped all together.

A surge of nausea gut-punched me so hard I gagged. The whole world seemed to jostle on its axis. Twin Russ groaned like it struck him too, and his face whitened almost to ivory. Aftereffects of the leap, I guessed, though this didn't happen the last two times. "What the hell?" Twin Russ asked.

Five-thirty p.m. Future Russ must've used the four o'clock leap into Marv Parker's office without any do-overs. He must've forced us onward to the next drop-off point. *No exit here.* Or else two Russes taking the same leap burned twice the fuel—I had no clue which was the right explanation.

Five-thirty p.m. My father might already be shot, again. If not, it would happen soon—any minute, any *second*—and we were too far away to stop it.

First, we had to find some covering. Impossible to think straight when you're naked. Then a phone. Then, don't get arrested.

I popped my head out of the waiting room. Nobody in the hall, closed elevator to the right, and an empty nurse's station down on the left. While I watched, a nurse rushed from one room to another, but she was way far off and didn't see me.

Another bout of nausea whacked me good. My head spun. Twin Russ pulled off the trash bin cap and puked inside. Something was badly off. Our fit inside this universe was wonky, unsettled, a toy train that kept wobbling because one wheel wasn't quite on the track.

My plan now was to ransack a nearby room for bed sheets we could use as makeshift togas. With two cots in each room, I had two chances to find an empty bed, or two possible patients to catch me in the act and scream for help. What's behind door number... 205?

"Wait here," I told Twin Russ.

My bare feet slapped rudely on the hall floor, but I slipped into the opposite room without trouble. The closest cot was empty, but in the dim light I could make out the shape of a patient in the next bed over. I froze—and heard the steady drone of snoring. I grabbed a handful of neatly tucked blankets and sheets.

Vigorous tugging got the blanket loose, but then came footsteps in the hall, approaching. When I turned to have a look, just that slight movement left me merry-go-round dizzy. I steadied myself on the cot's aluminum side rail, then the blanket I was grasping pulled back against me.

"*Mine*," squawked a voice from two feet away.

Five seconds ago, *there was nobody in this bed*. I would've bet my life on that fact, which meant even my perceptions were falling apart. Because *now* the cot was definitely occupied by a toothless old man with the grip of a professional arm wrestler. I cried out and lost my hold on the blanket.

The neighboring patient flipped on her light, and my tug-of-war opponent screamed through his pink gums at the sight of me standing naked by his side. He pulled his hard-won blanket over his head.

"Pervert!" The other patient screamed. You could say grannies look alike, but this one was the spitting image of the one who doused me with a hose, way back when this whole leap business started.

"Sorry!" I said, and backed out of the room just as empty-handed and naked as when I got there. Twin Russ shrugged questioningly at me from the waiting room doorway, but I zipped right past him.

Two nurses and a security guard jogged toward us, shouting

the usual pointless requests that we stop and perhaps answer a few questions. Elevator straight ahead, door invitingly open. It was a fluke I couldn't pass up.

I dove inside the elevator car and body-checked the back wall. Twin Russ, right behind me, swiveled and smacked the "close doors" button as our pursuers gained on us.

"*Woah, woah, woah*," the security guard said to the doors as they slid shut. His outstretched hand couldn't stop them in time, and Twin pressed the fourth floor button to get us moving.

"We're going up?" I asked through my heaving breathing.

"You want to show up in the lobby like this?" Twin asked.

"I think we're stuck between spaces," I said.

"No we're not. We're moving."

"No—not the elevator—I mean—"

Twin didn't have to ask why I stopped talking. He could see the ghost as well as me. It took shape in the center of the elevator car, forcing us against the back wall. It was the see-through outline of a woman, facing away from us. I reached out for her shoulder, but she was no more solid than a hologram.

"Holy crap," Twin said.

"This is what I mean," I said. "Stuck between spaces."

The ghost woman's image thickened enough that we could see clothing, a pair of scrubs. The vague outline of a rectangle in both her hands—which materialized into an electronic tablet. She was a random nurse, just going about her day at work.

She perked up her head, turned, and noted for the first time our naked double presence. We covered ourselves appropriately. She nibbled the edge of her lower lip. To a nurse, we were more a curiosity than a shock. "Um?" she said, sizing us up.

A perfectly reasonable question for a time like this.

The elevator dinged, the doors slid open onto the fourth floor, and the nurse flitted out of existence again. Vanished. No tablet, no scrubs, no nothing.

"What the?" Twin said.

"Yeah," I agreed.

5:40 P.M.

ON THE FOURTH floor, we hunched along the hall with our hands covering our privates. No telling when someone else would step out of a room, or appear out of thin air, and set off an alarm. Already, we were probably caught on security camera. We had to work fast.

The plan was, once we were decent, we'd split up, look for a phone to call Dad with and warn him, if it wasn't too late already. Inside a storage closet we found a stack of flimsy hospital gowns. We snatched two of them and draped them over bodies. They were decorated with a pleasant lilac motif, high fashion.

"I think they're on backwards," I said.

"Crap," said Twin Russ.

We both made the rookie mistake of slipping them on with the snaps in the front. You don't get good coverage that way, especially if you plan to make a run for it, but we had no time for a fix.

"I'll ask for a phone at the nurse's station," Twin said, and hustled up the hall. Now that we could pose as patients, we didn't have to sneak around anymore. I went for the nearest room, hoping there'd be someone inside whose cell phone I could borrow. But before I could leave the hall, somebody called my name.

A few rooms down, my broadcasting teacher, George Yesterly, stood in a doorway wearing a pastel blue gown and clutching a mobile IV, drip tube plugged into his wrist. "Russ," he said again. "Is that you?"

"The one and only," I said, nowhere to hide.

Yes wheeled his IV toward me. Still haggard, but he didn't look quite so ill as when we collided outside the school restroom all those hours ago in a world that used to be mine.

"What brings you here?" he asked, nodding at my gown.

"I, uh, my eye…" I said. "Headaches, after I got hit in gym, so my mom's a little knee-jerk about injuries. We came down to the hospital to get a concussion check—you know—a couple MRIs."

"Your mother is here?" Yesterly asked. He made a little show of glancing around for her. Weirded me out big time.

"Downstairs," I lied. "Conrad Bower's mom—she's a nurse—she let it slip that you were here, so I thought I'd come up and say hi, you know… would you happen to have a phone I could…"

Mr. Yes clasped one hand on my shoulder and gave me a fatherly grin.

"I'm glad to see you, Russ," he said. "You saved my life."

"Wait—what? I did?"

"This afternoon when you mentioned I wasn't looking too hot, well, it got me on alert. I tend to ignore these things, but because of what you said I cut out early, went to my doctor's, and he sent me straight over here in an ambulance. Heart attack! Could've killed me if I waited much longer."

"Wow," I told him. "That's great. I mean, that you got here in time."

One good turn among all my time-space screw-ups. Sure, I caused a medical emergency for Marv Parker, but I *saved* George

Yesterly from one—as if the universe was balancing itself out against my manipulations.

I didn't ask him about telling me he was a diabetic. No time. *This* Mr. Yes didn't say it, and besides, it was just a white lie he told to stop me from worrying. Nothing worth mentioning, compared to what I'd done.

"Of course, I've got some big life changes to make…"

As he spoke to me under the flickering fluorescents, the intermittent seasickness rolled in. The hallway swayed on huge but invisible waves. Mr. Yesterly's colors faded and his voice thinned, and then he turned transparent. The last I heard him say was, "…don't have to know what you're doing to do some good."

His see-through ghost stepped back from me, startled. Because I had just disappeared from his world, too.

Twin Russ rushed back down the hall, swaying from his dizziness. But he had a cell phone upraised in his hand. "Got one," he said, just as he stepped *through* Mr. Yes and disbursed the last of his lingering image.

"The nurse," he said, panting. "She asked where my ID bracelet was. Thought I was screwed. Then she just—"

"Disappeared?" I guessed.

"Yeah. And I snatched her phone off the desk."

"Something's different. We're sliding back and forth between realities."

"Isn't that what's supposed to happen?" Twin asked.

"Not uncontrollably, not like this," I said. "It's the same instant in time but it's different—spaces. Or the same space, but different. It's complicated. And we're carrying things with us, like these gowns and that cell phone you're holding. It's not a full-fledged leap. It's *worse.* I think we're jammed between more than one dimension at once."

"Where did Mr. Yes go?"

"Exactly. I don't know. Call Dad, for God's sake."

"I already did. Straight to voicemail." He pushed the phone toward me so I could hear our father's recorded voice droning on about being unavailable and if we needed to get a hold of him, please call…

I cursed louder than I probably should have.

"We might've screwed up the phone service," I said.

"Don't I have our phone right now?" Twin asked. "I mean the other me, from a few minutes ago, the me I was before I pressed that button."

God, how many of us were there now?

Virgin Russ, the one who always lived in this universe.

One O'clock Russ, the guy who survived the Rapide crash.

Then the two of us who just made the leap: me and Twin.

If the time line was intact here, 3.0 would've been "erased" by Bobby at Sliver Screens and Future Russ would've disappeared in the car wreck. That brought the Russ count to four, if my math was right: Virgin, One O'clock, Twin and me.

I snatched the phone out of Twin's hand and dialed our home telephone number, two-thumbed. It rang seven times before I gave up. Even the answering machine wouldn't connect, and now it was 5:45, way too late to save my father from that bullet.

But then, just before total black-hole despair kicked in, I realized something about Dad's cell phone voice mail message. It wasn't the same one I was used to. I knew Dad's recorded spiel by heart. Leave a name and callback number, blah blah blah. Hardly more inventive than the automated one they give you if you don't record your own.

But the message I just heard was not the same. So I called back.

"You've reached Kasper Vale," my Dad's voice said. "I'm away from my phone right now. You can either leave your name and number or select three to be connected directly to Pastime Productions for further assistance."

"*Dad* is Pastime Productions," I said aloud.

"What's Pastime Productions?" Twin asked.

"Our travel agent." I pressed three, waited for the connection.

Until now, the changes between realities had been small, at least in my realm of influence. YouTube/YouView. The resurrection of the Pastime Playhouse. But we'd just fallen into a universe where my father's route had taken a major detour. He wasn't wasting away in his attic office this time around. *This time*, he owned his own company— the people who brought you the Pastime Project.

Maybe this turn should've jolted me, but it all made sense, actually. If circumstances were just a tad different than in my home universe, Dad might've ditched Rush Fiberoptics and built his own start-up tech company *before* he invented the time-space program. As his own CEO, Dad wouldn't have had to fret about the moral implications of his work. Nobody else would be able to touch it. He could push the project past research, straight into development, and pull the plug whenever he felt the implications were getting too scary.

Too bad his son made a spectacular mess of his invention. Maybe the biggest fail since the Big Bang. Crap, maybe this was the sort of screw up that *caused* big bangs.

I was mulling over this minor implication while the phone rang and rang.

"Nobody's picking up," I told Twin.

"We'll have to find wherever Pastime Productions is and get there ourselves before—" He didn't have to say—*before Bobby Parker.* "What's the message say?"

"It just keeps ringing."

"Give me the phone."

There wasn't anything to gain, so I surrendered the cell.

"Wait, call Mom and tell her not to go home," I told him.

The reality wobble struck again. I braced myself against the wall and groaned. My heart pounded with the worry that if this didn't stop soon we'd be pulled to pieces or stuck in an empty zone between dimensions forever.

The trace amounts of food in my gut were surfacing this time. I dove into Mr. Yes's hospital room, angling for the toilet. He was solidly *there* again and seated on the edge of his bed, staring at a framed print of a pier at sunset.

"There you are," he called out. "I thought you disappeared."

"Sorry," I answered, between wretches. My voice echoed in the toilet bowl.

"You must've hit your head pretty bad," said Mr. Yes.

"I'll be okay," I groaned.

"Better get back downstairs, though. You know, it really seemed like you *disappeared*. I started thinking I was hallucinating from the medication they gave me, but it wasn't really anything that powerful..."

I came out of the bathroom, wiping my mouth on a handful of paper towels I got from the dispenser. "Mr. Yes, you wouldn't happen to have any idea where my father's company is located, would you? Pastime Productions, it's called?"

"Strange question," he said.

"Strange day," I countered.

"Drove by there the other day. Nice repurposing of the old lot." Yesterly didn't have to say more. If Dad was nostalgic enough to name his company after the Pastime Theater, it was no stretch to imagine he'd buy the empty lot and build his offices there. Should've guessed it myself.

On my way out, I asked Mr. Yes if I could borrow some money for the vending machine downstairs, promising I'd pay him back. All he had was a fifty, but he gave it over anyhow, thanking me again for the inadvertent life-saving warning. I wished I could tell him that he just saved my ass, too, but it would've taken too long to explain, and he never would've believed me. So I said goodbye and stepped back out to an empty hallway.

Twin Russ was nowhere to be found. I'd been ditched.

5:55 P.M.

TWIN MUST'VE OVERHEARD Yesterly tell me where Dad's business was based, or he got a hold of Mom on the phone and asked her, or he guessed the answer. Whatever the case, off he went by himself.

Because—you had to figure—if Dad named his own company after his groundbreaking science experiment, *this* might finally be one of those universes where our father achieved some actual results, maybe even an answer to our predicament. An antidote, of sorts. Twin Russ was angling to get there first, and cut me out. *Bastard.*

Part of me hoped Twin was stupid enough to take the elevator again. That way, if he slipped between dimensions mid-ride, he might find himself appearing where the elevator car *wasn't*. Going down fast. That'd handle the traitor—no witnesses, no cleanup.

No such luck, though. As soon as I entered the emergency stairwell, his barefoot steps echoed up from a few stories below. I shouted after him, but the response was a resounding door slam. So I followed.

Took the last few steps to the ground floor with my arms thrust ahead of me, pushed nonstop through the exit and into the lobby. I must've looked deranged with my backward gown and my wheezing, but nobody paid attention. A much more interesting show was already in progress.

There were five times as many people as when we showed up with Dad—dozens crowded around the admissions desk and the standing-room-only waiting area. A few shouted for attention, but most were subdued, scared. It looked like some crisis evacuation meeting zone.

Outside the plate glass window, ambulances and civilian cars clogged the emergency lane. Spinning lights swirled their colors across my range of sight. In the center of it all, just shy of the automatic sliding doors, three crouching security guards had wrestled a patient to the ground and pinned his arms behind his back. "*Let me go!*" the captive screamed. His voice cracked, not quite a man.

It was Twin Russ, dropped by the guards on his way to freedom.

"I didn't do anything!" Twin screamed at them.

A familiar nurse watched from the admissions desk, covering her mouth with one hand. She was the nurse from the elevator, the one we flashed indecently. It must've been her that alerted security.

Since I was still unnoticed on the sidelines of this circus, I slipped into an adjacent wing through a pair of swinging doors, huffing it fast toward a side exit.

I chanced a pit stop at the hospital gift shop to commemorate my visit. Shopping fast, I made a quick show of considering a tote bag and water bottle, then grabbed a Wright Beach t-shirt with jogging shorts and a pair of cheap knockoff Crocs, the only footwear they had in stock besides flip-flops. I blew the bulk of Mr. Yes's fifty bucks in one swoop.

The bored clerk didn't breathe a word about my patient gown or my fugitive attitude. Thirty seconds in a nearby men's room, I emerged in my getaway suit. The incriminating gown I kicked under one of the toilet stalls—good riddance.

I hurried out the side exit, and froze beneath the startling cloudless blue sky. Not atmospheric blue, but the solid electric blue of a crashed operating system. The Blue Screen of Death. It domed above the earth, or as much of it as I could see.

And the city was full of noise—hundreds of horns and alarms, sirens, angry shouts from the far side of the parking lot. *I did this.* I crashed the world. *Error* might as well have been written across the naked sky, followed by my name. Who could have guessed that some teenage twerp from a nowhere coastal North Carolina town could wreak this much havoc?

All that immense unstoppable power did nothing to make me feel mighty. I was an insect under the dead blue dome. It could fall and crush me the same as anybody else. I was nobody. All I did was wake a force I couldn't handle.

Azalea Taxi cabs circled the hospital, sharks around a sinking boat, so one of them caught me fast enough, right at the sidewalk. The driver was a scrawny man with deep facial lines, impervious to what was happening around him.

"Front Street, downtown," I told him.

"We waitin' on y'alls brother?" he asked.

"Huh?" I asked back.

The cabbie nodded at his rear-view mirror. A second later, the back passenger door swung open. There was Twin, still in his gown, panting and glistening with sweat. I had no choice but to scoot over so he could get in.

"What the hell?" I said.

"Security nabbed me," he said.

"Yeah, I noticed."

"Then thanks for helping."

"*You* ditched me *first*," I reminded him.

"They had me on the ground, then another of those dimensional shifts happened, and all of a sudden they didn't have me. I just got up and ran out here, and saw you getting into this cab."

If the driver could hear us, he didn't say so. He pulled around to the Oleander Street exit, facing a solid line of stopped traffic. People were out of their cars, hoods lifted open. Far down the road, black smoke billowed from somewhere unseen. I didn't want to think what it might be.

All these malfunctions... I imagined airplanes dropping from the sky by the thousands. Nuclear plants losing power, drifting into meltdown. The end of everything.

6:10 P.M.

OUR TAXI DRIVER plowed halfway downtown by weaving past stalled cars, skirting shoulders and jumping curbs. For him, this whole Reality Meltdown was the final challenge round. Then we hit an intersection where the cab stalled out and wouldn't turn back over, no matter how hard our driver cranked the key.

Twin was overwhelmed. He gawked out the window and said, "Is this even real?" to the Blue Sky of Death. Just then, five military Chinooks *thump thump thumped* their double rotors overhead. I hoped to hell their guidance systems stayed operational while they were up in the sky.

I got woozy again, braced myself for another shift. The taxi went ghostly. Our backseat lost its solidity, dropped out from underneath us. There was nothing but asphalt to break our fall. I turned sideways and landed on my ribs. Twin sprawled flat with such a crack I could almost feel the pain zap through my own spine.

A split-second to go and our shift would be complete—in the middle of snarling rabid traffic. I scrambled off the street, lost one

Croc, grabbed Twin by the arm as I went. We both rolled under a bus stop shelter, just as the last hazy glimpse of our cab faded out. In that other world, our cabbie was about to get mighty peeved that we ditched him without paying.

"What the hell!" Twin said.

"Dude, you should be used to this by now."

"Let's not get in any more disappearing cars," he said.

Lucky for us, traffic was at a standstill in this reality too. A truck eased into the space where the cab had been and ran over my Croc, but the footwear bounced against the curb, unharmed.

Had to focus now. Had to think—life or death. If we'd been sailing along at thirty miles per hour when the shift went down, we'd have ended up spread across the street like strawberry jam on toast.

I grabbed my Croc, slipped it back on. No worse for the wear. We took off running, Twin dangerously barefoot. We had to be skirting the next leap point, 6:15. Time was folding up and closing down.

6:15, 6:37, 6:56—even if we were reckless enough to make more leaps, the half-points were fast collapsing in to a meaningless blurt of minutes, then a handful of seconds, then no time at all. 7 p.m. was the monster climbing the staircase, closer and closer.

We turned onto Front Street, both of us out of breath after a four-block sprint. Twin bounced on one foot, clutching the bare heel of the other in his hand. Across the street, past a gridlock of cars, was our end zone—the former site of the Pastime Playhouse.

But there was nothing former about it. The theater was *there*. A brick-faced 1930s Public Works project, the tube shaped ticket booth under the marquee awning with its dead and dusty light bulbs, and the readerboard letters explaining that the place was TEM OR RILY CLO ED.

No sign of my father's headquarters.

"I thought you said it would be here," Twin said.

I stepped off the curb into the choked standstill of vehicles. I tuned out the crisis and kept my eyes glued on the building, staring it down, willing it to change. I didn't blink. My eyes watered from the cloud of exhaust fumes around me.

But there it was: the ghostly mirage of another building, superimposed on the theater. A newer, sleeker sign transformed the words Pastime Playhouse into Pastime Productions. Above it, a clock the size of a monster truck tire had hands that turned counterclockwise. My father's headquarters was there, just past the veil of this dimension.

"This is the place," I said.

Twin and I reached the three sets of entrance doors. We yanked on two handles simultaneously, and both of them clapped against their deadbolt locks. I didn't hold out much hope for the third, but Twin dutifully gave it a yank. No dice.

I shielded my eyes with my hand and peered through the glass door. The lack of sunlight dimmed the lobby, but I could make out the same old marble floor, the extravagant gilded faux-gold frames that used to contain the "coming soon" posters. Hand painted murals behind the concession stand showed iconic scenes from *Casablanca* and *The Wizard of Oz* and *Gone With the Wind*. A lost memory reclaimed. I could almost smell the popcorn.

Out of that shadowed fantasy past, somebody was coming toward us. A lanky teenager with a screwy look on his face. I had to step back, thinking it was a reflection. But no, it was him, Virgin Russ. He stopped at the door and glared at us through the glass. The kid was a mess—mussed hair and a clammy cast to his skin.

"Let us in!" I said.

After inhaling another few seconds of doubt, he twisted the bolt lock and pushed open the door. "I guess I should've expected you... both," he said.

Inside, our voices resounded in the dusty front lobby. The glass displays at the concession stand were empty of candy, the popcorn machine purged. The cold was sharper than it should've been, and it made Twin in his flimsy gown hug his own shoulders. There was a pervasive whiff of gas, like when you overfill a lawn mower tank.

"Can you tell me what I'm doing here?" Virgin asked us.

"What do you mean? Don't you know how you got here?" Twin asked back.

Virgin glanced cockeyed at Twin's hospital gown but didn't ask for details. He said, "I was in my dad's office upstairs, and then suddenly—"

"You shifted," I butted in. "You're stuck on this ride with us."

"This place—this theater—it burned down years ago—but..."

I wasn't all that surprised to learn that Virgin Russ was bound to us with our inter-dimensional field trips. He rode the same shifts because his nature was identically coded. Whatever programming malfunction was capturing us in its loops was capturing him too. He *was* us.

"We're in another dimension. Dad's office is still here—just—not—accessible, at the moment," I explained, or tried to.

"Don't call him *Dad* like we're brothers," Virgin said. "He's *my* dad. You left yours behind in some other... whatever. Don't you dare forget that." Evidently, *this* Virgin Russ had been given plenty of opportunity to get bitter about our existence before we even arrived on scene.

"Listen to me," I said. "Set all that aside right now. You need to understand that everybody here is in danger."

"From what?" Virgin asked.

"Bobby Keene-Parker," Twin and I said.

That bomb was a total dud. Virgin said, "You're kidding, right?"

"The guy's a maniac and he's got a gun. If he finds you..."

"How would he find us here?"

Even as Virgin asked the question, the past began to slip from us again. The murals of Bogart and Bergman and Garland turned to shimmering afterimages, then they were gone. In their place was a metal staircase with Plexiglas steps lit by a pale blue glow. Small mood lights dotted sheet metal walls between rivets. Every decorative touch in the place reflected Dad's *Brave New World* futuristic utopia kitsch. We had arrived at Pastime Productions.

Twin doubled over and gagged from the vertigo, nothing left to vomit.

The receptionist's desk was unstaffed, the waiting area with its Swedish weird-posture chairs was empty. And at the far end, where the theater itself used to be, an elevator waited, door shut.

I made for the stairs, wasting no time.

"What are you doing?" Virgin said, and grabbed my arm. His eyes widened when he realized his rash move had caused us to make physical contact, but there was no cataclysm. I knew it, but Virgin was making all these discoveries anew.

Virgin, the *real boy*, wanted to shut out all the troublemaking wooden Russ puppets dancing around him on their strings. He wanted to avert his eyes and pretend we didn't exist.

"You want us out of here, right?" I asked him.

"Hell, yeah."

"Then let me go talk to Dad. He'll have the solution."

Upstairs, the Death Star decor gave way to unfinished drywall, floors dusted with sanded compound powder. It was a simple hallway, two doors on either side and the elevator gleaming at the far end. Dad must've heard us because he popped out of a doorway on the left and said, "There you—are." He lowered his chin to get a clear view of three Russ Vales over his reading glasses.

"My God," he added, with a wistful smirk on his face that was almost embarrassing, like he was admiring his own handiwork. What he'd only been able to produce once with his biology, he'd now replicated with his technology. Nothing to be proud of, Pops. It was a holy mess, like multiplying Gremlins by getting them wet.

More than that, I wanted to rush down the hall and hug him, breathe him in, celebrate the fact that he was alive and well and un-shot. Heck, he was even dressed in khaki pants and a pressed button-down shirt. Clean-shaved and self-employed.

"What the heck is that?" I asked him, nodding at the strange piece of equipment he was cradling in his hands. It looked like a Vietnam-era walkie-talkie, the size of a shoe box and outfitted with a nest of antennas, one of them as long as a fishing pole and bobbing, even as Dad tried to hold it still.

"This," Dad said. "Is a Flux Stabilizer. It'll fix everything. I think."

6:20 P.M.

DAD'S NEW OFFICE was a junkyard of gadgetry, wires and gutted computers—the contents of his office back home crammed into a room a fraction of the size. He and Virgin fit snugly inside, but we two replicas had to watch from the hall.

The Flux Stabilizer's long antenna prodded and scraped the wall no matter how Dad adjusted the angle. It was a monstrosity of chips and hinges that seemed bound together only by the winding of its own wires. Dad explained, "If the stabilizer is used in conjunction with the program, then in theory it will recalibrate any variables that have been thrown off track. It would send you back where you came from."

"In theory?" I asked.

Dad slumped into his office chair with a sigh. He nodded at the bank of computer screens, all of them stone dead. The lights overhead flickered, threatened to die completely. These widespread technical malfunctions had screwed with his progress, and maybe even his calculations, I realized.

"I haven't been able to replicate the program exactly," Dad admitted. "Obviously, I succeeded in some other universe, but not here, not yet. But it may not matter because I can bypass the problem. This stabilizer will interact with the program after it's been downloaded onto the cell phone."

He pointed to an empty slot in the center of the Flux Stabilizer. It had the basic dimensions of my cell phone and a connection jack.

"Plug and play?" Twin and I said together. Our echo was getting annoying.

"Sure," Dad answered. "And these circuits will reroute the program through patch software. Sorry for the bulkiness. I didn't have time for sleek product design—or for a trial run, for that matter."

"But you're sure it'll work?" Twin asked.

Dad looked down at his wacko device, then back at us. "Sure as I'll ever be. Call it a full reboot. It'll send the user back to his own universe, to his own body, probably at the exact point he left it. At the same time, any other—versions—who are still separated from their home dimensions will be…"

"Deleted," Virgin Russ said, staring us down.

"What about you?" I asked Virgin.

"Nothing. I'm where I belong, so I get to stay."

Dad nodded and said, "It's just how the math works out. The firm boundaries will have to be reestablished. I wouldn't have predicted it, but this propagation of identical code is likely what's causing all these anomalies, and a full reboot is the only thing that will stop…" Dad looked to the ceiling, the flickering lights, the implicit Blue Screen of Death sky just over our heads.

"You mean too many Russes spoils the world," I said.

"I'm afraid so. Nature is a delicate equation. The universe is a complex program."

And you are a virus, were the words left unsaid.

Twin got morose, staring at the Flux Stabilizer. I understood his hesitation. For me, a reboot was a no-brainer: back to a life with the same crappy letdowns any kid my age had to deal with. Ask forgiveness of a few people, and things went back to normal. But *Twin's* home life was a tragic mess, with Dad possibly dead. Even in this reality, there would be serious fallout from the incident at Silver Screens, the crashed Aston Martin, all of it. It was a rigged lottery where I would be the only winner, and I felt like crap about that.

"Can more than one of us use it?" I asked.

"I didn't expect there to be two of you…" Dad admitted.

"Actually…" I said, because a key player was missing from the scene. One O'clock Russ—the guy who walked away from the car crash and went home to find Bobby in his living room. If Bobby ambushed him this time around, there might be no One O'clock left at all.

Except I hated to think of the other Russes like they were dispensable CD-Rs with *The Worst of Russ Vale* copied on them. We thought, therefore we *were*. My fear for my existence meant I was real, not a glitch, and the same was true for each other Russ.

Besides, the chance of One O'clock already having been "erased" by Bobby Parker would be no stroke of good luck. No way. Because One O'clock Russ had the key ingredient here: the cell phone where the Pastime Project would be downloaded. Without that phone, Dad's reset device was nothing more than the most ridiculous skin ever designed.

"One last thing," said Dad. "Very important. You're going to need some serious bandwidth to get enough power for the transference. You're going to need the best receiver in town."

In other words, we were going to need the WCPF radio tower. Back to the scene of the crime.

Dad offered the stabilizer to Twin and I, though he must've realized that only one of us could take it. He didn't want to have to make a choice like that himself. We hesitated, and from down the hall came a pleasant *ding*.

It was the chime that announced the arrival of an elevator car. I let myself get distracted by the noise and the sliding aluminum door, long enough to give Twin the edge. He took the device into his arms.

Then the elevator door smacked into place and Bobby Parker stepped out, his gun already aimed. He shouldn't have found us, but here he was, relentless.

Twin dove for cover inside Dad's office, while I fell off guard and stumbled backward against the drywall and collapsed to the floor.

Bobby approached me stiff and determined. He steadied the gun with two hands as he reached point blank range, and then he didn't shoot.

"Which one are you?" he asked. "Tell me, *now*."

"Killing me won't make you a star," I said.

Bobby dipped his aim and asked, "What?"

I took my opening, propelled off the wall in a cloud of white dust, straight through my father's office door. I body-slammed Virgin Russ by mistake so we *oomph*ed in stereo and crashed into a house of cards made of spare circuit boards.

Suddenly this was a craptastic plan, getting jumbled up with myself and trapped in a dead-end closet. All Bobby had to do was pivot and he had his own shooting gallery made of one regretful inventor and three identical reckless teens—bonus points for the triple play.

A sputtering blue light flashed. Calm voices were talking somewhere. Twin hugged the Flux Stabilizer and shrank in fear from the gun. Bobby smirked at him and said, "What you got there?"

My throat clutched shut. Bobby's question was rhetorical. It was clear that somehow he knew what the stabilizer was for, just like he knew where to find us. He was ten minutes ahead of me, at least, on everything. Bobby knew the rules of the game. Bobby knew what we were and what needed to be done. Bobby was the antivirus.

"Now wait a minute," Dad said, stepping forward.

Bobby elbowed Dad's jaw and knocked him aside. He turned and put the gun to Twin's forehead. I pressed my hands to my ears an instant before the blast. The noise pushed through anyhow, skull-rattling. Then, pure quiet, except for those strange and oblivious voices in another room, the voices I'd heard a moment before, calmly discussing whatever it was they were discussing, now magnified and echoing.

Here was no longer my father's office. I was in the projection room at the Pastime Playhouse. A pulsing blue light shined off a small glass window. It was the light from a digital projector casting a movie onto the screen down in the theater. The voices I'd heard were the actors in the movie being shown.

I sat up and took stock of what had just happened. Bobby killed Twin, clearly enough, and Twin's death had stabilized realities again. Fewer Russes meant no more inter-dimensional flip-flop. By the luck of a coin toss, I touched down in the movie theater instead of my Dad's office.

The Flux Stabilizer sat safely in my lap, just where Twin dropped it the instant he died. My salvation—I lifted it in my hands, heavier than I expected. Parts of it were hastily soldered together with steel elbow joints, an alien thing of interchangeable parts. But it was still missing its cell phone heart.

And those voices, still sounding out from the theater speakers. I recognized those voices. Savannah and Bobby, speaking lines from my movie, "Take the Leap."

I peered through the glass at the theater screen below. It was in fact the movie I taped in the Silver Bullet diner—a short-reverse-shot sequence, miraculously edited together by someone else. My actors sat in their diner booth, playing the parts of the doomed motorcycle daredevil and the love of his life.

This was final page in the script, where the girl volunteers to reject her college scholarship and stay behind, marry the daredevil, if only he'll promise not to risk the jump that killed his father. This is where Bobby nails his climactic line:

"I ain't gonna let you toss your whole life to save mine, girl. You've got a million more leaps of faith, and maybe I got less, but we're just going to have to let go and see where it is we fall."

6:30 P.M.

I HEADED BACK down to the theater lobby, where magic hour sunlight bathed the glass entrance doors and lit the dancing dust motes. Real sunlight from a natural sky. The street outside was thick with traffic, but it moved at a steady pace, like any normal Friday evening. With fewer Russ Vales, the world was right again.

The empty concession and posterless frames told me the place was still defunct, but that fact hadn't stopped *somebody* from screening a movie in the theater. I carried the Flux Stabilizer against my shoulder so the longest antenna wouldn't scrape the swinging door. Then I pushed through into the dark. The sound of cheering and clapping hailed from the speakers, but it was not meant for me.

And the smell of gasoline was so noxious in here I could taste it. The white vinyl surface of the screen was marred with blooms of mold, but still the scene in progress was clear:

A tween girl on a pitcher's mound, red hair sprouting from under her cap. She winds up her pitch and throws, and the amateur video swish-pans to where the batter takes a foolish swing at a curve ball.

This wasn't the footage I'd shot in the diner. It was amateur home video from several years ago, our little league championships.

Strike three for the win, and the team swarms the diamond to pile the star pitcher with their love. The last to mope out onto the field is a scrawny little Horace Vale. By then, the others have already got Paige Davis hoisted onto the tallest teammate's shoulders. A triumphant moment captured forever, a moment that *never happened.*

I understood that what we were watching was actual found footage from another universe. Digital video shot years ago, probably by some kid's parent, then archived in their home movie collection, only to be salvaged in the present, smuggled into some other reality, and spliced into this film. And here was the final showcase screening.

"What the hell is this?" a girl from the audience said aloud.

I hadn't expected a test audience, not with the theater's shutdown status and the gas fumes. But a handful of viewers sat clustered together in two rows, dead center. Silhouettes in the dark, except the one who stood to ask her question. Her freckled, skeptical face and baseball cap were lit by the reflection from the screen.

My chest heaved at the sight of her. The guy I used to be, just hours ago, in another world, would've never believed I could have such a visceral reaction to the sight of Paige Davis.

On screen, the video cut to another scene: more amateur video footage of a line of soldiers ushering duffel bags through the security checkpoint bypass, into a crowd of waiting friends and relatives in an airport lobby. Kids hurtling forward to jump their uniformed parents.

There's young Conrad Bower, mugging for the camera, doing a spastic interpretive dance to show his excitement. Must've been his mother recording. For no apparent reason other than pent-up glee, Connie strikes a mock bodybuilder pose—nothing you'd ever catch him doing in this life.

And then somebody calls to him, and he turns, and a man in

civilian clothes drops to one knee and widens his arms. Connie and his father hug like they just won the game show grand prize. His father, alive and well. Another miracle that never happened.

One last shot showed Paige again, older now. The video might well have been recorded a few days before. The camera tracks her as she runs across a stretch of Wright Beach, leaps in the air and catches a Frisbee. She turns on her heels and whips the disk back, laughing maniacally, and the camera follows to where Paige's older brother catches it *smack* between his hands.

"Turn it off," I said. "What's wrong with you?"

My *voice* said it, but I didn't, actually. Because another Russ Vale was in the theater audience. As my eyes adjusted I recognized my father, Conrad, Savannah, Paige, and two more variations of me. I counted six figures until the screen went black and they fell into darkness.

A few seconds later that bright blank wall of blue overtook the screen and the house lights slowly brought me a clearer view of my friends, family, and facsimiles. One Russ was wearing the cargo shorts I still had on when this all began. I could assume he was our innocent Virgin, the one to be protected at all costs. Process of elimination meant the other was One O'clock Russ. Which one of them had the cell phone I needed—I had no idea.

"Oh, crap, *another one*," Paige said, flicking a hand gesture at me, her proof of an infestation.

"How can y'all stand this gas smell?" I asked them.

"That's what I'm saying," said Virgin, with a cough.

"What are you doing here?" Paige asked me.

"I should ask you the same question."

"We were invited," One O'clock proclaimed.

"By who?"

Savannah directed my attention to the highest seats, just below the projection booth. Someone was there, crouched so low in his seat

I hadn't noticed him at first. Bobby Parker, grinning, hands laced together behind his head.

At the sight of him I screamed, "Everybody get out!"

But none of them moved. Not even Bobby himself. Well, Connie, who was hunkered in the crash position against the seatback ahead of him, briefly lifted his hands from his face and flashed a tortured expression at me. That was it.

They had to sense the risk. The gasoline stench alone, making my eyes water fierce—

"Where did you get that?" Dad asked me, sidestepping along his row. When he reached the end, he came down the landing, drawn to the Flux Stabilizer. "Is that—I mean, the design—"

My dad recognized his own handiwork, I guess, even though he hadn't actually invented the device in this reality. With the theater still intact, Kasper Vale's mad scientist laboratory was still just an item on his Christmas wish list.

No time for show and tell here. Bobby was surely armed and could start blasting any second. Dad flinched when I screamed again: "You have to get out! Bobby Parker is a maniac. He trapped you here, and *he's got a gun!*"

They all blinked at me, turned to Bobby for a second opinion. Bobby stood up. His hair took on a blue glow from the projection beam behind him, and the shadow of his pompadour was writ large on the movie screen. He shrugged and showed both his hands. *Who me?*

"I got nothing, folks," he said. Lifted his shirt to expose his bare waistline, did a three-sixty, modeling his total lack of a firearm. "Alls I did was bring y'all down here for a show like I was supposed to."

"It's a trap," I said. "Savannah, you saw him aim a gun at his father."

Savannah hugged her purse to her chest and moved farther down her row, away from me, the crazy guy with the weird contraption in his hands, even though we were already on opposite sides of the theater. She was closest to the emergency exit—two seconds away if she turned and sprinted.

"At Silver Screen Studios," I told her. "You went there—"

Savannah shook her head, refusing my story.

One O'clock tried to calm me with his upraised hands. "You're confused, bro," he said. "I don't know what happened where you came from, but whatever you're talking about, it didn't happen here."

I couldn't keep my eyes off Bobby. He was headed down the landing now, just behind my father, and I refused to accept that he was anything less than a maniac, in this world or any other.

"Where'd you get this movie?" I asked Bobby.

Bobby shrugged. "Why don't y'all tell me? *You* made it."

"You know what's going to happen before I do," I said. "You've known all along, maybe even before you came into the diner. You're in on this, whatever it is."

"Alls I know," Bobby said, flapping his fingers on either side of his head, "is there's like a dozen of you dudes swimming around in my head, all telling me a different story. Can't keep it straight anymore. I'm through with this gig, is all I'm saying."

"You had a gun," I said. "From the shooting range."

"Yeah, I left it in my—" Bobby's words caught in his throat. His eyes bulged like he needed the Heimlich. Just behind me, another surprise visitor had arrived. This one was the cause of Bobby's shock.

I turned, fully expecting to find another factory-line model of myself. Instead, there stood a second Bobby Keene-Parker, Clone Trooper, pistol aimed on his target, who, naturally, was me.

6:35 P.M.

FRESH ON THE scene, Bobby Parker Part Deux had the murderous look of a carnivore let loose from its cage. He was shirtless, wearing red breakaway track pants with the seams unbuttoned from the knees down. A hasty costume change, it seemed.

The implications here zipped through my mind. Somehow, Bobby Parker Deux took a turn with the Pastime Project. Most likely stole my 6:15 wormhole ride, in fact. Somehow, once 7 p.m. rolled around, Bobby was going to get the prize cell phone and make a leap of his own. I didn't know how, but the details hardly mattered. All it meant was that *bad deeds* were about to go down.

Nearly everyone I loved gathered together. *Corralled* was a better word because this setup was no accidental fluke. It was intelligent design.

"Give me that," Bobby Deux ordered—meaning the Flux Stabilizer.

Meaning Bobby knew the value of my wonky walkie-talkie.

It was clear now that our child-actor friend (any version) was

242

in the business of killing Russes. I'd seen it done. So I had a pretty dark prediction for what would happen if I gave him what he wanted. The space I currently occupied would be empty air in less than three seconds.

"I think I'll keep it, thanks," I said.

"Give it," he repeated, and raised his aim toward my face.

Original Bobby spoke up, "No way! No way! You are *not* here. I didn't do this. I ain't going through any time warp."

"Chill out," Bobby Deux told his prototype. "Trust me."

Original Bobby shook his head—*hell no.*

"Look—" I said, but Bobby cut me off.

"You can't make me do this, too, you sick freak. I've had enough of y'alls games." He wasn't addressing his clone-self anymore. His eyes were flitting back and forth—me, Virgin, One O'clock, me, Virgin, One O'clock. He'd lost track of which of us he was supposed to be talking to.

"Shut up," Bobby Deux said. "God, I can't even look at you. It's like you're some loser fan dressed as me for Halloween. You're such a fake." Deux wasn't aiming at anyone in particular now.

"Screw you," Original Bobby said, then he did a magic trick. Flashed his father's lighter out of nowhere. Thumb on the igniter, gave it a flick. He held the finger-high flame just inches from the back of the nearest red plush theater seat. It didn't seem like much of a threat, until I realized—emitting from the seats, the ruffled red curtains on the walls—

"The place is doused with gasoline," I said aloud.

Savannah took her cue. With a high-pitched screech she darted for the exit door, shoved the bar two-handed, and escaped. She never even looked back, and I couldn't blame her.

The rest of us, we'd get enveloped in flames if Original Bobby touched his lighter to the seat.

"No—*not yet!*" Redux screamed at his old self.

The fire trap was all part of the plan—*former* plan. Bobby probably brought the gas can himself, dribbled it around, all in preparation for our arrival. If it wasn't Bobby, it was whoever was using him to carry out this plan.

"You ain't real," Bobby said. "Just a voice in my brain."

"It's the other way around," Redux replied.

Calmly, One O'clock offered his open palm to Bobby, strained his reach across two rows of seats. One O'clock said, "Give me the lighter, man. You don't want to do this anymore. Plans have changed."

Bobby trembled. His lighter flame trembled. Finally, he flinched his thumb away. He snapped the lighter shut and slapped it into One O's hand.

"*Shoot him,*" One O'clock said, cold and clear.

Redux fixed his aim and pulled the trigger. If he was targeting me, I'd have been dead before the idea of it even occurred to me. But instead I had time to crouch and cry out, just like Dad and Paige nearby.

Further up the landing, Bobby Parker lurched backward from the force of the bullet. He tumbled into a seat, one leg draped over the armrest, and gawked down at the red flower blooming dead center on his chest.

Redux lowered the gun and slapped a hand over the top of his head, stunned. However he thought shooting another Bobby was supposed to feel, he clearly wasn't feeling that way. And he had no idea the worst part was coming next. If he'd known, he never would've fired the gun.

Draped in his theater seat, Bobby Parker went limp. We didn't need a medic to diagnose him dead. Didn't even need a pulse check. Bobby's death was official the instant the gun thumped on the carpeted floor, and the empty track pants gently folded down on top of it. Redux had killed his original and, in doing so, erased himself.

I wished I could feel relieved. Bobby Parker was just a pawn in a game I played with a hidden opponent. Not just chess but that crazy three-dimensional chess where pieces could jump from one plane to another, appearing and disappearing, attacking where they wouldn't be expected.

And my opponent knew all the moves ahead of time. The greatest Game Theorist ever to plot a military strategy, especially with inter-dimensional time travel at his disposal. *Careful not to trust*, the knight said, just before he was captured.

"We gotta get out of here," One O'clock told us all. He moved onto the landing, brushed aside the track pants with his shoe and grabbed the gun from the floor. Just his thumb and finger on the hilt. For a guy who'd only taken one leap, he acted very much in control of the variables here.

Dad gripped my shoulder to steady my shiver. I was too wiped out to think through even the simplest logic—but something was wrong here.

"It's quarter to seven. We have fifteen minutes to use the device or we're screwed, forever," One O'clock insisted. "Our last shot."

Paige said, "And what're we supposed to do when you two disappear? How do we explain a dead actor shot by his own clone?"

"Why did you tell him to shoot—himself?" I asked One O'clock.

He flashed me the same sneer I used to deflate other people when they asked stupid questions. "To trick him into canceling himself out, and it worked, right?"

"But why would he *listen* to you?" I persisted. "All along, I thought I was playing Bobby, convincing him to shoot the movie and all that. But really, he was manipulating us. He lured us to Silver Screens, he showed up at my Dad's office, but there was no way for him to know—"

"Time's wasting," One O'clock reminded me. He pulled our cell phone from his pocket and showed off the readout. Of course he would've taken it from Virgin, knowing what it was worth. All we had to do now was insert that phone into the Flux Stabilizer and get to the radio tower in time. But I couldn't think about that now.

"Everything that's happened," I said. "It's a way to make me keep jumping across dimensions. More leaps. More Russes. And the more Russes there are, the more—"

"Unstable the system," Dad concluded along with me.

"Yes, like a viral attack, which makes the system—"

Connie let loose a barrage of coughs, probably from gas fumes.

"Susceptible to infiltration," Dad finished for me.

"*The black*," Connie choked out, gripping the seat ahead of him.

"What?" I asked.

"The black *eye*," Connie said.

The mere mention of my injury brought the throbbing back to my face. I dabbed the tender flesh just above me left cheek, and as I did, One O'clock slipped his finger through the gun's trigger guard.

"Woah—wait a second," I said. "I got hit at school and—"

"But where is *his?*" Paige interrupted.

Because One O'clock, who was supposed to have caught the same schoolyard smack down I did, should've sported an identical shiner. But his face was clear and clean of all but a few whiteheads.

This Horace Vale wasn't One O'clock at all. Too late, I finally knew what Future Russ was going to say: be careful not to trust *yourself.*

6:42 P.M.

"WHO ARE YOU?" I asked—whoever he was. The one I'd been calling One O'clock. The one who could not have actually been a former manifestation of me, who was lying to us, who was way more in control than he should've been. Let's call him *Wrong Russ*.

"Come on," he said. "Questions like that make me look stupid."

I saw the differences now. A trace of fuzz on his lip that would've taken me months to grow. And he looked ten pounds lighter than any other Russ, face stretched thin, like those before-and-after PSAs about meth addicts and how human they used to look.

"You're him—the one who sent the first video," I said.

Wrong Russ sighed. His gun wasn't necessarily aimed at anyone, but the threat was there. He said, "Just give me the device."

"You point that gun at me and I'll break this thing," I said. "Nobody will go anywhere, and your whole plan will be screwed."

"Fine, then just come with me. We can both use it."

"Tell me what's going on," I said.

"We're running out of time."

"Where's One O'clock Russ?"

"Come on… there's no sense in—"

"*Where*?"

"Gone. Erased."

"You killed him," I said.

Dad and Virgin positioned themselves at my sides. They were betting Wrong Russ wouldn't risk hurting them with a wayward bullet—but they didn't know that his schemes resulted in Dad getting shot once already. Not to mention, he'd arranged for so many Russes to die, I couldn't keep count. If I had him I.D.ed correctly, he was the first cause, the designer of all this chaos.

"Sure," Wrong Russ said. "I broke through into this reality and replaced him right after the car crash. Assumed his identity, you could say. The only real one here is him." He nodded at Virgin. "The rest of us are eight-bit characters. You know that. We're as real as Super Mario falling into a lava pit. There's always an extra life."

"*I exist*," I insisted.

Wrong Russ scoffed at me. "I used to think that, but I've been stuck in this game so long, I lost count how many times, how many leaps. All I want is to find my way out. Maybe I was the first Russ to use the Project. I'm not even sure about that."

"How did you get a hold of it?" Dad asked him.

"You—or another iteration of you—thought it was a secret, but I found it," Wrong admitted. I could almost see the moisture in his eyes when he spoke to our father. "The first time I leaped—it was an accident—a joke. I didn't think it would work, but then I was lost. I've lived this day… God. Five hundred takes of the same scene. You can't even tell one from the next anymore. You know every line, every angle—but you still can't get it right."

"But the clock—it runs out at seven," I said.

"Which is why I've had to jump to a new track before the end. I sent messages to other versions of myself, like you, across dimensions.

Get them to make enough leaps, destabilize the boundaries, you can break clean through and start over again. I don't know how many times anymore. But now we've got a way to end it for good. Finally. This is what I've been waiting for. A Flux Stabilizer. Like I said, all I want is out."

I realized aloud, "It was you—the techno-vortex, the knife—you're the one who screwed with Bobby's head and lured us here and killed Paige."

"He did *what*?" Paige asked.

"In another world," I said.

"That was an unstable wormhole," Wrong Russ said. "I could only get partway through. When you're stuck halfway, there's all sorts of interference and feedback. But I had to do something to make you leap again."

"So you murdered your own friend?"

"These worlds are dreams, you understand? No more real than dreams, except you keep waking up from one into the next. But I want to wake up for good, and so do you."

"Don't tell me what I want," I said.

"Don't pretend I don't *know* what you want," Wrong said. "The only difference between us is time. I've had more time to realize who I really am."

Time—all this time, repeated time—and not a second to think, to consider how Wrong Russ played me like an X-Box hero using every available cheat code. He recorded the invitation and mailed it through space and time. He duped me into thinking he was me from some glorious future.

One shot, he promised, but that was his first lie, because from the start he meant to shove me through the wormhole over and over again, enough times to bust a leak between dimensions and flush himself into this world.

He was the gremlin who tampered with Connie's video game and computer and telephone, who pushed me to go out and screw up my life so I'd have to make the leap again. And again.

I couldn't image what mindset would make him commit his betrayals—his murders and manipulations, driving Bobby crazy. People did horrible things all the time, but not people with my exact personality, my empathy, my memories and longings, my perfectly sane arrangement of brain and nervous system.

To him, every new universe was just a game. He could draw a blade across Paige's wrist and it was nothing more than a trick blade, a movie prop, and the blood was chocolate syrup, and Paige was just a scream-queen actress. Because how else could you—could *I*—do it? Press down and slice and watch the life fade out of her eyes? And do it for no other reason than to lure me into leaping again?

Alternate selves discarded, with no more thought than when you toss out a dulled disposable razor. Russ Vales picked off at random when the sheer number of them threatened reality itself. And Bobby Keene-Parker of all people had been sent to take them out, except the original of course. That's why Bobby asked who I was at the point of a gun. He didn't want to shoot the wrong Russ.

This was me. This was who I was.

Loser and winner, cheated and cheater, victim and monster.

Virgin Russ stepped forward, held out his hand to Wrong Russ.

"You're not going to hurt us," Virgin said. "Give me the gun."

Wrong cowered back, twitchy-eyed, panting. He tucked the gun into the back of his waistband. Something else was in his hand now—Bobby's lighter.

Next came a deafening blast. I thought it was an explosion, but it was the emergency exit door, slammed wide open. A dark figure dove in, hunkered low. Police, more and more of them spilling in. A battering ram. Helmets, face shields, Kevlar vests. Demands growled out.

Wrong Russ did not obey them. He flicked his thumb on the

igniter, and the lighter flame came alive again. As Virgin reached out to snuff it, the flame seemed to leap for the gas-drenched seats, eager to spread. An instant inferno enveloped the rows and crawled up the curtains. A wall of heat and light rushed against our bodies. I reeled, coughed, couldn't see, and someone wrenched the Flux Stabilizer from my hands.

Wrong Russ, of course.

The air was too hot to breathe. I choked and coughed and tumbled down the landing toward the theater entrance ramp. Somehow, I had Paige's wrist in my grasp and we rushed away from the heat, Virgin and Dad close behind.

But Conrad? I couldn't find him through the fire and confusion.

Uniformed police crowded the lobby exit doors in full raid mode. Dust kicked up so thick it lingered. In the midst of it, Wrong Russ was a gray shadow, gun in one hand and the bulky stabilizer in the other, like a homemade bomb.

Lobby doors swung back, a mad rush for the box office. Police swarm: "Drop it! Drop the gun!" The weaponless among us halted in our tracks, ducked low, kept our distance from Wrong Russ and the onrush that was about to take him down.

Then gunfire. I don't know whose. Uncountable reports. The glass concession case shattered. I shoved Paige behind a Ms. Pac Man machine and dove for cover beside her. She grunted from the impact and swore at me, but she was safe for another instant at least.

Then quiet. A few guttural shouts. Official commands. The syncopated stomp of a dozen boots, heavy breathing. The castle overrun with marauders.

Rough hands lifted me off the floor and twisted my arms behind my back. Handcuffs cranked into place. I was given a hurried escort through the choking dust and smoke, toward sunlight.

My steps kicked metallic debris—remnants of the Flux Stabilizer, now scattered scrap parts. A tossed-aside pile of Wrong Russ's clothes. He had been taken out by police. Deleted. Time winding down to zero hour. My only escape hatch, slammed shut and locked.

6:58 P.M.

MY HANDCUFFING SEEMED to be a case of mistaken identity. I tried to plead with my arresting officers, but the patrol cops weren't listening. They told me to zip it. I was not under arrest, just detained until the details were clarified.

I was alone and still cuffed in the backseat of a parked cruiser two blocks from the burning theater. Windows opened a crack for fresh air. Forced to watch the smoke filling the sky. Flashes of orange fire.

My temporary holding tank was parked in front of a vintage clothing store. The mannequin in the window, wearing a 1960s dress that looked more like a curtain, glared at me accusingly.

Most of Front Street was cordoned off, with emergency vehicles of every stripe hoarding road space. I'd managed to make a disaster zone of downtown Cape Fear twice in less than ten minutes, but at least this time the pandemonium didn't run so deep that it screwed with the laws of nature. There weren't enough Russes left for that.

A pulsing red light cut through the smoke. It was the beacon at the top of the radio tower reminding me of the chance I lost.

In the front seat, an open laptop mounted on the console told me it was 6:58. Two minutes left to go, but I fretted over the immediate past instead. I'd seen Paige and Virgin and my father leave the theater, but Connie—I didn't know. He was trapped in the center of all those seats when they went up in flames. Maybe the cops had time to grab him, but that fire, it came on so furiously. And the flames would've struck him with such a paralyzing fear...

So much carnage and all for nothing. Because Wrong Russ was dead and gone, just minutes away from his salvation. After however many hundreds of leaps and reboots? It was almost a shame for him to have failed, and almost a blessing that my defeat came much more quickly.

Wrong Russ was proof that time and temptation would twist my mind in ways I couldn't at that moment anticipate. He was the end result.

I didn't see Paige coming until she was outside my window. Her cheeks were smeared with soot. She wrapped her fingers into the inch of window space. Then I saw: she was pressing something against the window. Our Curt Schilling baseball card.

"How'd you get out here?" I asked her.

"There's a lot going on. I probably won't be missed."

"Conrad..." I said.

Paige dropped her eyes. She didn't have to say it out loud. What she said instead was, "Take a look at this card, Russ. You remember it?"

"Yeah. My *lucky card*. You fished it out of the garbage to remind yourself what a failure I am."

She hitched her lip at me. "Who said that?"

"You did. In another life."

"I admit, it sounds like something I'd say. But it's a lie."

"I should've gone back for him," I said.

"The real reason I took this card," she went on, ignoring me, "is to remind myself about sticking with it, about missed chances and redemption and all that corny stuff."

"*Please*," I said. I imagined them pulling the burned husk of a body from the theater wreckage, backpack still strapped to his bones, smoke still rising from the char.

"Okay, so it's sort of ironic," Paige explained. "Y'all sucked at baseball, but I've seen your heart, Russ Vale. You need to quit tossing out your cards."

"I don't have any more cards," I said.

The clock on the police laptop blipped to 7 p.m.

And I heard it, the chime of my cell phone.

Paige reached into the belly pouch of her sweatshirt and took out the phone to verify what I'd heard was true. She had my cell phone, kind of battered and scratched, but otherwise intact. She said, "I grabbed it off the floor, just before they got us out. Figured you might want to have it back."

"You do it," I told her.

"Uh-uh, James Cameron. No way I'm jumping into y'alls weird sci-fi fantasy. This is yours to fix. That's why I showed you the baseball card. A reminder."

"Nothing will change here. Connie will still be dead."

"It's something me and the other Russ have to live with. This is our world. But you, you don't belong here." She eyed me for a second, then lowered her voice to recite: "*I ain't going to let you toss your whole life to save mine, girl.*"

A line of dialog from my movie, used against me. The sting of it threw me off guard, like Paige knew it would. Handcuffed, I could only watch as she slipped the cell phone through the window crack and aimed its screen at me.

"Take care of Virgin," I said.

"Virgin? What virgin? What does that mean: *take care?*"

"I didn't mean..." I started, but she pressed the blue icon.

DAY ONE
(TAKE FIVE)

6:37 P.M.

I POPPED BACK into awareness, hands still behind my back, though nothing bound them together anymore. I wasn't in the cruiser, either. I was in some tricked-out muscle car, my bare butt propped on some massive speaker that took over the whole back seat. It cranked out rap so hard my bones rattled.

The dash clock said 6:40. Set a few minutes fast, I figured. The burly driver's bald head, red-flame tattoos and all, bopped to the beat of the music. I hunched low, but his lazy eyes caught me in the rear view and burst open wide.

"What the—" he said, swiveling around to face me.

"I'll explain later!" I yelled. Why not?

Burly Dude grabbed for me. I dodged his meaty grip, shoved the door, and rolled onto the sidewalk. The grit of concrete bit my skin, but it was better than chancing Burly's wrath.

Nearby pedestrians gasped at my public indecency. The sky was natural blue with scattered clouds, and reality seemed generally stable. Good news. Not enough Russes here to screw with the coding.

Four of us, by my count—Wrong Russ, Virgin, me, and the *me* from five minutes back. One O'clock and Twin would already be dead, murdered by Wrong and Bobby. *Five* alien intruders seemed to be the magic number for total interdimensional meltdown. The fifth must've been that surprise Bobby clone, or the extra Russ I hadn't known to count.

Burly Dude laid on his horn. I found my feet and lunged hands-first into the consignment shop. That damn window dummy watched me with that same judging glare she would give me again, twenty minutes from now.

Inside, somebody called out, "Hi, there—let me know if y'all need any help." Obviously, the shop owner couldn't see me past the overstuffed racks and linen piles, clothes hanging literally from the rafters.

I snagged the nearest pair of jeans and shimmied them over my hips. Great: pink hearts stitched down the thighs, flared bell-bottoms. Even greater: waistline too tight to button.

I might've looked for a better fit, but the time bomb was ticking down, and just outside the display window, Burly Dude was finally rising from his car, snarling at me. I found a bland gray sweatshirt and went on my way. Zig-zagged through the bulging clothes racks to the back of the store like navigating a mosh pit to reach the stage. Behind me, Burly stepped in with a welcoming overhead jingle.

The checkout counter came into view. A woman with rat's-nest hair lowered her knitting to get a look at me.

"I'll pay you back, I swear," I told her, and swiped a pair of scuffed black electrician's boots from a shoe rack. I dropped them into my path and stepped inside as I went.

Burly was over six feet, so I saw his glistening bald head coming at me through the clothes. I took an alternate route, ducking low so he couldn't catch sight of me. The clothes were almost suffocating, but then I saw the light, and dashed through the exit.

Down the street, the Pastime Playhouse was intact. No fire, no smoke curling into the sky. For the moment.

My oversized boots clomped off beat as I ran toward the theater. Every muscle in my body was jelly from hours on the run, but I still had to push.

I was almost there when Savannah shot through the narrow alley between the buildings and headed straight at me. She ran with both hands in front of her face, thumbing manically at her phone. This was when she fled from the showdown inside, another angle on the moment.

"Savannah!" I said.

She jolted, fumbled the phone, and it skittered across the concrete ahead of her, jettisoning the battery as it went. A newspaper box broke her stride. She slumped into it, red-faced, purse dangling from the crook of her elbow.

I had to squeeze her shoulder to get her to truly see me.

"Listen—I'm going in there. Don't call the police," I said.

She shook her head. "Don't call the—why?"

"They'll ruin everything. Just trust me. I'll stop what's happening."

"They—they kidnapped me—Bobby and the other—you—and I had to sit there and watch—inside the theater—I don't—you—who?"

"I'm a good one," I assured her.

Her head kept shaking but her eyes seemed to believe. That was the best I could do. The dismantled phone would buy me a few seconds of time, at least, if Savannah decided to ignore my pleas and call the cops anyway.

I rushed in through the lobby, alone. Kicked off my boots for the sake of stealth. No real plan in my head. I didn't have the time for strategy like Wrong Russ did. All I could do was bumble in and hope to cause enough chaos to offset his careful calculations.

Inside the theater, Wrong recited his justifications once again, the second daily staging of a local play: "These worlds are dreams, you understand? No more real than dreams, except you keep waking up from one into the next. But I want to wake up for good, and so do you…"

Former me was supposed to say, *Don't tell me what I want,* but this time I leaped from around the corner instead. No way Wrong Russ could've forecast my appearance. This was all new territory. None of his hundreds of leaps had ever brought him to this new string of events.

But… the bastard got the best of me anyhow. Dodged my grappling arms and whacked my skull so hard I saw white flashes and reeled into the gas-soaked theater seats.

His gun went off. More screams and scrambling. I wasn't dead. The throb in my skull assured me of that. When my eyes refocused, Wrong Russ had control of the Flux Stabilizer, just like last time. He stepped backwards, warning everybody off with his firearm. Near his feet, Former Me was nothing but a wicked-witch pile of hospital gift shop clothes on the floor. Five seconds flat, and a miserable failure.

All I did was get another version of myself killed again, and now we were spiraling toward another crash. Wrong turned the gun back on me. One last bit of tidying up before he scrammed. I was wedged on the floor between two rows of seats. Easy target, defenseless and dazed.

"No!" somebody screamed. It was Connie, ten feet behind me.

The shadow of a fat wingless bird arced overhead. It looked like a turkey taking awkward flight. Wrong Russ did a double take at the incoming projectile, raised his eyes and his aim to meet what was hurtling his way. Connie's backpack, stuffed almost to bursting.

Wrong decided not to fire. Instead, he sidestepped, and the pack flopped onto the landing, gushing all its contents. Books and action figures and Magic cards, everywhere.

Wrong Russ coughed out a laugh, swiped Connie's emptied pack off the floor, and shoved the Flux Stabilizer inside. He turned to make his escape, no longer interested in picking me off, it seemed. This time, there'd be no police raid to stop him.

After he fled, I tried to stand, but my latest head wound took its toll. Everything popped black, a fuse blown in my brain, and I was out cold.

6:53 P.M.

I WOKE UP with pain sizzling through my forehead. Someone tipped bottled water into my mouth and got me coughing even more. No clue where or when I was, but the information trickled in as I recovered from my stupor.

A moving car, Dad's to be exact, the backseat, me in the middle with Virgin almost on my lap. I would've told this other me to give *me* me some space, but Paige and Savannah flanked us on either side. We were packed pretty tight.

And my best friend Conrad Bower was manning the wheel. Connie, *driving.* I blinked, suspecting a brain injury (mine or his), but there he was, hunched forward, hands at ten and two on the wheel. Yeah, he looked frightened, but not *petrified.* Not helpless, not anymore.

We were cruising Front Street at a reasonable clip.

Dad in the shotgun seat, navigating.

"Stop sign," Dad told Connie.

We all lurched when Connie stomped the brake, but nobody

complained. Forget about *driving*: last time I even saw Connie inside a car was never, in this world or any other.

"Connie," I said. "You're *killing it!*"

He gave a quick nod—concentrating too hard to chit-chat.

Virgin said, "He wouldn't get in otherwise, so we had to let him take the wheel."

"He saved my life," I said, mostly to myself, remembering that fat-bird backpack soaring overhead, what it must've taken Connie to make such a bold move at gunpoint.

"You might have a concussion," Paige announced.

She was the nurse with the water, getting more on the front of my shirt than in my mouth. I grumbled and nudged the bottle away, even if I would've preferred to wrap my arms around her and forget everything else.

"I'll be okay," I said. Because, hey, in a handful of minutes I'd be pain free. Gone to oblivion, just as soon as Wrong Russ activated the Flux Stabilizer. I'd be nothing but a memory, and maybe not even that.

"How long was I out?" I asked.

Dad turned in his seat, slapped a reassuring hand over my knee. "Just a couple minutes. It's seven minutes to seven now. We had to carry you out of the theater. People are going to have some questions when all this is done."

"All what?" I asked.

I got my answer when Connie turned a sharp left into the WCPF station parking lot. The backseat occupants grunted as we crushed each other. Straight ahead, the radio tower spiked the sky like vast scaffolding for something better in the future.

They'd brought me here for the final showdown. Me, the worthier Russ, if only because I didn't kill anyone.

But Wrong Russ wasn't where we expected him to be, stationed at the tower base waiting out the clock. At first, I thought we must've beat him rushing over here, but then I saw the gate swung open, half the padlock dangling busted from the latch. He must've shot the lock to gain access.

And then I looked up. He was scaling the center ladder, just like I did twelve hours before. Halfway to the top already, with Connie's backpack strapped on his shoulders. The Flux Stabilizer's antenna sprouted from its open pouch, ticking back and forth with each new upward lurch.

I didn't have a clue what Wrong's deal was. Maybe he wanted to get closer to the satellite dishes and receivers at the tower top, thinking they'd give a stronger signal. More likely, he was fortifying his position—out of range of anyone who came to stop him, like us.

"Does he still have the gun?" Paige asked.

"If he's smart. And he is," I said.

If any of us tried to climb after him, Wrong Russ could take pot shots with his pistol all he wanted. I pictured the gruesome fall. He'd pick us off, one by one, and nobody would get close to him.

"I'll go," Virgin volunteered. "He won't hurt me."

True: killing Virgin would be suicide for any clone, but—

"He's desperate," I said. "He'll shoot you out of spite if you stop him from taking the leap. He's run out of chances."

"Or you might just slip and fall, even if he doesn't shoot you," Connie added, eternal optimist. He'd brought the car alongside the gated base. Wrong was too high up for us to see him at this angle, and we were closer than was safe. I worried he'd start firing at the car to scare us off.

"It has to be me that goes, even if I don't make it," I said.

Nobody protested, especially not Virgin. I was the stranger in these parts, the one who wouldn't be missed no matter the outcome.

Savannah was hunched in a fetal ball against the door. She hadn't offered an opinion or even a word since I regained consciousness. I wondered how they lured her into the car in the first place. Maybe they told her Bobby was still on the loose and looking for her to be his co-star for eternity. Or maybe she felt a *smidge* of obligation to see this through. Who knew? She just sat there, clutching her purse. *Her purse.*

"Savannah, I need some of your makeup," I said.

I lifted my butt off the seat and struggled the jeans down to my knees. No time for modesty. Paige covered her eyes with her forearm and said, "Woah, wait a second—not cool."

To Virgin, I said, "Dude, take off your clothes."

"What?"

"I got a way to beat Wrong Russ."

"Wrong *what*?"

"Never mind. Y'all have nicknames."

"What's mine," he asked.

"Classic Russ," I lied. "Like Classic Coke. Give me your pants."

6:55 P.M.

IN VIRGIN'S BORROWED clothes and shoes I climbed the tower. My arms and thighs were so weak, I worried they'd just give out. The roof of Dad's car down below looked like a kiddie pool for a daredevil high jumper. Down there, Kasper Vale stood beside his car, hands in his pockets, my only spectator. Our final words for each other weren't much, but then I wasn't exactly his son.

There he was anyhow, absorbing all the mystery of my existence, the way you'd contemplate a snapshot of yourself you don't remember being taken.

Further above, Wrong Russ clung to the ladder. He was an even stranger enigma—one that none of us wanted to ponder. The backpack was repositioned on his chest for easier access. He gripped the pistol firmly, hanging one-handed. I could practically see down the gun barrel.

He wasn't moving anymore. He was waiting. For me. All he had to do was wait and he'd win, simple. And if my ploy didn't work, if I couldn't fool him, then I was a dead man, hopefully before I hit the ground.

My arms would barely cooperate with the climb. All the thrill I might've felt before was gone. My hands were sweaty on the rungs. Each footstep reverberated through the tower structure like an amped-up laser gun blast.

Wrong shouted something down, but the wind disbursed it. Either he was stalling for a better shot, or my impersonation of Virgin Russ was working so far. The trick wasn't so much the clothing swap as the hasty patch job to conceal my black eye. Foundation and powder and a bunch of other beauty product from the stockpile in Savannah's purse.

Just before I left the car, Paige passed me the Curt Schilling baseball card, and this time she didn't have to tell me what she meant by it. I wanted to bestow some final wisdom on Virgin, but all I could think was "take care of these people," knowing now they could mostly take care of themselves.

I got another ten feet higher and Wrong said, "Don't come any closer."

"You're not going to shoot me."

"What are you coming up here for, anyway?"

"To convince you."

"Convince me of what?"

"To climb down and share the leap with the other Russ."

"Lost his chance."

My climbing dragged to a crawl. I had some dumb notion if I moved slowly enough, he wouldn't notice.

"Nobody's stopping me this time," Wrong said. He stirred from his perch, turned away from me and went for further heights. The satellite dishes were clustered just a few yards over his head.

Cape Fear sprawled out below and spun of its own accord. Wrong had to be feeling the vertigo too—or maybe not. Maybe all he felt was the rush. We were leaps apart, different to the cores of characters.

269

I was still desperate to keep myself wrapped in the humanity he already shed.

"I have to know," I called up to him.

"Yeah?"

"How'd you get Bobby Parker to do all your dirty work?"

"Bobby was a certifiable nutso. You could steer him off a cliff with the right argument. All it takes is a good director."

"He shot Dad."

"The only real Dad is the one waiting for me on my home turf."

"This sure as shit is real."

"From your point of view, I guess," he said.

"Tell that to the people down in that car."

"Collateral damage. What can I say?"

"Why'd you show them those movies in the theater?" I asked.

Wrong stopped and glanced up toward the red beacon light. I could sense it—his nerves wouldn't let him go higher. We were maybe ten rungs apart and I wished we could keep climbing, just a few more seconds to put off the confrontation.

He looked down at me through the V of his armpit. "I didn't want any of this," he said. "When I get back—to my real life—everything I did and saw will be erased. I'll be Regular Russ again. But I wanted someone—I wanted *them*—to see what I could achieve, what was possible. I wanted to see their faces. That's why I showed them. All I ever wanted was to make them happy, so I gave them what they lost, even if it was just in a movie."

Then Wrong Russ did what I never would've dared. He reached out one leg and planted it against a horizontal steel brace, grabbed a diagonal lattice and pulled himself from the safety of the ladder. Out on a limb, betting I wouldn't follow. Luke at the end of *Empire*, with no Falcon to save him. Except not, because that would make me Vader again. Seth, not Sith, damn it.

"All you did was make them grieve all over again," I said.

The mention of the ones we left below made us both chance a look back down. Sure enough, they were all out of the car now. They were craning their necks to watch us, two boys lost out of time and space, settling this major mess we made.

"I showed them better lives," Wrong said.

"All this extra time and you couldn't figure it out?" I asked.

"Figure what out?"

"They never needed your help. You needed theirs."

We were level with each other now. Three of me, arm to arm, could've reached him, but not me alone. The steel brace where he was balanced groaned when I tested my own foot on it. This structure wasn't built for the jungle gym antics of two hundred-and-fifty-pound teenagers.

Wrong anchored himself to a lattice and kept his gun on me. He held the backpack by its coat rack loop, unzipped too far so the Flux Stabilizer jutted precariously out the side. "I'll shoot you," he reminded me.

"And erase yourself," I said, playing my Virgin Russ role.

"One way or another, I'm off this ride." The stubborn set in his jaw was just as mine would've been if our situations were reversed.

I was right beside him, ready to leap. When I grabbed a lattice beam, the strain on my wound made me hiss. The cut across my hand was torn open again. Blood dribbled down my forearm, bright enough to catch Wrong's eye.

He'd made that slice himself, the mark that betrayed me.

His eyes widened, and I knew I was caught. "*You—*" he growled.

7:00 P.M.

INSIDE THE BACKPACK, our cell phone chirped cheerily. The Pastime Project, coming to a close.

I lunged at Wrong before he could shoot me. A lunatic suicidal move, but I didn't have a choice. He reared back and almost lost his footing. I caught empty air and learned how badly gravity wanted me. But I kept clinging with a finger hold.

The gun smacked steel, triggered a shot that spark-pinged a bullet off metal just beside my head. The recoil jerked the gun from his grip, and down it went—to be dashed on the ground or swallowed by the Cape Fear River.

While Wrong considered his loss, I took another fast grab and caught hold of one backpack strap. But my fingers lost the lattice and I was swinging midair over a long span of space. To his credit, Wrong held fast, even when my full weight snapped his arm straight down, hard enough to dislocate a shoulder. Credit Connie, too, for choosing an accessory that could withstand a human clip-on ornament.

I dangled. Nothing but sturdy vinyl and Wrong's determination keeping me alive. He was all teeth, holding fast to his strap, and the backpack was a high-stakes wishbone stretched taut between us. I knew our strength. He'd last another few seconds, tops.

Then I heard it, the rip of a zipper slowly prying itself apart. The long antenna on the Flux Stabilizer bent its aim straight down, toward me, as the bulky equipment slid free from its protective pouch and readied for a sky dive.

"*No!*" Wrong screamed.

I made a blind grab as the device geronimoed. At this instant, in a million other realities, my reach was not quite right. In those worlds, the device tipped off my fingertips and fell away forever, but this was not those worlds. Here, I managed to catch the thing. It smacked firmly into my hand.

The arc of my full-body swing brought my sneaker toes against a lower beam. But the back swing sent me out over open space again. Because I had the device and there was still a chance to recover it, Wrong Russ kept his job as my anchor and my pivot.

Momentum brought me forward again. I locked a crossbeam in the crook of my arm. The backpack fluttered away, empty and exhausted.

A five pound chunk of tech like the Flux Stabilizer weighs at least a hundred when your muscles are frayed. But I wasn't going to give it up now. Our cell phone was safely housed in its heart, just where Wrong Russ inserted it.

It flashed the final minute: 7 p.m.

Poised on the next beam above me, Wrong said, "Aim it up at both of us. We'll both go through."

No harm done, I supposed. But I vetoed the plan. Because this final wormhole would send Wrong Russ back to a world where the Pastime Project was a constant reality, where every day he'd be tempted to use it again—*one last shot to get everything right*—and how seriously long would a guy like him hold out before the urge took over, until he threatened all of existence again?

Because I was him and he was me. I'd zap myself back to my bed, safe and sound, no harm done, but in twelve hour's time the call would come to me again. Another invitation to make the leap.

I didn't have to take this trip anymore. This world was as solid as any other, and it was the end of the line. I reeled back, assumed the best possible stance I could manage, and pitched the device out over the Cape Fear River.

Who knows if an ump would've called it a ball or a strike? Accuracy didn't matter, as long as I was tossing it for good.

Above me, a scream and a clatter, and then a blank space where my double had been a second before. Wrong Russ's body rushed past. A quick eclipse over the falling sun. He jumped and was falling, falling, reaching out for that spiraling chunk of metal and wires already far beyond his grasp.

His final failed leap.

There is no victory in watching your own death, though you can't turn your eyes away. My stomach thought it was *me* in free fall, and I cried out with despair that wasn't mine to feel.

A disturbance on the surface of the water far below. A brief blue flash, an almost imperceptible split in the current, swallowed again instantly. Wrong Russ was gone, but I clutched for dear life to someone else's existence. And held on tight.

INTO THE FUTURE

SEVEN P.M. PASSED me by, and I still *was*. Still I am. Maybe not in the solid, anchored way that Virgin Russ is, but we're both still flesh and bone and blood, both the captains of our own thoughts and personalities.

He's more impulsive than me, go figure—still that full-throttle energy. After what I went through, I'm more of a stop-at-all-the-stop-signs-and-look-both-ways sort of guy.

I'm not convinced my friends and family were relieved when I climbed down from that tower alive. I was like the loser who gets too drunk at the party and crashes on the couch, and the next morning I'm still there, snoring away, and it's awkward for everybody.

They put on smiles, gave hearty hugs, but maybe they would've preferred my disappearance, one way or another. It would've been tidier, easier to explain, and easier to live with.

The cover story we first concocted in the Silver Bullet was still our official statement to the public. So *as far as you know*, Russ Vale had a reclusive, home-schooled twin named Seth, and I got cast in the part, go figure.

You've probably seen it on *Evening Entertainment* or read about in *People*. How the Vale Brothers were running an elaborate ruse, pretending to be each other, in preparation for a documentary that never really got off the ground.

After the business with Bobby Parker, we were forced to "admit" our mistaken-identity game and apologize. Turns out, when you're mired in an explosive international scandal, people ask questions. And there were repercussions: like both of us had to take last year's final exams all over again, just to prove we didn't tag-team the first time.

Never mind that reporter who found no birth records for Seth Vale. I mean, you could stand us side by side and see we were twins, you could do genetic testing to prove it scientifically, so what difference does some missing paperwork make?

Yeah, you've heard our story, but not everything you read on BuzzFeed is true, except maybe a few of the nutty trolls speculating in the comments section: "prolly got a Dyad Institute cloning lab in their basement, yo" or "this some syfy shiznit gowin on here." That dude with the Caillou avatar wasn't too far off the mark, after all.

You can fool your public, but you can't pull one over on the woman who vividly recalls giving birth to just one kid. Madeline Belmont-Vale had to learn our secret after the fact, and it was a delicate procedure, much like snipping the right colored wires in the right order to avoid detonation.

Mom's Big Surprise went down sooner than we hoped. She got tipped off to the Pastime Theater crisis and actually showed up amid all the cop cars and cordoning tape. Seated in the back of an ambulance, I heard the *clack clack* of her high heels a few seconds before she rounded the corner and grabbed both sides of my face, demanding to know if I was okay, and what happened to my hand, and why was I wearing stage makeup over a black eye?

"Madeline?" Dad said, Virgin standing next to him. Oops.

Congratulations, Maddy, it's twins!

Mom looked back at me, then yanked her hands away. She got a little non-verbal for a few seconds—mostly *wha* noises. Then she pressed her fingers to her forehead, found her cool, and said to my

Dad, "Kasper, what did you do?"

Because this kind of M.C. Escher upside-down logic? The only man who could make a working beta test of something like this was my father. Later, he sat her down and laid out the equations that got us into this mess. Or what he could figure, at least, because this universe's Kasper Vale had not yet actually cracked the time-travel code. Took about a dozen hours of talking to make her believe.

I don't want to pretend Mom was easily convinced, but she's a woman who needs to compartmentalize things in her life. Something like an extra, identical son? She can't let that kind of puzzle go unsolved for too long.

Ultimately, after she thought she understood enough of what happened, Mom gave Dad an ultimatum: erase every file and burn every notebook with the slightest scribble about the Pastime Project. It was either that or divorce. Dad had already dealt with the nasty repercussions of time-space tinkering, and he knew it wasn't nearly as bad as Mom could make his life. He moped and stalled for a while, and I knew his agony, having to ditch your dream for the reality of other people.

But it's like giving up sugary soda or social media. You feel alive and full of promise again soon enough. You feel cut loose from your own tight knots. Within a week he was plotting other, equally secretive projects. Some people you can nudge in the right direction, but you can't change them.

We had a nice backyard campfire, all four of us Vales, tossing notebooks to the flames. Burning every bridge that might've one day led me astray, into another universe again.

SKIP AHEAD TO six months after that day, the longest day.

The hoopla eased off long enough that our town could appreciate something else besides the salacious details of the Bobby Parker tragedy for five minutes.

So the local state university branch did a screening of an award-winning film called *Shelter*, directed by a homegrown ingénue who spent close to a year documenting the trials and triumphs of a few women living at a local halfway house. Raw and moving, the film won spots at more than a dozen festivals around the country and earned its director a statewide grant.

Not to mention the Young Auteurs award at Silver Screen Studios. Paige Davis's was the only entry submitted from Port City Academy, and an obvious shoe-in for the win. I mean, if the doc was destined for HBO or Netfilms, it could certainly beat out a bunch of jumpy, blurry, horror flicks from the Cape Fear local public school kids.

Paige never told me she was submitting an entry. Never even let on she was making a movie, not seriously. But in the end, watching for the first time in the UNC-Cape Fear auditorium, I realized her doc would've kicked my movie's ass if I actually managed to submit it.

I won't lie—a little pride swelled in my chest, for my friend's sake. After the post-screening ovation and the Q&A, Paige needed some air, so together we slipped out through a back exit and strolled the campus. For once we didn't talk about "that day."

Just off the university quad there's a pond with a spewing fountain, bobbing lily pads on the perimeter, arched pedestrian bridges running across the narrow points. We leaned on a wooden bridge rail and watched the sun glint on the water, and then our eyes met and obviously I tried to kiss her.

I'd been waiting and wondering for six months, while Virgin Russ went hounding stupidly after Savannah. She and Virgin even went out a few times before those flowers went limp, Savannah jetted off the California, and Virgin remained a virgin. It made sense: she was sizzling and they'd been through the wringer together, but not the way I had with Paige.

So what did Paige do about my kiss attempt? Our lips never even touched. She turned and laughed quietly, politely, against her shoulder, and I just about melted into a pool of shame.

"I take it back?" I said.

"I'm sorry if I gave you the wrong idea," she said.

"No—I mean, *you* kissed *me* once, in another life. Shocked the hell out of me, to be honest, but after a while it didn't seem so strange. It seemed, I don't know, *natural*, for us. But you were right."

"About what?"

"Just before you kissed me you said I didn't get it."

"Get what?"

"I don't know. I still don't get it, but I *know* I don't."

"I have a girlfriend," she blurted. "You don't know her. She's not from our school."

"Oh, wow," I said.

"Is that so strange?"

"No—I mean—yes—I mean—"

"Whatever I did or said, I don't know what I meant," she said. "That was another me, and I wasn't there, even if I, well, *was*. I'm complicated, just like you. That's the way people are, Scorsese. You can't pin them down, you know?"

I nodded. Considering I'd run into a dozen possible takes on Horace Vale while I voyaged through time-space, I knew Paige was right, as always. Nobody was predictable. Maybe there was a Paige somewhere who would've kissed me back, there on the bridge with the croaking frogs—but that's my fantasy, and I can't rewrite the world.

In this life, I'm content to be her friend, and to potentially kick her butt someday when we both go up for the same film award, preferably an Oscar, or at least a Golden Globe.

THE OFFICI/L STORY goes, I killed Bobby Keene-Parker. Took the rap, at least. Nobody could claim Bobby shot himself, though it would've been a cleaner story, and the truth.

A lengthy investigation determined that I acted out of self-defense, because he was threatening to burn the whole theater down, my friends and family inside it. My story was corroborated by the others on the scene—Paige and Conrad and Russ and Dad. Not to mention the clear evidence that Bobby (or someone) doused the theater with gasoline some hours before our arrival, proving premeditation.

More likely Wrong Russ poured the gas, but he was never part of our story. Several dozen good folks down at Silver Screen Studios also attested to Bobby Parker's berserker turn: how he threatened his father and crew members with his gun, vowed to hunt down the Vale brothers and kill them, stole the prop cop car. Case closed, even if the door wouldn't exactly latch tight.

Granted, we took some heat for leaving the theater before the police showed up. But I caught the blame for that one, too. Claimed I was so freaked after I shot Bobby that I ran, and my people had to go find me, talk me down from the radio tower, bring me back to the scene of the crime.

Our various interpretations of what went down got rather convoluted. We didn't always give the sanest answers. Savannah claimed she saw *two* Bobby Parkers, but let's face it, the girl was under tons of stress—witnessing a shooting, getting kidnapped. Eventually, the district attorney had to shake his head and admit our story was destined for the Greatest Unsolved Celebrity Freakouts of All Time.

It didn't hurt that Marv Parker and his team of lawyers was there to help with the smoke-and-mirror special effects. Movie Marv didn't have a clear memory of what happened, distracted as he was by a near-fatal heart attack, but the one fact he was sure about was who pulled the gun on him. In the interest of sullying his son's memory as much as possible, Marv gave us all the legal help we needed.

Still, unanswered questions kept the news outlets buzzing for way too long: What made Bobby snap? Why'd he target these local nobodies? Why'd he bring them to the theater? Imagine a world where I made the real story public. *Vale Brothers Concoct Sci-Fi Fantasy for Publicity! Seth Vale, Star-Killer, Exploits Tragedy!*

Right, nobody would believe me, which is why I'm telling this story to myself, mainly. To understand why I didn't make that last critical leap back to my own quiet, anonymous life. Sometimes I forget what I was thinking. Sometimes I want to go back and decide differently, and then I remember that final decision on the radio tower was all about removing the temptation. I couldn't trust myself not to turn out like Wrong Russ. He was living proof of how easy it would be to slip into that kind of character, just by tapping an icon too many times.

Whenever I second-guess myself, I consider that there is a Russ Vale somewhere who actually *did* take the final leap, who woke up that Friday morning again with a foreknowledge of almost everything that would happen for the next twelve hours. I'm sure he couldn't help himself, playing the puppeteer. And I'm sure he's miserable now.

Somewhere there are other Wrong Russes whose horrible

schemes worked out, Wrong Russes who twisted up a bundle of realities so bad they're just thick knots in the fabric of the multiverse.

I just have to hope he never finds his way back to this reality again. The chances are in my favor. I don't like to dwell on the *almost-was* or the *could-possibly-be*, although those worlds do prod the back of my mind every now and then. A sense of some elsewhere nudging at me, disguised as a memory, though it never actually happened.

It's what other people call déjà vu.

Conrad felt it, that original Friday morning on the sidewalk, when he looked back at his bedroom window, even though I wasn't there. A feeling slips through the thin space between worlds, just for a second. *I've done this before.*

My friend Conrad Bower never made the leap like me, but he got a glimpse of another life—his father, alive and well, greeting him at the airport after a long flight from Afghanistan. We've talked about that moment on the theater screen so many times since then. The welcome on his father's face, it lives inside him now. Connie can access the memory of that video whenever he needs it most. He might've lost a better life, but he got his strength back.

Wrong Russ did one thing right after all.

That video of spliced-together alternate realities was never recovered from the Pastime Playhouse projector, by the way. My best guess was that Wrong Russ uploaded it from a source in another reality, just like he'd done with the videos he sent. The bastard learned some clever tricks in all that extra time he spent surfing through the universe's endless channels.

There *was* another video, though. Eighty million YouView hits, so I guess you've viewed it, too. It went *viral*, as they say, though I'm not as fond of that word as everybody else seems to be.

The final footage of Bobby Keene-Parker, a dialog with a young actress named Savannah Lark, recorded by an amateur filmmaker. I just *love* when they say *amateur* and forget to mention my name.

Well, Russ's name.

Police recovered the busted camera from the Aston Martin. They found the memory stick intact and pored through it a hundred times for evidence. Finally, they gave the video back to us, but not before somebody leaked it online.

People assume it was me, desperate for publicity, but if attention was my game I would've sold it to the highest bidder. Really, after a while Virgin Russ and I were sick of the scrutiny. *Celebrity Scoop*, VH-1, even the CW was eager to recoup their Cape Twilight losses with a made-for-TV biopic: *Bobby Keene-Parker, Unhinged*.

We wanted show business, but not as sidekicks in an exploitation flick. Okay, I *did* have to talk Russ out of offering to write and shoot the TV movie.

Savannah, on the other hand, she flew with it. Jumped that plane first-class to Hollywood, riding on the attention she got from the video of her and Bobby. You probably saw her in *Think Tank 2* with Mark Wahlberg, where she plays his daughter in one scene. She's also been in a couple Polar Ice Caps music videos, and I guess she's dating the drummer. I would've warned Russ, but some things you have to learn for yourself.

Let's face it, nobody watches our short video because of our virtuoso film making. It's not even edited or finished. The allure is the same as rubbernecking at the car crash, fixing to catch the crazy in Bobby's eyes, just about to burst loose. Sometimes I imagine a world where Bobby quietly ate his burger, flirted with Savannah, and went back to his life. Maybe in that life, he kept his rage locked away. Maybe he channeled it into his art instead.

In a way, I took that away from him. But there's nothing you can do about regrets except look ahead.

EVERY NOW AND then there's a blip. A quirk. My laptop freezes more than it should. My new cell phone makes random calls to strangers. A shadow in the corner of my vision isn't really there. I know what my "brother" will say even before he steps in the room.

Maybe your life's not so different, but you've always been a grounded part of this reality, while I'm still getting used to it. The small adjustments. Popcorn doesn't taste quite as good here, but Silver Bullet burgers are even better.

I'm still wrapping my head around the fact that *Wall-E*, one of my favorite movies, now only exists in my imagination. You'll have to take my word for how great it was. Then again, there's the brilliance of Heath Ledger's encore performance in the third Christopher Nolan Batman movie, which was way better than the one from my world. Most people here still pay for their music. And poor Miley Cyrus... man, oh, man.

I'm stranded, and somewhere I'm missed, but I like to hope I've found a new life that's just as real and unpredictable. Don't get me wrong. In the basement of my mind, I know if something happens to Russ first, then I'm a goner. Just a *poof* and a pile of clothes, like I never existed. Freaks me out to think about it sometimes.

But, you know, that's life for everyone. You don't know when your fade out is coming. Russ will leave behind a shell when he's gone, but otherwise we're the same. We'll both be memories some day. How we live before the end is how you'll tell us apart.

ACKNOWLEDGEMENTS

My wife and children always deserve the biggest thanks for giving me time and encouragement while I hide in the office to write. I love you, Nikitases.

Invaluable feedback on this book came from my son Gavin (I know, I know, a divided worm does not actually become two worms, no matter what Russ thinks). Also Craig Renfroe, David Hale Smith, Lizz Blaise, and Ryan Doody, who helped to shape the book. And especially Andrea Coleman for her YA expertise. Her extensive comments were a huge help.

Many thanks to educator Liz Prather and her team of beta readers in the SCAPA writing class at Lafayette High School in Lexington, Kentucky. They read an early draft of *Extra Life* and gave some great tips from the teen perspective, including which of my pop cultural references were the most egregiously out-of-date. Those students were Mattie Graff, Kirk Hardy, Jackie Knight, Shelby Lawhorn, Maura Reilly-Ulmanek, Anna Smith-Sargent, Gram Welch, and Aidan Ziliak. I wish them all the best of luck as they enter the wacky maze of adulthood.

For their inspiration and advocacy throughout the writing of this book, I want to thank Christopher Rowe, Russell Helms, Michael Mau, Josh Russell, Roger Jones, Travis Roman, Bill Mullen, Doug Brewer, Ashley Mullins, Tyger Williams, Gwenda Bond, Jeff Parker, Julie Hensley, Robert Dean Johnson, Young Smith, Maureen McHugh, Jim Keller, Peter Covino, and Mary Cappello.

For help in delivering *Extra Life* to readers, I thank my agent Yishai Seidman at Dunow, Carlson & Lerner, and the mastermind behind Polis Books, Jason Pinter. I'm deeply grateful to everyone on Jason's team at Polis, including Lauren at The Cover Collection; Sara Rosenberg, David Ouimet, Kim Wylie, Tara Marsden and David Dahl with PGW; Emily Tippets; and Carol Thomas for some sharp copyediting.

I won't pretend to understand all the science I glossed over in this book, but if I've sparked your interest in the possibilities or impossibilities of time travel, I highly recommend the pop physics books of Brian Greene and Michio Kaku, which were important resources for me.

ABOUT THE AUTHOR

Derek Nikitas is the author of two thriller novels, *Pyres* and *The Long Division*. His debut novel *Pyres* (St. Martin's Minotaur) was nominated for an Edgar Award for Best First Novel, and *The Long Division* was a *Washington Post* Best Book of the Year.

His short stories have appeared in *Ellery Queen Mystery Magazine*, *Thuglit*, *The Ontario Review*, *Chelsea*, *Plots with Guns*, *New South*, and more. He has written stories for the *Killer Year: Stories to Die For* anthology (St. Martin's Minotaur, 2008) and for the zombie anthology, *The New Dead* (Griffin Books, Feb 2010).

Derek was raised in New Hampshire and Western New York. He earned an MFA in Creative Writing from the University of North Carolina at Wilmington and PhD in English from Georgia State University. He teaches creative writing at the University of Rhode Island.

Extra Life is his first novel for Young Adults. Visit him on Twitter at @DerekNikitas or online at www.dereknikitas.com.